SKYFLASH

A Novel
By

Lee Gimenez

RRP

River Ridge Press

SKYFLASH

by
Lee Gimenez

This is a work of fiction. The characters, incidents, and dialogues are products of the author's imaginations and are not to be construed as real. Any resemblance to actual persons, living or dead, is entirely coincidental.

Printed in the United States of America.

Published by
River Ridge Press
P.O. Box 501173
Atlanta, Georgia 31150

First edition.

Cover photo: Copyright by Ella Hanochi; used under license from Shutterstock, Inc.
Cover design: Judith Gimenez

ISBN-13: 978-0692454039

ISBN-10: 0692454039

Other Novels by Lee Gimenez

Killing West

The Washington Ultimatum

Blacksnow Zero

The Sigma Conspiracy

The Nanotech Murders

Death on Zanath

Virtual Thoughtstream

Azul 7

Terralus 4

The Tomorrow Solution

SKYFLASH

Chapter 1

J.T. Ryan was certain he would die today.

Ryan stared down the barrel of a gun, his heart pounding. He was strapped to a chair and his hands were tied behind his back.

"How the hell did you find out about me?" the swarthy man standing in front of him spit out, as he shoved the muzzle of the large handgun to Ryan's forehead. The metal felt cold and stank of gunpowder. "Tell me, or by God, I will blow your head off!"

A trickle of sweat rolled down Ryan's face. He had to pick his words carefully – they could be his last. The man holding the gun, Jose Garcia, was a Colombian drug-lord with a reputation for brutality. Garcia had murdered his own son when he suspected the younger man cheated him out of drug profits. Before he killed him, Garcia had cut off his tongue and stuffed it down the man's throat. And to emphasize the point, he had his son's wife and three children murdered as well.

His mind racing, Ryan desperately tried to sort through his options. He was being held in the basement of Garcia's estate, and besides the drug-kingpin, there were four other men in the room, guards armed with AK-47 assault rifles. Although Ryan was big and rugged, he was securely bound to the chair. His body was racked with pain from the savage beatings he'd taken over the last week. The odds of escape were dim.

"Answer me, damn it!" Garcia shouted.

"Does it matter how I found out?" Ryan responded. "The thing you should worry about is I'm here, and I know all about your plan."

Garcia's face showed contempt, then he barked out a harsh laugh. "I should worry? You're the one with a gun to your head."

"You think I'm the only one who knows what you're up to?" Ryan said. "I work for the FBI. They know I'm here."

"You're lying!" Garcia yelled. "You know nothing." To prove his point, he struck the gun across Ryan's face.

When Ryan came to seconds later, he felt a burning, white-hot pain all over his face. Blood trickled from his nose and lips. The coppery taste of blood filled his mouth.

Garcia was still standing in front of him, now holding the large handgun at his side. "I don't believe you. You don't work for the FBI. You're from one of the other drug cartels. Which one? It's probably one of them in Mexico. Which one?"

"I know all about Skyflash."

Garcia stepped back, a surprised expression crossing his face.

"I know about Skyflash," Ryan repeated. "The FBI knows about it, and that you're behind the whole operation." The searing pain in his face intensified and he gulped in a deep breath. When the ache subsided, he tried his bluff, "Teams of agents are on their way here. They'll be arriving soon." This part was a lie. The FBI knew about Garcia, but they had no idea where Ryan was. There were no teams of agents nearby.

Garcia stood stock still, glanced at his men, then back at Ryan. It was obvious he was brooding over what the FBI operative had said. The drug-lord was a dark-complexioned man, with jet-black hair and a short beard. A long, wide scar ran down the whole left side of his face. He was built like a fireplug – short, stocky, and heavily muscled. His piercing black eyes were hooded and he had a cruel, menacing look that spoke volumes.

Ryan felt more blood trickle from his nose. He took a breath, smelled the blood's distinctive scent, plus the other rancid odors in the basement – urine and feces and vomit. No doubt Garcia used the place to interrogate and torture his enemies.

Suddenly Garcia laughed, the harsh sound reverberating in the concrete-walled room. "You lie. The FBI isn't coming. And you're no FBI agent – I've dealt with them in the past, and they broke after a third of the beating you got." He chortled, and his men joined in the laughter. "No – you're no FBI. You're a worthless piece of shit. Shit I scrape off my boots. Now tell me the truth. Which of the other drug cartels are you with?"

Ryan swallowed hard. His ruse hadn't worked.

A cold grin settled on the drug-lord's face. "I'm tired of this game. It doesn't matter to me if you talk or not. You're a dead man either way."

"Want me to kill him?" one of Garcia's lieutenants asked.

Garcia shook his head. "No. I want the pleasure to be all mine." He raised his pistol and pointed it at Ryan's head. "Do you know what kind of gun this is?"

The FBI operative stared at the large handgun. It was a Smith & Wesson .44 caliber Magnum with the eight-inch barrel, the same type of weapon made famous in the Dirty Harry movies. Clearly, Garcia used it as a way to further intimidate his enemies.

Ryan nodded.

The drug-kingpin laughed. "Then you know one bullet from this will blow your head clean off." He slowly pulled back on the gun's hammer and the weapon cocked on the double-action notch.

Garcia paused, the cold grin spreading on his face. It was clear he wanted to savor the moment, wanted Ryan to know he was about to die. "Say a prayer, because it will be your last."

It all happened in a split-second. Ryan heard an earsplitting roar and felt a blinding pain.

Then everything went black.

Two Months Earlier

Chapter 2

Atlanta, Georgia

"Take a look at this," Lauren said, glancing up from her laptop's screen.

J.T. Ryan walked across the kitchen and stared at the computer. It showed a detailed itinerary for their long-delayed vacation to Rome.

"Looks good," he said, taking a seat across from her at the table. They were in Lauren Chase's home north of the city. "But I'd rather look at you."

"Be serious for once," she replied. "We've been talking about this trip for a while, and now that you've got a break in your schedule, we're going to Italy. You promised, remember?"

Ryan gazed at Lauren, a smile spreading on his face. Though they'd been together a long time, she still took his breath away. A petite woman in her early thirties, she had sculpted good looks, long auburn hair, and hazel eyes. The freckles on her pretty face were highlighted by the reddish tone of her hair. She was also highly intelligent, with a PhD from Stanford. Now she was a professor of computer science at Georgia Tech.

Ryan and Lauren had just gotten up, and they were both dressed in bathrobes. Watching her, he admired how her curves filled out the garment.

"I know what that smile means, John Taylor Ryan. And the answer is no."

"How'd you know what I was thinking?"

She closed the lid on the computer. "Because I know you, J.T. I know all you want to do is get back into bed, and ...." She blushed, as if she'd just remembered the details of last night's lovemaking. Lauren was fairly shy, especially when it came to discussing sex.

His grin widened. "If I remember correctly, you were the aggressive one."

She crossed her arms in front of her and her face turned a darker shade of crimson. "Stop that. Get serious will you? What did you think of the itinerary? I want to call the travel agent to book it."

"Go ahead. Book it."

"Really? You're not just kidding around?"

"When do I ever do that?"

She shook her head slowly, but a smile lit up her pretty face. "Since always, J.T. But just because you look like a young Tom Selleck doesn't mean you're as witty as he is."

"That's true, but I still make you laugh." It was one of the many reasons he loved her. She laughed at his jokes, even when they weren't that funny.

"Yeah," she replied. "You're right."

"Just let me know the cost of the trip, Lauren. I'm paying for the whole thing."

Her smile turned into a frown. "No you don't – I make money too – and anyway, this Italy trip is going to be expensive."

"I appreciate that, hon," he said, holding up a palm. "But I'm paying, no more arguments. I've got money from the bonus I made on my last assignment. And anyway, you deserve it. We haven't been on vacation in a long time."

"All right," she said, finally relenting. "I'll call the travel agent later today."

"Good. You know how we could make this trip more special?"

"How?" she asked, a puzzled look on her face.

"It could be our honeymoon."

"We've talked about getting married before, J.T."

"And you've always said no."

She reached across the table, took his hand and held it tenderly. "I love you very much. I want us to get married. And I want to have children too. But kids need a father around. Are you willing to quit your job?"

"I can't give that up, Lauren."

She frowned. "It's too dangerous. Every time you go off on assignment to some God forsaken place, I expect to get a call telling me that ...." Her voice trailed off into a whisper, and she didn't finish the sentence.

His work had been a long-running argument between them. One that didn't have a good solution, he realized. The status quo: Lauren had her home, and Ryan had his mid-town apartment. They spent a lot of time together when he wasn't working.

Ryan smiled, trying to lighten the mood. "I'll make some breakfast. Then we can climb back into bed."

She grinned. "You? Cook? I want to live. Anyway, I don't have time for breakfast. I've got to go work."

"It's Saturday – you don't teach classes today."

"Staff meeting, J.T. We just picked up a new grant. Doing research on programming for nanotech robotics."

He rolled his eyes. "I don't even know what that means."

"You're good at detecting," she replied, "I'm good with computers."

"That's not the only thing you're good at, Ms Chase." Ryan got up from the table, came around her side and stood behind her. He parted her long auburn hair and began rubbing her shoulders. Her skin felt soft and warm and sensual. He breathed in her scent, the lavender perfume reminding him of last night, arousing him even more.

"Stop that," she said in a throaty whisper, but she made no move to push him away.

Bending down, he kissed the back of her neck. Goosebumps rose on her skin.

"I've got to get ready for work, J.T...."

"You said that already." He went back to massaging her shoulders, and after another minute of this, pushed aside the front of her robe and gently caressed her breasts.

She moaned.

Then she got up from her chair, turned and faced him, her robe falling to the floor. With a mischievous grin she said, "You're incorrigible, you know that?"

He pulled her towards him, wrapping his muscled arms around her sensuous body. "Is that good or bad?"

She laughed. "Both."

Bending down, he kissed her on the lips, and they stayed that way a long moment. She tasted salty and delicious. When they pulled apart, he asked, "How long have we got?"

She glanced at the kitchen clock on the wall. "Half hour."

"Plenty of time, for now. But I want a rematch tonight."

"You're insatiable, J.T."

"I don't know, Ms Chase, you're the one that couldn't get enough last night."

Lauren blushed. Then she smiled, took his hand, and led him to the bedroom.

***

They had just finished when Ryan's cell phone buzzed. Lauren, who was lying in bed next to him, picked up the phone from the night table and glanced at the screen.

Ryan, his breathing still labored, admired Lauren's nude body, which was pink and flush from the sex.

Lauren made a face, and handed him the phone. "It's what's her name," she said, her tone icy.

He took the cell. "Hello?"

"It's Erin," he heard the woman say. Erin Welch was an FBI Assistant Director in Charge, overseeing the Bureau's office in Atlanta. As a private investigator, Ryan had done consulting work for the FBI many times before.

"What's up?" he replied, watching as Lauren hurried into the bathroom to get ready for work. Their half hour session had turned into an hour, and Lauren was running late.

"I don't think your girlfriend likes me very much," Erin said.

He laughed. "That's because you're a good-looking blonde. She'd rather you were old, fat, and frumpy. She doesn't believe me when I tell her you're cold as ice, and twice as hard – all business, all the time."

There was silence on the line, and Ryan said, "You still there?"

"Yeah. You make me sound like a real bitch."

He chuckled again. "You said it, not me."

"Don't be a wiseass, Ryan. You're not as funny as you think."

"Probably right. Is this a business call, or did you just want to listen to my charming wit?"

"Spare me. Listen, I've been working on a case and I want to bring you in."

"What kind of case, Erin?"

"A murder."

"Where did it take place?"

"Right here in Atlanta."

He rubbed his jaw, felt the heavy stubble there. "Local PD involved?"

"Of course. They asked for our help."

"Must not be a routine case then," he replied.

"It's not."

"How many FBI agents do you have working for you?" he asked.

"Twenty-five. Why?"

Ryan sat up in the bed and leaned back against the headboard. He had always looked forward to working with the FBI in the past, since they always paid well and on time. But this time he was already thinking about the pending vacation with Lauren. *I've postponed that too many times before.* "Why do you need me, then?"

"Because of your unique talents, J.T."

He laughed. "You mean you need someone who's willing to get his hands dirty to get the job done."

"Something like that. The case is of a sensitive nature. But I can't give you details over the phone. You'll have to come in and sign a contract first."

"My usual fee, Erin?"

"I think you charge too much. But you do deliver." She sighed. "Yes, your usual fee."

"Good. I'll take the case then. But only because the crime was committed locally. Lauren and I are planning on going to Italy, and I'm not screwing that up. When do you want to meet, Erin?"

"Right away. This morning, if you can."

"Okay. Your office downtown?"

"No, Ryan. I need to show you a corpse. Meet me at the morgue."

Chapter 3

The Fulton County morgue is located on Pryor Street, south of downtown Atlanta.

J.T. Ryan had just arrived and was now sitting in the stark, sparsely furnished lobby, waiting for Erin Welch. The lobby was deserted, save for the security guard at the door and the receptionist behind the desk.

Although Ryan had been to the morgue many times before and had seen his share of cadavers in his line of work, he still found the place bleak and depressing. But the grimness was understandable, considering the local Medical Examiner and his staff of forty processed an average of 2,500 deaths a year. The appearance of the place didn't help. It was all dull green painted walls, worn linoleum floors, and overhead fluorescents that provided harsh, overly bright lighting. But the smell was the worst. It was a combination of cleaning solvents and the pungent aroma of formaldehyde, along with something underneath, the subtle hint of human decomposition.

He found a year-old copy of *Sports Illustrated* among the stack of forensics magazines on the table in front of him and leafed through it, killing time.

He looked up and saw Erin Welch enter the lobby and walk towards him. The striking blonde wore a Burberry raincoat and toted a leather briefcase.

"How's my favorite FBI Assistant Director in Charge?" Ryan said with a smile.

"Cut the crap, Ryan. I'm in no mood for it."

They shook hands and sat across from each other.

"Sorry I'm late," she said, taking off her raincoat. "Traffic sucked."

"Fall weather in Atlanta," he responded. "If it's not rain, it's ice."

Ryan studied the attractive woman as she rifled through her briefcase. In her mid-thirties, Erin was stylishly dressed as usual, wearing a Christian Dior black pantsuit with a white blouse. Her long, straight hair, parted down the middle, cascaded past her shoulders. High heels, Louboutins he noticed, completed her attire. He had met models who weren't half as good-looking as Erin. *No wonder*, thought Ryan, *that Lauren doesn't like her.*

The ADIC pulled a thick document from her briefcase and handed it to Ryan. "Sign this," she said, giving him a pen.

"Can I read it first?" he said with a chuckle.

"Don't worry ... it's the standard agreement."

He scanned it quickly, made sure his fee was stated correctly. "The fine print in the back has grown – it's twenty pages now."

"Like I said, don't worry about the legalese. It just says I can lock your ass in jail if you screw up."

He smiled. "And here I thought we were close friends."

Erin rolled her eyes. "I hire you because you do good work. It's as simple as that."

"Don't worry, you're not my type. Lauren's all I need."

A sour look came over her face at the mention of Lauren's name. "So, you're finally taking her on that vacation you promised her. It's about time."

"I would have done it sooner, Erin, but the Bureau's kept me busy."

The FBI woman nodded, knowing he was talking about some of the recent assignments. "That's true," she said in a low voice, as if she didn't want anyone to hear. "If it hadn't been for you, I may not have solved those cases."

He laughed. "Is that a thank you I'm hearing?"

"Don't let it go to your head. You've already got an inflated ego."

Ryan chuckled again and signed the document. He handed it back and she stuffed it in the briefcase. She stood, and grabbing her coat and case, strode toward the reception desk.

"FBI ADIC Welch to see case number B374472," she told the male receptionist as she held up her badge. The man, who obviously recognized her, didn't look at the ID, but simply nodded and pressed a buzzer, unlocking the interior door to the morgue.

Ryan followed her through the maze of corridors, past closed doors that led to the morgue's autopsy rooms. It was cold in this part of the building, much colder than in the lobby, the temperature kept low to retard decay. The floors here were industrial tile so they could be hosed down after the postmortems. Erin's heels clicked on the surface, the only sound other than the buzzing of saws from the autopsy rooms.

When they reached a wide corridor at the far end of the building, Erin flagged down a technician in a stained lab coat. Holding up her badge, she said, "FBI. Case number B374472."

The technician was a thin, hollow-faced young man with pasty skin. Although he looked to be in his twenties, his eyes had the weary, old-man look that comes from seeing too much death.

"This way, Ms Welch," he replied. Like the receptionist, the technician obviously knew Erin. He led them into a cavernous warehouse-like room, lined with metal lockers on all of the walls. This part of the morgue was even colder than the rest. After the autopsies, the corpses remained here, waiting for transport to the city's mortuaries. Ryan knew the room was nicknamed 'the meat locker' by the employees. It was eerily quiet here. Only the whirring of the industrial-capacity air conditioning, which attempted to suction away the aroma of decomp, could be heard.

After consulting a clipboard hanging on the wall, the technician strode to the end of the room and opened the door of one of the lockers. Ryan and Welch followed him and watched as the tech pulled out the metal tray and removed the sheet covering the cadaver. Without a word, the technician turned and left the room.

Ryan studied the body and almost gagged at what he saw and smelled.

The nude corpse was female. Beyond that it was difficult to determine her physical characteristics, due to the intense beating the woman had suffered. Her face was totally mutilated – it resembled raw hamburger meat. Her upper torso had also been beaten. Below the coroner's Y-incision, in the abdomen area, Ryan noticed what appeared to be a gunshot wound. Bruising was also evident on her genitals, thighs, and legs. He had seen a lot of DBs as a private investigator, and before that when he was in the Army's Delta Force in Afghanistan. But this cadaver was among the worst.

"This was no simple homicide," Ryan said, shaking his head slowly. "Whoever did this was full of rage."

"I agree, J.T.," Erin replied.

Ryan pointed to the gunshot wound in the stomach. "Is that the COD?"

"The Medical Examiner said the cause of death was indeterminate. It could have happened as a result of the GSW, or the severe beating. Either one would have been enough."

Ryan nodded. "The coroner run a tox screen?"

"Of course," Erin said, arching her brows. "You think he's incompetent?"

"He's a government employee, isn't he?" he said, trying to lighten the moment from the grim scene in front of them.

"I'm a government employee, damn it," Erin snapped. Then she must have realized he was making a joke because she shook her head. "Gallows humor. I should have known you'd try that too. To answer your question, the ME ran a toxicology analysis. It showed alcohol and cocaine in her bloodstream."

Ryan turned back to the cadaver. "The genitals are bruised."

"They ran a rape kit too. Semen was found in the vagina. But it'll take time to identify the source."

One of the dead woman's eyes had the typical blue-white haze brought on by the lack of oxygen after death. The other eye was gone from the socket – only a bloody, bruised hole remained. Ryan's hands closed into fists, as he thought about the violent way the woman had died. *Whoever did this has to be caught. No one deserves what this woman suffered.* Anger boiled in him and he took a couple of deep breaths to calm down. He said a silent prayer for the woman, then turned to the FBI agent. "I want to catch the animal who did this."

"So do I," Erin replied.

"Do you know who the woman is?"

"We do. That's why I brought you into the case."

"Who is she, Erin?"

"The governor's wife."

Chapter 4

J.T. Ryan glanced out the floor-to-ceiling windows of Erin Welch's corner office. On the 15th floor of the FBI building, the office had a panoramic view of downtown Atlanta. In the distance he could see commercial jets circling Hartsfield International, waiting for their turn to land.

Erin pulled a thick file from a wall cabinet, went back to her desk and sat behind it. She slid the folder across the desk and Ryan picked it up. "This is the coroner's report," she said, "plus all the other information on the murder from Atlanta PD. The lab is still working on the semen found – it takes time to identify and then match the DNA."

Ryan didn't open the file, instead leaned forward in his chair. "I heard on the news a few days ago about the governors wife's death. But there was no mention of a murder. How was APD able to keep that quiet?"

Erin tucked her long blonde hair behind her ears. "Like I told you at the morgue earlier today, this is a sensitive case. It could involve the top elected official in Georgia. Until we know more, the Chief of Police wants to keep this off the front page. That's why he called the FBI and got me involved."

He nodded. "I understand. Everybody's covering their ass – nobody wants to screw up and lose their highly-paid, cushy jobs."

"You've been around the block, Ryan. You know how this works."

"You assign one of your agents to work on this?"

"Of course. Several in fact. But I want you to work independently of them."

"Why?"

Erin gave him a hard look. "Because I trust you." She leaned back in her leather executive chair. "Let me give you some background. As you know there's a new Director at the Bureau in Washington. I had a good working relationship with the previous FBI Director. Unfortunately, my new boss and I have some bad history. I pissed him off on a case years ago and he's been gunning for me ever since. Now that he's in charge, I'm sure he'll try to get rid of me."

"I get it," he said. "You're not sure you can trust your own agents?"

"Maybe yes, maybe no. Female ADICs are still rare in the Bureau. Not everyone likes working for a woman."

Ryan smiled. "I'm guessing your warm, charming personality hasn't won them over, huh?"

Her face reddened and he could tell he'd angered her. Then she shrugged. "I'm working on that. I know I have to be more diplomatic. But ... this is a tough job. I have to be a hard-ass sometimes to get it done."

Ryan nodded, feeling sympathy for the woman. He guessed most of her agents considered her a bitch on wheels. But he saw her as a tough, no-nonsense kind of person, the type he liked dealing with on a professional level. "I get it, Erin. I see what you're up against. And you're right. You can trust me." He looked down at the file, then back up at her. "I want to spend time reading this thoroughly," he said, pointing at the file. "But can give me the broad strokes on the case, no pun intended."

She ignored his attempt at humor. "How much do you know about Liz Cooper, the governor's wife?"

"Not much. Just what I've read in the papers. She was estranged from Governor Cooper, right?"

"Yes. The two have been separated for a year and lived part. As I understand it, they ran in different social circles. He's devoutly religious. She was much younger and liked to party. That's what caused the rift in the marriage."

Ryan rubbed his jaw. "Is the Governor a person of interest in the murder?"

"He has an alibi."

"That's not an answer, Erin."

"Like I said, he has an alibi for the time of death, but he hasn't been ruled out completely. When you read the file, you'll get a better sense of the case."

"Okay. Any other suspects?"

"Several. Mrs. Cooper ran with a fast crowd. And the tox screen showed alcohol and drugs in her system. There's a couple of people who could be good for it, all high profile. That's where you come in. I want you knee deep in this, regardless of what you uncover." She leaned forward. "I want the killer or killers found and put behind bars, no matter who they are."

"Even if it's the governor?"

"Especially then. But I need your utmost discretion. You report to me, and me alone."

Ryan's thoughts flashed back to Liz Cooper's mutilated corpse at the morgue, and his blood roiled in anger. *If I find the murderer, he'll never get to jail. When I get through with him, he's going to look like Liz.*

"Got it, Erin. I report only to you. Anything else?"

"Yeah. Let's go find the bastard who did this."

Chapter 5

Ryan had turned one of the empty rooms in his mid-town apartment into a gym, and he was there now, pounding on the heavy bag. The large punching bag hung from a hook on the ceiling, and it swayed from the right jabs, left hooks and uppercuts he delivered in quick succession. Ryan felt the sharp sting from the blows, even though he was wearing boxing gloves. He'd been at it for thirty minutes and sweat poured off him.

After reading the reports Erin had given him and making calls on the case, he'd changed into gym clothes and came in here. It was a routine he followed consistently. Hard exercise, the tougher the better. It kept his body and mind sharp, and he always felt exhilarated afterwards.

It was a habit he'd developed in Special Forces. He would have loved to do it every day, but it was difficult, especially when he was out of town on a case.

He stepped away from the bag and wiped perspiration from his forehead. After taking a couple of breaths, he went into a martial arts stance and began a series of powerful side kicks on the punching bag. He followed that with several front kicks and finally a roundhouse kick. He kept at it for another fifteen minutes, until his legs, aching from the effort, signaled him to stop.

He took off his gloves and left the room, anxious to grab a shower before dinner. But the doorbell rang and he went to the door and opened it.

Lauren, wearing business attire and carrying a paper sack, stood there.

"You're early," he said, with a smile. "Figured I had plenty of time to get ready."

She went up on her tiptoes and gave him a quick kiss. "I brought Chinese," she said, holding up the bag. "Hope that's okay."

"That's great," he replied, closing the door behind her. They headed toward the kitchen where she began to unpack the food.

She looked glum and he said, "Everything okay?"

Lauren shrugged, then turned toward him. "I guess. We'll talk over dinner." She pointed to the bathroom. "But you need a shower." She wrinkled her nose. "You're stinky."

"Yes, ma'am."

He showered and changed, and by the time he got back to the kitchen she had dinner set out on the table. After pouring her some wine, and getting a beer for himself, they began to eat.

"Why the sad face?" he said, after tasting the moo shoo pork.

Lauren sipped the merlot. "Something happened at work today."

"Not good, I gather."

She looked pensive, and after a dainty bite of her food, she pushed aside her almost full plate. "Not good at all. One of my students died."

"Sorry to hear that, hon. What happened?"

"Drug overdose. The strange thing is, you'd never suspect he was a drug user. He was one of the brightest students at the university."

Ryan put his fork down, reached out and took her hand. "You just never know."

She stayed quiet and after a few minutes he tried to lighten the mood. "How's the trip planning going?"

Lauren's face lit up. "I booked it with the travel agent!"

"Great."

"Before we know it, J.T., we'll be on our way to Rome. By the way, the new case you're working on ... please tell me it won't interfere with our plans ...."

He took a long swallow of his Coors beer. "Not a chance – I know how much this means to you."

"Good to hear. What's the case about, anyway?"

"A murder, and it may involve some high profile people."

"Like who?"

"It's confidential – you know I can't talk about pending cases."

She scrunched her pretty face and stuck out her tongue at him. "You and that FBI bitch keeping secrets from me again."

"You know that's not true, hon."

She laughed. "I know that, J.T. Got you, didn't I?"

For once it was her making a joke. But it was good to see her in a better mood. He smiled back. "Yeah, you did. If you don't watch it, I'm going to have to spank you later for that."

Lauren gave him a mischievous smile. "Promises, promises."

Chapter 6

The Georgia Capitol Building was called the 'Gold Dome' for a reason. The gilded, 75-foot round dome elegantly capped the stately, four-story building on Washington Street. The structure housed the state's government offices and was the most distinctive building in Atlanta's skyline.

Ryan parked his Acura in the lot across the street, and after locking his handgun in the glove box, walked over and entered the building. He went through the security checkpoint, then took the elevator to the governor's office. Yesterday he had talked to Governor Cooper's chief of staff, who had primly informed him that the governor was a very busy man. After reminding the staffer that this was a murder investigation, the man grudgingly agreed to set up the appointment.

Ryan was shown into the governor's spacious office and asked to wait. As he waited, Ryan studied the room. He had never been there before and was impressed with the elegant furnishings. There was a credenza on the side wall, displaying family pictures. One of the photos showed a young man in Army fatigues.

Just then a side door opened and the governor walked in. Ryan had never met the man in person, although he'd voted for him in the last election. In his early seventies, Cooper was tall, thin, and a bit stooped. His silver hair contrasted sharply with his ruddy cheeks.

"Mr. Ryan," the governor said, extending his hand. "Good to meet you. Please have a seat."

After the two shook, the governor sat behind his wide, ornate, desk while Ryan took one of the burgundy wingback chairs that fronted it.

"I understand you wanted to speak with me," the governor began, "regarding my ... wife's death." The man had a reedy voice, and it broke a little when he mentioned her.

"Yes, Governor. As I explained to your chief of staff, I'm assisting the FBI with their investigation."

"Yes, yes, I know. But I've already spoken to the police and the FBI. Although my wife and I were separated, her death hit me very hard." A pained expression was on the man's face. But Ryan was used to dealing with people who often lied to him and put up a false front.

Cooper pointed to one of the photos on the credenza. "That's my son. He's an Airborne Ranger, currently posted at Fort Bragg. My staff checked you out. You're former military."

"Yes, sir."

"You have an impressive background, Ryan. Army captain. Delta Force. Tier 1. Not many Special Forces soldiers achieve that."

"Yes, sir. Now, about the case."

"Of course. As you probably know, I was out of town when she was killed – in D.C. in fact. There's twenty people who can vouch for me, including several senators. In addition to that, I ... still loved her very much. But ... she was a free spirit, much more into partying than I. To tell you the truth, we probably should have never gotten married – she was half my age." His voice broke again. "But you know what they say, love is blind ...."

Ryan had read the file and knew about the ironclad alibi. But still, Cooper could have hired someone to kill her. As the governor spoke, he studied the man's mannerisms and inflection, looking for any tells – tell tale signs that the man was lying. So far, he hadn't spotted any. Cooper seemed genuinely saddened by his wife's death.

"Anyone you think may have been responsible for her murder, Governor?"

"Liz liked to party, and from what I've heard, she was working her way through a long list of men."

Ryan nodded. "Anyone in particular?"

"Her current fling was with that crazy painter ... what's his name."

"Yes, sir, I know who you mean."

Ryan asked him more questions over the next ten minutes, and eventually the governor looked at his watch. "I have a cabinet meeting to attend. Anything else I can tell you, Mr. Ryan?"

"No, sir, that'll do for now. I appreciate your time."

"I identified her body at the morgue, Ryan. I saw what the killer did to her. Promise me you'll find him."

"Yes, sir, that's what I plan to do."

Chapter 7

Erin Welch was having lunch at her office, when her phone rang. Placing the sandwich on the desk, she picked up the receiver. "This is Welch."

"It's Ryan," she heard the man say.

"Glad you called, J.T. How'd your meet with Cooper go this morning?"

"Productive."

"Yeah?"

"I've questioned hundreds of people in my line of work and he's not the killer."

"You're sure?" she asked, pressing him. "Maybe he ordered a hit."

"Don't think so. He seemed genuinely distraught."

Erin reflected on her own conversation with the governor. "I've talked with him too. And I agree – he's not the guy. I just wanted your take."

"Tell me more about the painter. I read about him in the reports; what's the deal with him?"

"I have a bad feeling about that guy," Erin said, as she clicked open the case file on her laptop. She quickly scanned the list of persons of interest and began reading out loud from the notes. "Steven Morgan. 43 years old. Lives in Atlanta; Buckhead to be exact. Famous painter – has a worldwide reputation. Quite wealthy. He's also eccentric. Rumored drug user. He and Liz Cooper were an item ... the *Atlanta Journal* ran news articles about them. They were photographed together at quite a few social events."

"You talk to him, Erin?"

"Wanted to, never got the chance. After his initial questioning by local PD, Morgan lawyered up. His big money buys lots of expensive legal talent. We'll get our chance to question him, but it won't be soon."

There was a pause from the other end, then she heard Ryan say, "Maybe I'll have better luck."

"I was hoping you'd say that."

"Kind of why you hired me, isn't it Erin?"

"I won't confirm or deny that statement," she replied. "Just one thing. If you do get a chance to speak with our famous painter, don't get too rough. I don't want the FBI sued for harassment."

"Don't worry – I'll keep you out of it – in fact I won't even mention the Bureau."

"Good."

He laughed. "Anyway, I'll treat him with kid gloves."

"Bullshit. We've worked together before ... I know your MO."

"I'm offended," he said with a chuckle.

"Yeah, I bet."

"So, if I get him to talk, do I get a bonus, Erin?"

"Damn you," she yelled, her anger flaring. "Your fee is set!"

She heard him laughing and realized he was making a joke. "You're a wiseass. You know that, J.T? I'm hanging up now."

Erin ended the call and shook her head. *That man is insufferable sometimes.*

Chapter 8

Ryan put his cell phone in his pocket, still smiling from his conversation with Erin. He was driving north on I-75, and spotting the North Avenue exit, took the off-ramp and headed toward the Varsity for a quick bite.

After parking, he got his food order from the counter and looked for a place to sit. As usual, the iconic restaurant was packed, but he finally found an empty table that overlooked the Interstate. He munched on the greasy but delicious chili dogs and onion rings. The Varsity was his favorite lunch place, had been since his college days. Lauren always laughed at him for going there so often – said she preferred 'real' restaurants. But he always reminded her that the diner was an Atlanta institution, dating back to 1928. She replied that the faded signs, ancient chrome seats, and chipped Formica tables of the place were the same as when the diner opened, making them over 80 years old. And she was probably right.

After finishing his lunch, he took out his phone and dialed Lauren's number. It rang for a long time, then went to voicemail. Remembering now that she was attending a conference, he hung up.

Back in his Acura moments later, he studied the GPS map on his car's screen. He'd made appointments for this afternoon with two suspects in the case. Neither one was as promising as the painter, but he'd been a PI long enough to know that you have to chase down every lead.

He fired up the car and drove off.

***

Ryan was in a deep sleep in his apartment when his cell phone rang.

Waking, he turned on the bedside lamp and glanced at the alarm clock. 1:07 a.m. He picked up the cell and held it to his ear. "Hello?"

"Is this John Ryan?" he heard a male voice say.

"Yeah. Who is this?"

"This is Dr. Archer, from the ER at Grady Hospital."

Ryan sat up on the bed, his pulse quickening. It was never good news when you receive a call at night from a hospital. "What's going on?"

"Do you know a Lauren Chase?"

He stood, pressing the phone closer to his ear. "Of course. What the hell's going on?"

"You better get down here, Mr. Ryan. She's in critical condition."

Chapter 9

Ryan gunned the Acura well over the speed limit, ran every red light he came to, and when he got to the hospital's ER parking lot, parked haphazardly in front of the building. He sprinted into the emergency room, and after a few moments, located Dr. Archer. The doctor was a tall man with thick-lensed eyeglasses, which gave him an owlish appearance.

"What the hell happened?" Ryan demanded, his heart pounding.

Dr. Archer held up his palms. "Calm down, Mr. Ryan. We're still trying to sort that out."

"How's Lauren?"

"She suffered a serious concussion and a broken leg."

"I want to see her!"

"Of course, as soon as that's possible," Dr. Archer replied in a comforting voice. It was clear the man was used to dealing with anxious relatives. "If you'll have a seat in the waiting room, I'll take you to her soon."

"Tell me what happened, Doctor."

"I talked to the EMTs that went to the scene. Ms. Chase, along with several other people, were attacked by a man who went berserk."

"What? What are you talking about? Lauren was at a conference, at the Hyatt Hotel in downtown."

"That's right," Dr. Archer said, "That's where it happened. The guest speaker, right in the middle of his presentation, became very agitated, jumped off the stage and began clubbing the nearest attendees with the microphone stand. The stand was one of those heavy, metal ones and it caused a lot of damage. People rushed in to stop him, but unfortunately Ms Chase was sitting in the first row, and along with several others, was badly hurt. One of the victims is dead."

"Jesus, that's crazy. How could something like this happen?"

The doctor shrugged. "We see it more frequently than you think. The cops have the attacker in custody – he's being held in a secure area of the hospital. We're running blood tests on him. We suspect a drug overdose caused his bizarre behavior. Possibly methamphetamines."

Ryan thought about this. "I know meth can cause this. But Lauren told me about this guy. He's a well-known computer expert – no way someone like that would take meth – that's a street drug for low-lifes."

"I know, Mr. Ryan, but these days, you just never know ...." The doctor glanced at his watch. "I've got more patients to see. Have a seat, and I'll come get you."

Archer hurried away, and Ryan found an empty chair in the waiting room. The Grady ER was the go-to place for the city's downtown urban core, and as expected at this time of night, the place was crowded. Screaming kids, anxious-faced mothers, coughing seniors, and tough-talking teens wearing gang colors packed the room. The noise from all of the conversations created a shrill racket. Ryan tried to shut it all out as he sat and worried about Lauren.

Two hours later Dr. Archer returned. "You can see her now, Mr. Ryan. Follow me."

"What took so long?"

"There were complications. Unfortunately, Ms Chase has lapsed into a coma. She's in Intensive Care."

Ryan tried not to think about the implications of this news as he followed the physician out of the ER and up to the ICU on the second floor. The large room was long and narrow, with the hospital beds separated only by curtains. All the beds were in use. Nurses and med techs bustled about and the beeping of medical monitors blended with the groans of the patients. The scent of antiseptic hung in the air.

"She's right over there," the doctor said, as he strode to the far side of the room.

The doctor led him to the last cubicle and stepped aside, allowing Ryan to enter.

"You can only spend five minutes with her, Mr. Ryan," the physician said in a kindly voice, "but no more. She needs rest."

Ryan had never seen Lauren look so frail or pale, and it terrified him to see her this way. She lay motionless on the bed, which was surrounded by multiple monitors. Her head was heavily bandaged, and a thick breathing tube was in her mouth, held in place by medical tape. Bruises covered her face.

Pulling a chair over, he sat next to her, his stomach churning.

Lauren's hands rested on the sheet that covered her and an IV tube was attached to one of her arms. Her skin was ashen – it was drained of color, appearing the same shade as the white gown she wore.

He reached over and touched one of her hands. Her skin felt cold.

"Lauren," he said, "it's me."

There was no response.

Besides the slight movement of her chest from the breathing tube apparatus, it was difficult to tell if she was alive.

Ryan sat there, caressing her hand and talking to her. He was desperately trying to get a response. The rest of the world melted away as he focused on the woman he loved.

Suddenly he heard the rustling of curtains and an ICU nurse came into the cubicle. “I’m sorry, Mr. Ryan. Your time’s up. You need to leave.”

He looked up at the nurse. “How long will she be like this?”

“It’s difficult to say. Each case is different.”

“But she will come out of the coma, right?” Ryan said, the fear twisting his stomach into knots.

The nurse, a matronly woman in her fifties, said nothing for a moment. Then a sympathetic smile crossed her lips. “In many cases, yes. But if you’re a religious man, Mr. Ryan, it wouldn’t hurt to pray.”

Chapter 10

Erin Welch had just pulled her car into her assigned parking spot at the FBI's underground garage, when her cell phone rang. She turned off the Lexus and answered the phone. "Welch here."

"It's Ryan," she heard the man say. "I need your help." He sounded brusque, his usual levity absent.

Erin had watched the early morning news on TV, instinctively knew why he was calling. "Sorry to hear about Lauren, J.T. I saw the news and I talked to APD – they filled me in on the details."

"That's why I'm calling. The bastard who did this is under protective custody at Grady. A couple of uniforms are posted there. I need to get in his room and question him."

"Rip off his head, you mean?" she said.

There was no response, and after a moment, she said, "You're out of luck, Ryan. The guy's dead."

"What?"

"That's right. The lieutenant who's handling the case for Atlanta PD called me a short while ago. The guy died – appears to be a drug overdose."

"They do a tox screen?"

"Yeah. They thought it might have been meth or cocaine. It wasn't. But they did find trace elements in his bloodstream."

"What was it, Erin?"

"Some new chemical substance – something they'd never seen before."

"Damn it. I should have gotten to him sooner. I should have pushed past the uniforms and got him to talk."

"What ... and get arrested? You're not invincible, Ryan, even though you think you are."

"Damn it! If you'd seen Lauren at the hospital, you'd know what I'm feeling right now ...."

"I'm sorry," she replied. "I know it's tough." Her briefcase was resting on the passenger seat and she clicked it open, took out a report. "Listen, J.T., I've got some info on our prime suspect in Liz Cooper's murder."

"Steven Morgan, the artist?"

"Yeah. As I told you before, he lives in an exclusive townhome in Buckhead, but as I understand it, he spends a lot of time at his loft a mile away from his home. Morgan does his painting there." She read off the address. "You may have better luck finding him at his loft."

"Thanks, Erin."

"One other thing. Morgan has a bodyguard who shadows him everywhere he goes. A thug by the name of Bruno. Long rap sheet. And from what local PD tells me, he's armed and dangerous. So be careful."

Chapter 11

Ryan hated the Buckhead area of Atlanta. Described as the place where old money lived and new money partied, it had started long ago as a genteel, upscale neighborhood filled with Southern mansions. It had evolved into a destination for high-end nightclubs, elite restaurants, and exclusive boutique shops at Phipps Plaza and Lenox Square Mall. Ryan found the *nouveau-riche* set that frequented the area pretentious, and he avoided it as much as possible.

Steven Morgan's loft was located on the west side of Buckhead, just off West Paces Ferry Road. As Ryan pulled into the long gravel driveway bordered on both sides by magnolia trees, he realized the term 'loft' didn't do the place justice. It was actually an old Southern mansion, replete with a colonnaded portico. The left side of the house had been expanded and converted into a glass-and-steel monstrosity that Ryan guessed cost more than the PI would earn in a lifetime. Erin was right – Morgan was exceedingly wealthy.

He parked the Acura in the semicircular driveway that fronted the mansion and, getting out, rang the door chime.

A young woman in a maid's uniform answered the door a moment later. "May I help you?"

"Sure. Is Steven here?"

"Well ... yes, Mr. Morgan is here," the woman replied uncertainly. "Do you have an appointment? He doesn't see anyone without an appointment."

Ryan waved a hand in the air and smiled. "My name's J.T. I'm an old friend of his. If you'll point me in the right direction, I'll find him." He smiled more broadly. "I'd like to surprise him."

Her eyes nervously darted toward the glass-and-steel part of the house, then looked back at him. In a firm voice she said, "If you'll wait here, I'll check with him first," and began closing the door.

Ryan laughed, then pushed past her into the mansion. "Why ruin the surprise?" Wasting no time, he strode quickly through the vestibule, and took a long corridor toward a closed door at the very end, while the maid trailed behind, loudly asking him to stop. He opened the door and stepped inside.

The loft was one big open space, its high ceiling at least two-stories high. The tall windows overlooked a heavily wooded area. Abstract paintings on large canvasses were stacked against the walls, while other half-finished canvasses rested on easels around the room.

"I'm very sorry, Mr. Morgan," the maid said, "this man just barged in. He said he was a friend of yours."

A balding, heavy-set man wearing a stained painter's apron stepped out from behind one the canvasses. Ryan recognized him from the photos in the case report – it was Steven Morgan. Taking a dangling cigarette from his lips, Morgan barked, "Who the hell are you?"

"J.T. Ryan. I just need a few minutes of your time."

"Should I call the police?" the maid asked.

"No. Go find Bruno," Morgan ordered, "I want him in here now."

"Yes, sir," she replied, hurrying away.

Morgan turned back to Ryan. "If you know what's good for you, you'll leave now, before Bruno gets a hold of you."

"Like I said, my name's J.T. Ryan, and I'm investigating Mrs. Cooper murder."

The artist took a step back. “Are you a cop?”

“Private investigator.”

“Listen, whoever you are, if you want any information, contact my attorneys.” He dropped his half-smoked cigarette on the floor and ground it out with his shoe. Then he pulled out a new one and lit it up. Taking a long pull from the cig, he let out a cloud of smoke. Pointing to the door, he snarled, “Get out! Now!”

“Don’t make this hard on yourself, Morgan. I just want to talk.”

Just then Ryan heard the door open and he turned, saw a large man with a high-and-tight crew cut step inside.

“Bruno,” Morgan barked, “take this piece of trash out. And hurt him in the process – I want to teach him a lesson.”

“Yes, Mr. Morgan,” Bruno replied, closing his meaty hands into fists. “With pleasure.” The bodyguard was built like a Mack truck – big, brawny, and all muscle, from the looks of it. Ryan was 6’2”, muscular, and weighed a fit 200, but Bruno towered over him, at least 6’6” and over 260 pounds. This wasn’t going to be easy, the PI realized. He could draw his weapon, but the last thing he wanted was a gun going off and the cops being called. No, he had to do this the hard way.

With a sneer, Bruno advanced, holding his fists up in a classic boxing stance. Closing the distance between them in a split-second, the bodyguard delivered a roundhouse punch, but only hit air as Ryan quickly sidestepped the blow.

Not wasting time, the PI struck the man with two jabs to the kidneys, and followed those with an uppercut to the jaw. Bruno staggered, let out a grunt, and went down to one knee.

“Get him, Bruno,” Morgan ordered. “Do your fucking job!”

His eyes blazing with hate, the bodyguard sprang off the floor and rushed Ryan again, swinging wildly with both fists. One of the punches caught the PI in the face and another in the stomach, and Ryan, gasping for breath from the agonizing blows, staggered backwards.

Bruno chortled. "You're dead meat now."

The bodyguard advanced, his muscular arms outstretched, intent on throwing the PI to the ground.

Ryan struck him with a well-placed kick to the man's crotch, stopping the giant in mid-stride. Bruno groaned, his eyes went wide and, going to his knees, clutched his groin with both hands.

The PI lashed out again, this time with a side-kick that smacked Bruno's face. Ryan heard the *crack* of broken cartilage as the big man collapsed to the floor, blood seeping from his bent nose. After checking to make sure Bruno was unconscious, Ryan turned back to the painter.

"Ready to talk now?" Ryan said.

Morgan put his hands on his wide hips. "You can't do this! I'm calling my lawyer right now." He pulled a cell phone from his pocket, but before he could dial, the PI took it away from him.

"This phone's defective," Ryan said with a chuckle. "You'll have to get a new one." Then he threw the phone full-force against the nearby wall and the device split into several pieces.

Morgan ran for the door, but before he reached it, Ryan grabbed him by the shoulders and spun him around.

"Okay, Morgan. I don't have time for more bullshit. Are you going to talk, or do I have to get rough?"

Now that Bruno was down for the count, Morgan didn't seem nearly as cocky. In fact, he was sweating and his face was flushed. He unbuttoned the top buttons of his shirt. "Christ, it's hot in here. Can I at least sit down?"

Ryan pulled over one of the stools and pointed to it. "Go ahead."

"What do you want to know?" the man said, sitting down.

"You and Liz Cooper were close, right?"

He shrugged. "Yeah. So what? There were a lot of men in her life."

"I've read the reports – you two were an item on the social circuit."

Morgan smirked. "Liz was a coke whore – she spread her legs for any guy who got her the stuff."

Ryan visualized Mrs. Cooper's mutilated body and in a rage slapped the man hard across the face. Morgan howled and tried to get off the stool, but the PI grasped him by the shoulder and pushed him back down.

"Where were you on the night she was killed, Morgan?"

The man rubbed the bright red mark on his cheek. "I already told the cops. I was here, in my loft, painting."

Ryan rolled his eyes. "And your alibis are Bruno and your maid, right?"

"That's right." He pulled at his collar. "Damn it's hot in here. Can I get a drink of water?"

"So you can have the maid call the cops? I was born at night, but not last night."

Morgan frowned. "So if you're not a cop, what are you doing here?"

"This is how this is going to work – I ask the questions, you answer them. Got it?"

The man glanced around the large room, as if trying to figure a way out.

Ryan grabbed Morgan's shirt front and hauled him to his feet. "You killed her, didn't you?"

"No," he sputtered. "Of course not. Yeah, I fucked her and we scored dope together, but no, I didn't kill her. Why would I do that?"

"I don't know why, but I know you did it. You're the slimy kind of bastard who would do it. Why else would you refuse to talk to the cops? I've interviewed several other suspects, as have the police and FBI, and you're the only one who's lawyered up. Why is that, I wonder?"

Morgan shrugged, said nothing.

"You're testing my patience."

"I know my rights – you can't do this to me – it's illegal!"

Ryan laughed. "That's funny." He pushed the man back down on the stool and grabbed his throat with both hands. "I'm going to start squeezing. I figure you'll last, what, 30 seconds before you croak? Let's test out my theory, okay?"

The man's eyes went wide as Ryan squeezed, cutting off the man's air supply. He struggled, trying to push the PI away, but he was no match for his superior strength.

"When you're ready to talk," Ryan said, "just nod your head."

The painter's face turned bright red as the pressure increased. The look of raw fear intensified and after half a minute, Morgan nodded his head furiously.

When Ryan let go, the painter fell to the floor, gasping and sucking in lungfuls of air. The man sat up and started coughing. After a moment he glanced up at Ryan with a desperate look. "You're crazy, you know that?"

The PI squatted in front of him. "And don't you forget it. Now talk."

"I'll talk, you crazy bastard. But it won't matter. It'll never hold up in court. It'll be your word against mine."

Ryan gave him a hard look. "Tell me what happened. You killed her didn't you?"

Morgan shrugged. "It was an accident. I didn't mean to do it."

"I don't want an editorial. Just give me the facts."

"God it's hot in here," the painter said, rubbing his upper torso. "And my chest hurts."

"Fuck that. How did you kill her?"

"All right, I'll tell you, damn it. It was an accident, like I said. Liz and I were up all night, drinking, doing drugs, fucking, it was a wild night, man ...." He stopped, clutched his chest again. After gulping in more lungfuls of air, he continued. "Anyway, we both got wasted. She fell asleep, but I got a second wind and decided to paint. I kept some canvasses and supplies at her place." Morgan rubbed his arm. "God, I don't feel well."

"You're going to feel a lot worse if you stop talking."

"All right, all right. Anyway, like I said, I left her bedroom and went into the spare room where I kept my stuff. I took a hit from my stash and started painting."

"Then what happened?"

"The drug had a weird effect on me that night. Normally it just makes me paint faster and better. I've done great work on that stuff."

"So what happened that night?"

"I went crazy. I was angry and frustrated; the painting I did was pure crap. I took a knife and slashed it, I was so angry."

"Then what?"

"I went back to the bedroom – Liz was still asleep – I woke her, cause I wanted to fuck again – but she started cursing me and pushed me off – then it's all hazy. I think I grabbed a fireplace poker and hit her with it, but like I said, it's all a blur."

"Liz Cooper wasn't just beaten – she was also shot. You do that too?"

"Who knows … I have a gun, so maybe ... I was in a rage, I didn't know what I was doing ...."

Ryan recalled the police report. "There was no one at her place when the cops found her corpse. If you were in such a fog, how did you get out of there?"

"Bruno was waiting for me in the limo parked on the street. After I woke up, I called him and he came up cleaned up the place and got rid of the evidence ...."

"Figures."

Morgan was perspiring heavily and he continued rubbing his chest. "I don't feel well. I need a doctor." He tried getting to his feet, but Ryan pushed him back down to a sitting position.

"We're not done yet, Morgan."

"I've told you everything. What else do you want to know?"

Ryan's mind raced. He needed more from the guy, something to incriminate him, because he knew the painter was right. It would be Ryan's word against his, and that would never hold up in court. When the DNA from the semen was identified it would show it was Morgan's, but the man would claim it was from earlier that day. "Let's go through it again. You and Liz spent the night drinking and doing cocaine, and she fell asleep. Then you snorted more coke and started painting."

"No, man, I didn't do more cocaine before I painted. I've tried that, and all I get is shit art. No, man, I used Skyflash."

"What the hell's Skyflash?"

"It's a new drug. Skyflash is the full name, but everyone calls it Flash. That drug is like no other narcotic I've had before – it's the greatest high I've ever been on, better than heroin even. It makes you feel like a God. You can see heaven when you're on it. But that's not the best part ...."

"What do you mean?"

An awed look came over the man's face. "I've never painted so well, or so fast before. Flash is the perfect drug."

"Where do you get this stuff?"

But before the man could answer, he clutched his chest and his eyes rolled white. Then his body slumped to the floor and went still.

Chapter 12

Erin Welch awoke with a pounding headache. The new case was taking over her life, pushing aside all her other work. The governor had contacted her boss FBI Director Stevens, demanding answers on the case; in turn, Stevens had called her and read her the riot act – solve it quick, or pack your bags. And now she had a new problem to deal with – Ryan was at county lockup, pending assault charges by the ADA.

She rubbed her forehead, trying to push away the throbbing in her head, and after a moment, got off the bed and headed to her apartment's bathroom.

After showering and dressing quickly, Erin drove to Fulton County Jail, calling the Assistant District Attorney from her car. She had worked with the ambitious ADA before. She coaxed him into dropping the charges, after reminding him how useful it would be to his career if he had the Bureau on his side.

As she waited at the lockup's processing center for Ryan to be released, she made calls to her agents at the office.

Half an hour later she heard clanging metal from the far end of the waiting room. Looking up, she saw the barred door slide open and Ryan walked out. Putting her cell phone away, she waved him over.

"You look like hell, Ryan," she said, as the man approached and slouched on the seat across from her. The left side of the PIs face was puffy and strips of bandages covered several cuts, marring his rugged good looks.

The man grinned. "Yeah. But you should see the other guy."

Erin shook her head slowly. "What the hell happened, anyway?"

"It's a long story."

She checked her watch. "I got time."

"Morgan's bodyguard and I had a disagreement." He gingerly touched the side of his face. "He got in a few licks before I was able to take him down."

"I see."

Ryan pointed backwards toward the barred door. "Thanks for getting me out of there."

"You're lucky I know the ADA. He's agreed to drop the assault charges, along with the trespassing charges. Otherwise you'd be in there a lot longer. And it's a good thing Bruno has a long rap sheet; otherwise the district attorney might not have been so agreeable." Her anger flared as she recalled the police report. "You were supposed to question Morgan, not have him die on you."

The PI shrugged. "I had no control over that."

Erin took a deep breath to calm her irritation. "The post-mortem showed the artist died of a heart attack, so in that respect, you're right. Still – you pushed him over the edge."

"But I got him to confess."

"You did?"

"Damn right, I did. He killed Liz Cooper."

"What was the motive, J.T.?"

"He said he went into a rage after she refused to have sex with him – he beat her up."

Erin nodded. "He was our most likely suspect, so I'm not surprised he did it. The DNA results from the semen we collected from Cooper's corpse aren't back yet."

"Don't worry – they'll confirm Morgan had sex with her that night. By the way, you said Morgan died of a heart attack. Did he have a history of heart problems?"

"No, J.T. The coronary was caused by a drug overdose. The ME told me they found the same type of chemical substance they found in the corpse of the computer expert. A narcotic, he suspects."

"It's a new drug called SkyFlash," Ryan said. "The street name for it is Flash."

"What the hell's that?"

"Morgan told me about it, right before he died."

"Flash? I never heard of it."

Ryan nodded. "Me neither. According to Morgan it's something new. Really powerful. Gives you a rush higher than cocaine or heroin. And something else. The artist said it made him a much better painter and faster and more confident."

Erin frowned. "Sounds like bullshit to me. Drug addicts are always claiming they've found the perfect drug; the narcotic that turns their life into nirvana."

"Yeah, I thought the same thing too at first." He waved his hand in the air. "But I've had time to think, being in here for a couple of days. Morgan may have been telling the truth. Think about it – the dead computer guy, the guy who put Lauren in a coma, was a genius, a renowned expert in his field. He went into a rage and attacked a dozen people. Morgan went into a similar rage and killed the governor's wife." He paused a moment. "And there's something else. Lauren told me about another strange case. One of her best students at her university died of a drug overdose recently. A model student, one of the brightest kids at the school."

Erin nodded. "I'll check that out – see if they found the same chemical compound in the student's bloodstream."

"Good. The way I figure it, all these cases may be connected. Maybe Flash is the common denominator. These three – Morgan, the computer guy, the student, were all super bright, accomplished people. They weren't street thugs, common criminals smoking crack."

"You may be on to something, J.T."

He grinned. "It kills you, doesn't it?"

"What?"

"That I may have figured out this piece of the puzzle before you did."

Erin's face flushed, her anger flaring again. "Don't let it go to your head."

He laughed.

Standing, she said, "I've got to get back to the office. You want me to drop you off at your apartment?"

"No," he replied, a serious look crossing his face. "Take me to Grady Hospital. I want to check on Lauren, see how she's doing."

"Sure."

"You know, Erin, if this Flash drug is being used by prominent members of the community, this case is going to get a lot bigger than one homicide."

The FBI ADIC had been thinking the same thing. Her life was going to get lot rougher from now on. She rubbed her temple, trying to soothe the migraine that was growing with a vengeance. "I know that."

"What's your next move?"

She mulled that over a moment. "We find the bastards behind Flash, and do it soon."

Chapter 13

They had finally caught a break, Ryan thought, as he turned off the cell phone and placed it on his office desk. Erin had just called him with the good news. Now that the DNA evidence had come back confirming Morgan was Liz's killer, the FBI had searched the artist's home and found critical information. Among the stash of assorted illegal narcotics and drug paraphernalia the dead artist kept, they found a packet of blue powder.

Analyzing the powder, the Bureau techs realized it was not cocaine, heroin, meth, or any other narcotic they had seen before. Erin suspected the mysterious blue powder was Flash. And there was more good news the FBI woman told him. Besides Morgan's fingerprints on the container of powder, they found prints from another man, a sketchy character with a long rap sheet.

According to Erin, the internal politics in her office were intensifying – her boss, the FBI Director, leaked that she was probably on her way out, and the agents that worked for her sensed blood in the water. Deciding she couldn't trust them, Erin was bringing the info about the fingerprints to Ryan, giving him first crack at locating the man.

Ryan glanced at his watch and decided not waste another minute before tackling his assignment. His other cases could wait. Putting away the stack of reports he was working on, he grabbed his blazer and left his midtown office.

***

Vinny DeMarco owned a bar on a rough part of Central Avenue. It was a run-down place, bordered by other shabby establishments: a pawn shop, a bail-bondsman, and a massage parlor.

Ryan scanned the bar's seedy exterior. The name *Vinny D's* was painted above the front door, the color faded and peeling. A blinking Budweiser sign hung on the cracked picture window.

He stepped into the bar and scanned the dimly lit place, which stank of cigarettes and stale beer. A scarred wooden bar ran the whole length of the room, with tables and booths toward the front. Loud country music was playing from a jukebox in one corner. The place was nearly empty; the only customers were three black teens, no more than sixteen or seventeen, smoking at one of the booths, and an old guy at one of the tables hunched over a large mug.

The bartender, an overweight middle-aged woman, was wiping the counter and looked up as Ryan approached. She was wearing a stained T-shirt and jeans. The shirt was several sizes too small, stretching the fabric and leaving too much skin exposed. Her jeans rode low on her generous hips which accentuated her girth.

"What can I get you?" she drawled.

Ryan pulled out a bar stool and sat down. "What kind of beer do you have?"

She let out a long sigh. "We only got one kind, buster."

He chuckled. "Then that's what I'll have."

The woman filled a mug from a draft dispenser and set it in front of him. "That'll be five bucks," she said, her stained teeth showing.

He took a twenty from his pocket and slid it over.

Before taking a sip, he noticed the glass was chipped, and he pushed the mug aside. When she came back with his change a moment later, he said, "You always this busy here?"

She shrugged. "What do you expect – this place is a dump."

"Can't argue with that." *From the looks of it,* thought Ryan, *Vinny DeMarco didn't make money from the bar; probably used the place to launder drug money.*

"I'm looking for Vinny," Ryan said.

"You a cop? You look like a cop."

"No. I'm just looking for Vinny. I owe him some money, want to pay it back."

"Yeah, I bet," she replied, her voice dripping with sarcasm.

"So – is he here nor not?"

"Maybe he is and maybe he isn't." She gave him a crooked grin. "You make it worth my while and I'll see if he's around."

Ryan took out another twenty and slid it across the bar. She picked it up and tucked it away in a pocket. Turning, she said, "I'll go get him."

The waitress went into a back room, but when nothing happened, Ryan got suspicious.

He bolted out the front door and raced around to the back of the building, where he spotted a tall, wiry man getting into a late-model Cadillac. The vanity license plate on the front of the car read *Vinny D's.*

Sprinting over, Ryan jerked the driver's side door open and, grabbing the man by his lapels, pulled him out of the car.

"Going somewhere, Vinny?" Ryan said, throwing the man against the Cadillac.

DeMarco lashed out with both fists, one catching the PI in the jaw, and Ryan flinched, pulled back a moment. DeMarco may have been slender in build, but he packed a hard punch.

Ryan hit the man with a solid uppercut of his own, then followed with a powerful right hook. Demarco staggered and he collapsed to the ground.

Grabbing the unconscious man by both shoulders, the PI dragged him across the alley and toward the bar's rear entrance. Opening the back door, he pulled the body inside, and into an office area.

Ryan propped the man on a chair. Spotting a bottle of water on the desk, he unscrewed the top and poured the contents over Vinny's head.

The man sputtered awake and seeing Ryan standing in front of him, tried to take another swing at him. Grabbing the punch in mid-air, the PI twisted the arm behind the man's back and pulled it up. "I'll break it, you son-of-a-bitch, if you give me any more trouble." He pulled the bent arm higher to make his point.

Obviously realizing he was fighting a lost cause, DeMarco nodded. "All right, damn it."

Ryan let go of the arm and stood across from Vinny.

"Who the hell are you?" DeMarco said, rubbing his arm with his good hand. "You're no cop, that's for sure."

"My name's Ryan. And you're right, I'm no cop."

"What do you want?"

Ryan pulled a chair over and sat across from Vinny. He studied the man a moment before answering. DeMarco was olive-skinned, with a shaved head and a thick mustache. He had small, beady eyes with a furtive look to them – Ryan had seen the look before, mostly in ex-cons. The man smelled of garlic and Altoids.

"I know all about you, Vinny. You've got a long rap sheet – drug dealing, extortion, grand theft, running prostitution." Ryan waved a hand in the air. "You probably run a lot of it through this fine establishment."

The man shrugged. "Nobody's perfect."

"You're right about that."

"What do you want, Ryan?"

"The way I see it, you're a thug – a low-level drug dealer. You don't seem sharp enough to run a major drug operation."

DeMarco's face turned red. "What the hell do you know? I'm –" He stopped in mid-sentence, probably realizing he was about to incriminate himself. "I've got nothing to say."

"You've got plenty to say, Vinny. I just have to find the right way to motivate you."

The drug dealer shrugged again. "You know my rap sheet, so you know I served time. I've done stints in prison – if I survived the animals in there, you sure as hell can't frighten me."

"That may be true, friend, but you served your time at county. You were never convicted of murder before. This time you'll be going away to a Federal prison for a long, long time."

"What are you talking about? I never killed no one. Roughed people up, sure, but murder? Naw. Not my style."

"The FBI has you cold. They found your prints on Morgan's drug stash. Now he's dead. It's just a matter of time before they find your connection to the other high-profile deaths. With your record, it's not a stretch that you'll be the one left holding the bag. The FBI is already talking with the DA."

A worried look crossed DeMarco's face, then, after a moment, he smiled. "You're bluffing. If the FBI had the goods on me, why'd they send you? You said you're no cop."

"That's exactly why they sent me, Vinny. Because I don't have to follow any rules. I make my own."

Ryan stopped talking and stood. Then he stared down at DeMarco, grabbed him by the collar and pulled the man to his feet. "This is how this is going to go down. You tell me what I want to know, and I'll sweet talk my FBI boss to cut you a deal. If you don't talk, I'll beat the crap out of you, then turn you over to the Bureau. What's it going to be?"

DeMarco looked unsure of himself, and Ryan knew what the man must be thinking: *Fight? Run? Or Talk?*

To speed up the process, Ryan lashed out, punching Vinny savagely in the solar plexus.

The drug dealer groaned, folded, and slumped back on his chair.

"What's it going to be Vinny?"

After getting his breath back, DeMarco nodded. "What do you want know?"

"Tell me about Skyflash. The narcotic that goes by the name of Flash."

"It's a drug."

"I know that, you idiot. I know it's a drug you're dealing. Where do you get it?"

"What do you care?"

"From what I know about this narcotic, it's sophisticated. High-powered people are using it. A low-life like you couldn't have developed something like that on your own."

A glimmer of a smile lit up DeMarco's face. "So, I got something you want. Looks to me like I could write my own ticket – get the deal of a lifetime – immunity from prosecution, and more; maybe much more. Sure I'll talk. But not to you. I want a deal in writing. From the Feds."

Ryan realized Vinny wasn't the stupid thug he previously suspected. The man had street smarts.

The PI clenched his fists. "You'll talk to me, or I'll beat it out of you!"

"I don't think you will, Ryan. If this information is so important to the FBI, I think you'll turn me over to them."

Damn, thought Ryan, *the bastard is right.* Although the PI was itching to beat the hell out of the slimy thug in front of him, a new thought crossed his mind. Ryan had already been arrested for assault once this week. If he beat up this guy, he might get arrested again. And even Erin wouldn't be able to bail him out a second time.

Ryan took a deep breath to calm down.

Then, reaching into a pocket, he removed a set of plastic flex-cuffs and handcuffed the drug dealer to the chair.

Turning away from the man, he took out his cell phone and dialed a number.

When Erin Welch answered a moment later, he said, "It's Ryan. I got the package you wanted."

"Good," she replied. "Where are you now?"

"His bar, *Vinny D's*."

"Okay. I'll leave now – be there in twenty."

"Listen, Erin, after you pick this guy up, I'm going out of town for a couple of days."

"On this case?"

"No. This is personal. Something I've neglected for too long. Anyway, you'll need a few days to sweat our upstanding citizen here, get him some religion."

"Okay, J.T."

"Do me a big favor will you?"

"What?"

"Could you go see Lauren when I'm gone? She's still in a coma and I'd appreciate it if you could stop by the hospital and check in on her."

There was a sigh from the other end. "What, now I'm your personal assistant?" she said in an irritated tone.

"I wouldn't ask you, unless it was important. Lauren doesn't have any family."

After a long pause, she said, "Alright. But you'll owe me for this. Big time."

"Thank you, Erin. Don't worry, I'll pay you back. I'm going to catch the people behind Flash. That drug is responsible for putting Lauren in the hospital."

"See you in twenty," she said, and hung up.

Ryan put away his cell phone.

Turning back to DeMarco, he looked down at the man.

In a fit of rage, the PI slugged the man across the face, knocking him out.

"That's for Lauren," Ryan said.

Chapter 14

9/11 Memorial
World Trade Center
New York City

It had been too long, thought Ryan, as he crossed the plaza toward the south reflecting pool of the memorial. He had promised himself he would come here every year on his father's birthday, to commemorate his passing. His father, a financial planner, died during the tragic events of 9/11/01. The first terrorist plane to wreak havoc crashed into the south World Trade Center tower, killing him, along with thousands of other people. His father had worked on the 80th floor of the 107th floor skyscraper. The South Tower collapsed at 9:59 a.m., less than an hour after being hit by the hijacked airliner. That exact time had been inscribed into the PIs memory.

Ryan, constantly working on assignments that frequently took him overseas, had not been able to keep his promise. He'd missed coming here for too many years.

It was a cold, blustery November day, heavily overcast, which fit the somber mood of the place. Although the eight acre memorial plaza was filled with throngs of families and tourists, the area was eerily quiet, the people in attendance obviously choosing to murmur as a way of showing respect for those who died.

Ryan reached the south reflecting pool and looked out across the water. On the perimeter walls surrounding each pool were the names of the 2,983 people who died on September 11, 2001. The names were inscribed in bronze. The memorial park, which opened ten years after the Al Qaeda attacks, was composed of the glass-and-steel museum and the two pools built on the footprints of the original Twin Towers. Thirty-foot waterfalls cascaded into the pools, the water then descending into a center void. The sound of the rushing liquid was pronounced here, and was the only thing Ryan heard.

As he stood there he brooded about his father, who had died way too young. After a few minutes, his thoughts turned to Lauren. The mental picture of her in a coma filled his mind, and he said a silent prayer for her.

Just then, he heard the faraway away sound of a jet flying in the distance. He looked up, toward the gray sky. The memorial was surrounded by the newly built skyscrapers which towered over the plaza. The tallest skyscraper was the Freedom Tower. At 1,776 feet, it was the tallest building in the country. Its gleaming glass panels reflected the muted daylight, dispelling the gloom of the overcast day. The sight of the soaring, inspiring skyscraper lifted Ryan's mood, giving him hope for the future.

Chapter 15

FBI Offices
Atlanta, Georgia

Erin Welch entered the interrogation room and stared at Vinny DeMarco, who was sitting at the rectangular table. DeMarco's hands were shackled to the metal loop on top of the table.

She sat across from him, placed the thick file she was carrying on the table.

"So, Vinny," she said, "you ready to talk to me now? Yesterday you didn't have much to say."

"Yesterday," he replied with a grin, "you were full of bullshit. The way I see it, you got nothing on me."

Erin wanted to reach across and slap the slimy bastard in front of her, wipe the smirk off his face. *FBI assistant directors*, she fumed, *can't do things like that*. Not with this session being recorded and with a Bureau agent watching on the other side of the one-way view glass window.

She pointed to the folder on the table. "That was yesterday, Vinny. Today is a different day."

DeMarco glanced at the file, then at her. "What do you mean?"

"Before, all we had were your fingerprints on Morgan's drug paraphernalia. But now we've got much more. We have security camera footage of you delivering a package to Morgan's place the day he killed Liz Cooper. Which makes you an accessory to 2nd degree murder."

The grin faded from DeMarco's face.

"But that's not all, Vinny. We have a lot more." She tapped on the folder. "We matched your prints to more deaths tied to the Flash drug. Remember the computer expert who went on a rampage and killed a man? We found your fingerprints on his drug stash as well. And we have more."

The color drained from the man's face.

"We searched that dump you call a bar and found large quantities of illegal narcotics: heroin, meth, cocaine, and Flash."

"It's not mine," DeMarco protested, the shackles rattling on the table as he tried to motion with his handcuffed hands. "Someone planted that."

Erin smiled. "Save it. Your waitress already gave you up, told us all about your sleazy operation."

"That bitch! I should have fired her years ago."

"Too late for that, Vinny." She leaned forward in the chair. "Looks to me like we have you in a box. You'll be charged with two counts of being an accessory to 2nd degree murder, plus the narcotics charges. I've already talked to the DA. With your record, no jury's going to let you skate free. You'll rot in prison for a long time."

Erin paused, let that sink in a moment. "How old are you?"

"Forty-two. Why?"

"I figure you'll do a thirty year stretch," she said, "which would make you 72. If you live that long."

Erin picked up the file and stood. She turned and began walking toward the door.

"Wait!" DeMarco yelled. "Where you going?"

"We're done here, Vinny."

"No, wait a minute – that Ryan guy said if I told you my source for the Flash I'd get a deal."

She glanced at the man and grinned. "That was before. Before we questioned your waitress. She told us everything we needed to know," Erin lied. "She gave us the name of the source."

"She doesn't know that! I handle that end all by myself."

"I guess she's smarter than you thought." Erin replied, turning toward the door again.

"Wait. I can give more info than she'll ever know. Just give me some kind of deal, okay?"

When Erin heard this, she knew she had him. She'd planted the hook with the lie about the waitress, and Vinny gulped it down. *Sometimes*, she thought, *this job can be sweet.*

Grabbing a chair, she sat across from him again. "If you tell me everything you know, I'll have the DA give you a deal. Instead of doing 30 years behind bars, you'll do 10."

DeMarco shook his head. "Not good enough."

"Fine by me," Erin said, standing up. "I don't care if you do 30, you sorry bastard."

"Wait," he said, his voice pleading. "I'll take it."

"You sure? I don't want to waste any more of my time on a slimy son-of-a-bitch like you."

"Yeah, I'm sure."

"Okay, Vinny. I've got to take care of something – I'll be right back."

Erin stepped out of the interrogation room and approached the FBI agent who had been watching through the one-way glass. "I'll handle it from here, Stan. You can go back to your office."

"Yes, ma'am," the agent said. He turned and walked away.

Stan's a good agent, she thought. *But considering current office politics, could she trust anyone? Better safe than sorry.*

Once he left the area, she went to the control panel on the wall and turned off the recording camera. That done, she stepped back in the interrogation room and took a chair across from DeMarco.

"Okay, Vinny," she said, "Let's hear it."

The drug dealer spent the next twenty minutes telling her about his source for Flash.

Chapter 16

Stone Mountain
east of Atlanta, Georgia

After an hour's drive, J.T. Ryan found the sprawling ranch-like house.

Located off an unmarked dirt road, the secluded ten-acre property was nestled in the shadows of the massive granite outcropping known as Stone Mountain. The exposed rock peak towered over the whole county, providing a spectacular backdrop to the property. Even though it was well past midnight, there was enough moonlight to see the outline of the famous Confederate memorial carvings on the north face of the mountain.

Ryan drove past the home's gated entrance and kept going, doing a circuitous surveillance detection route, also known as an SDR, to make sure he sure he wasn't being followed.

Finally he pulled the Acura below a stand of trees off of the dirt road. He had seen no vehicle traffic for some time, and the only lights he spotted came from the flood lights that illuminated the outdoor areas of the ranch. The PI had purposely picked the late hour to maximize the element of surprise. According to what Erin had told him, Vinny's drug source was well armed and ruthless. Although Ryan's mission tonight was to incapacitate and interrogate Joe Miller, the narcotics middle-man, the PI knew from experience that things didn't always go as planned – sometimes they went south, and got ugly fast. The element of surprise was the key to increasing his odds of success.

Before getting out of the car, he pulled his pistol from his hip holster, checked the load, and added the sound suppressor to the weapon. Then he put on the night-vision goggles and the dim nighttime scene outside lit up to a green glow.

After waiting a moment for his eyes to adjust, he climbed out and crept toward the chain-link fence that bordered the whole property. As he zipped up his jacket to ward off the chill, he listened carefully for any unusual sounds, but heard only rustle of the wind through the trees.

When Ryan reached the seven foot fence he surveyed the scene on the other side. The sprawling ranch compound in the distance included a large main house, with several smaller structures around it. No one appeared to be outside.

Taking out his pocketknife, he pitched it toward the chain-link fence. It bounced off the metal, no sparks flew, and the knife dropped to the ground. *That's a relief*, he thought, realizing the barrier wasn't electrified. It would make his job a lot easier.

Putting the knife away, he took out a pair of wire cutters and cut a hole in the fence and slipped inside the property.

Using trees for cover, he advanced slowly and hid behind a row of shrubbery. Just ahead was the ranch. Floodlights illuminated the front entrance and the semicircular driveway. He heard no sounds coming from the interior of the structure. On the semicircular driveway fronting the home were two cars, a Mercedes and a BMW. There was also a black Chevy Suburban parked off to one side, on the grass.

He didn't see any sign of dogs, which was a good thing. Along with alarms and electrified fences, dogs were on top of his list to avoid. Once canines were alerted, they always eliminated the element of surprise.

Still crouching, he circled around to the rear of the house, looking for the back entrance. Spotting no one about, he sprinted to the door, and once there, hugged the wall. Squinting into the dim interior through the French doors, he realized the room was a large den, full of oak furniture and overstuffed leather couches.

The den was vacant – neither Miller nor his family was about. He inspected the door lock closely, saw that it had been pried open. A bad sign. *Had someone already broken in?*

With his pistol leading the way, he slipped inside, closed the door behind him, and crouched behind a sofa. His heart thudding in his chest, he listened for sounds.

Ryan heard nothing, save the ticking of a wall clock and the hum of central heating.

Then he heard something else, emanating from somewhere deeper inside the home: muffled *thuds*, several of them in quick succession. And right after that, loud screams, heavy footfalls, furniture being overturned. More *thuds,* then nothing.

What the hell's going on? he wondered.

Gripping the weapon with both hands, he stood and advanced toward the wide hallway to his left. Although the corridor was unlit, his goggles illuminated the area well enough for him to see.

Just then he saw movement out of the corner of his eye – a large man, dressed all in black, coming the other way. The guy was carrying a flashlight and a silenced automatic pistol. It was clear to Ryan the man was an assassin, and what he'd just heard was likely a hit.

In that instant, both men saw each other.

The man fired, and Ryan ducked behind a bookcase, the bullet missing and lodging into a wall. Ryan, momentarily blinded by the flashlight's strong beam, fired back, but his shot was off the mark.

The assassin crouched and continued shooting, the rounds splintering the bookcase.

Ryan, his vision restored, aimed and pulled the trigger in quick succession, the revolver spitting out four rounds, hitting the man in the arm and leg. The smell of gunpowder filled the room.

The PI felt a burning sensation on his temple and knew he'd been hit, but before he could continue shooting, blacked out and collapsed to the floor.

Ryan came to sometime later, the pain in his temple intense. Spotting his weapon on the floor next to him, he picked it up. He quickly sat up, crouched behind a sofa and scanned the room, now vacant. There were blood stains leading out of the room to the rear door, which was now open. He knew he'd shot the assassin, so that was probably his trail of blood.

Cautiously, he stood and looked out through the open doorway – the black Suburban was gone.

Gingerly touching the side of his forehead, he felt a trickle of blood – luckily it was only a graze. After reloading his weapon, he began searching the home for Joe Miller, although he had a bad feeling about what he'd find.

He located the first body in one of the bedrooms. The corpse was that of a small boy, no more than six or seven. He'd been shot in the back of the head, by the ear, execution style. The kid's pajamas were blood-soaked.

Ryan found Joe Miller moments later, in the master bedroom. He recognized the corpse from the pictures Erin had given him. Miller must have awakened right before he was killed, because there were signs of a struggle. His nude body was on the floor, and there was blood everywhere. His wife's corpse, also nude, was still on the king-sized bed.

The scene made Ryan sick to his stomach. Not for Joe Miller, who was a drug dealer and probably deserved to die, but for his wife and son, who were most likely innocents.

The PI continued searching the house, but found no one else, dead or alive.

After putting his pistol away, he took out his cell phone and dialed a number.

The phone rang for a long time, but eventually the other side picked up and he heard Erin's groggy voice. "Hello?"

"It's Ryan," he said. "I found Joe Miller."

"That's good, J.T. Did you get him to talk?"

"No. Unfortunately somebody got to him first. Miller's dead."

Chapter 17

St. Croix, U.S. Virgin Islands
the Caribbean

Jessica Shaw stared at her husband, trying to keep her anger in check. "I told you we should have never trusted that bastard."

"It couldn't be helped," Paul Shaw replied calmly, in between sips of coffee. The couple was having dinner at their palatial estate in a secluded part of the island. "Garcia was our best option at the time."

Jessica pushed aside her unfinished plate of linguini, disgusted with the whole situation. She was a petite, athletic woman in her thirties, with shoulder-length black hair and striking good looks. Men found her extremely attractive, but her piercing black eyes burned with such cold intensity that one look told them to stay away.

Jessica leaned forward in her seat. "If this contract falls through," she said, venom in her voice, "we're screwed."

She waved a hand in the air. "All this – this house, the cars, the money, all of it ...." She didn't have to finish the sentence. She didn't have to. Both of them were keenly aware of the repercussions.

"I know that, dear."

"Don't dear me, damn you," she hissed.

Her husband shrugged his shoulders. Paul Shaw was a tall man in his fifties, with a slight build and bookish, wire-frame eyeglasses. Nothing to look at, she'd always thought. But his appearance wasn't why she'd married him. Jessica did so because he was highly intelligent, unscrupulous, and was willing to put up with her domineering personality. He was also exceptional in bed, something you'd never suspect considering his non-descript appearance.

"Have you at least dealt with our latest problem?" she asked.

"Yes. The man I hired called me a while ago. He's contained the situation."

"You confirmed it?" she said with a glare.

"Of course. He sent me a photo of the body."

"Good," she replied, feeling a bit better. She stood and began pacing the dining room. "Still, this thing in Atlanta has me worried to death. The situation is completely out of control." She halted suddenly, scowled down at him. "Ever since Garcia went rogue and started selling Flash to others, it's put our operation in jeopardy."

"Stop worrying, Jessica – our plan is still on track."

"Easy for you to say," she spat out, her tone icy. "I'm the one who has to deal with the general." She began pacing again, her thoughts turning to the upcoming meeting. It would be a difficult one.

"I'm working on finding a replacement for Garcia."

"So you keep telling me, Paul. How's that coming?"

He took a bite of the linguine, then a sip of coffee before answering. "It's coming."

Jessica stopped in front of him, placed her hands on her hips. "That means you haven't found a replacement yet."

"Like I said, I'm working on it."

Jessica's face flushed, her anger boiling over. She stabbed a finger in his direction. "Remember our deal when we started this, Paul? I handle the sales end and you handle the production. Looks to me like you're not holding up your end of the bargain."

Paul shrugged. "I'll get it done. In the meantime, we have to put up with Garcia."

"When you find the replacement, you know we'll have to eliminate him."

"I'm aware of that, Jessica."

"And that won't be easy."

"I'm also aware of that."

"Damn it, Paul! How can you stay so calm?"

Paul gave her a thin smile. "We're different that way. You know that."

She glared at him, knowing he was right. She was the hot-tempered one. Still, it irritated her that he was so composed during this crisis. Jessica gulped in a few deep breaths, trying to calm herself. But it didn't work, her nerves were raw.

"We need to fuck," she stated flatly, knowing it was the only thing that relaxed her.

Paul took another forkful of pasta. "I'm not done with dinner yet."

"Screw that. You can finish later."

He gave her a long look. Obviously realizing she wouldn't take no for an answer, he nodded.

Turning, she left the room and strode up the wide, marble-step stairway to the master bedroom. She undressed, and once done, lay on her back on the king size bed, her legs dangling over the side.

Paul came in a moment later and began taking off his clothes.

"That won't be necessary," she said, "for what I had in mind." She spread her legs wide.

He nodded, and still fully clothed, knelt by the edge of the bed in front of her.

"You know what to do, Paul."

Leaning forward he began, his skillful tongue teasing and stroking her deliciously. A shiver of delight ran through her.

Jessica moaned from the pleasure, the tension of the day melting away. She realized once again why she'd married him, in spite of his many faults.

Using both hands, she grasped the back of his head and pressed it forward, forcing his tongue deeper inside her.

Jessica let out a guttural growl, as the waves of pleasure and pain washed over her in one long rush.

After catching her breath, she glanced at Paul. He wiped his mouth with one hand and stood up.

"It's my turn now," he said.

"Not yet," she replied, still hungry for more. She spread her legs wide again. "Get back here. I'm not done yet."

Chapter 18

FBI Offices
Atlanta, Georgia

J.T. Ryan looked out the floor-to-ceiling windows of Erin Welch's corner office, as he waited for the woman to return. It was a bright, sunny day with no clouds, and the city's impressive skyline spread out in every direction. From this vantage point on the 15th floor, Ryan thought, the gritty back streets of the city seemed very far away. It was an illusion the Chamber of Commerce continually emphasized. But he knew better, having dealt with the seamier side of the area for some time.

He heard the office door open and he glanced back, saw Erin enter the room and sit behind her desk.

"Sorry about the wait, J.T." She waved a hand in the air. "Damn meetings, you know how it is."

"I do," he replied as he sat on the visitor's chair fronting the desk. "That's why I never wanted to be in the Bureau."

"Lucky you."

The attractive woman looked frazzled. Her expensive black pants suit was wrinkled and her long blonde hair was carelessly pulled back in a pony tail.

"Bad day, Erin?"

"They're all bad days, now that the Director's gunning for me."

"How's that going?"

She tucked a loose strand of hair behind her ear. "Don't ask."

Ryan was about to make a wisecrack, then thought better of it – the woman was under a lot of stress – no sense in adding to it. He admired her, even if he didn't always like her.

"So," he said, "were you able to find any leads after searching Joe Miller's home?"

"Not yet. The lab guys are still working the forensics." She paused, rubbed her temple as if she had a headache. "Too bad you didn't get to question him."

"Yeah. But there's no doubt in my mind it was a professional hit."

"I agree. The assassin was a pro."

Ryan nodded. "The question is, who hired him?"

"Miller had a long rap sheet, and he was in a rough business – no doubt he had a lot of enemies."

"Get anything from the computer I found in his house, Erin?"

"Not yet. The files were encrypted – our tech guys are still working that angle."

The PI leaned back in the chair. "So we got nothing on nothing."

Erin's face flushed and her hands, which were resting on the desk, formed into fists. "Damn it, J.T., you don't have to state the obvious. I feel like shit as it is."

He chuckled. "Yeah. But you're the cutest FBI Assistant Director I know."

She stood up abruptly, her face a darker shade of crimson now. "Jesus, J.T., you're insufferable!"

Then she slouched back down on her chair and a minute later, began to laugh. After another moment, Erin shook her head slowly, trying to suppress a smile. "All right – enough with the jokes, okay?"

He grinned, knowing she felt better, even if she didn't want to admit it.

"Okay, Erin. How soon before we get something from the tech guys?"

"Maybe later today, more likely tomorrow."

Standing, he said, "Call me when you do."

"Don't worry, J.T. I've got you on speed dial."

***

Ryan drove to Grady hospital, and after spending time visiting Lauren, went to his mid-town office. Lauren was still in a coma, and it saddened him to see her this way. But it reinforced his resolve to solve the case and catch the bastards responsible for her condition.

He spent the next several hours at his office, doing paperwork, paying bills, and doing all the minutiae of running a small business. It was drudge work. Usually he hated it, much preferred being out in the field. But today he found the paperwork not as bad, taking his mind off Lauren at least for awhile.

When Ryan was done he went to the gym, worked out, and after a quick shower, headed home. On the way he stopped at a deli he frequented often, got a takeout dinner, and returned to his car, which was parked in the lot in front of the place.

Parked nearby was a black Ford sedan. He'd noticed a very similar car at the gym's parking lot. *A coincidence?* Ryan was always suspicious of those.

Taking note of the Ford's license plate, he climbed back in his car and fired it up.

His apartment was a short distance away, but instead of heading directly there, he took a circuitous route, stopping at a Kroger supermarket to buy food items he really didn't need. When he exited the market, he once again spotted the Ford sedan, parked by the curb a short distance away. The car's windows were tinted, and he couldn't make out who was driving, other than it was a man.

Ryan realized he was definitely being tailed. Normally he would have approached the car and confronted the driver, but the make and type of car gave him pause. That particular model was the vehicle of choice of government agencies.

He ignored the Ford and drove straight home.

After putting away the groceries, he pulled out his cell phone and dialed Erin's number.

"It's Ryan," he said, when she picked up. "Someone's been tailing me. I need you to run a plate for me."

"Okay," she replied, "What is it?"

He told her and he heard the tapping on a keyboard. A moment later she said, "You sure about the license number?"

"Of course."

"Shit, J.T. It's one of ours."

"What do you mean it's one of ours?"

"Just what I said," she repeated. "That car is from our FBI motor pool."

"Why the hell are you having me followed?" Ryan snapped.

"That's just it. I'm not."

"Christ. Things are worse than I thought at the Bureau. You hire me, and agents are tailing me without you knowing about it."

"God damn it, J.T. I'm starting to hate this job." Then Erin went into a rant, letting loose with a long string of curses.

When she was finished a minute later, he said, "Do you know what agent was driving the car?"

"Oh yeah. That's the worst part. I thought I could trust him."

"All right, Erin, at least we're wise to it now. I'll be on the lookout and do an SDR every time I'm working the case."

"Okay. Listen, the tech guys found some useful information from Joe Miller's laptop."

"Yeah? You found out where Flash is being produced?"

"No. They're still trying to break through the files, since most are encrypted. But they did uncover a lead. It appears Miller had a mistress on the side – a high-end hooker, actually. Looks like he frequented her place often."

"Got a name and address?"

Erin told him and he wrote it down.

After he was through with the call, he glanced at his watch. Not wanting to waste any time, he decided to eat quickly and head back out tonight to find the mistress.

***

Two hours later he pulled into the driveway of the upscale town-home in Dunwoody, an exclusive area north of the city. He would have been there sooner, but he'd taken a long, roundabout way to shake his tail. Confident he'd succeeded, he located the town-house.

Getting out of his Acura, he approached the entrance and rang the buzzer. Lights were on inside, and he could hear loud music coming from the place.

A tall, statuesque blonde wearing a white terry-cloth robe opened the door a moment later. She smelled of booze. Although she was attractive, she had a tired, almost haggard appearance. Her eyes were sunk in their sockets and had a glazed look. Ryan had seen that look before in drug addicts.

"Hi. Are you Margo?" he asked, over the din from the earsplitting rock music.

The blonde looked confused by the question.

"Are you Margo? My name's J.T., and I'm a friend of Joe Miller."

At the mention of Miller's name, the woman staggered back and slumped on a nearby sofa. She buried her head in her hands, and he heard muffled sobs.

Stepping inside, he closed the door behind him.

He scanned the living room quickly, saw no one else. As he waited for the woman to cry herself out, he went to the stereo on the bookcase and lowered the volume. Seeing that her crying jag continued, he left the room and quickly searched the rest of the town-home. Finding no one, he returned to the living room.

After wiping her tears, Margo said, "You ... knew... Joe? ... I ... loved ... him ... he was ... so good ... to ... me...." She spoke very slowly, as if in a fog. Her eyes, now red-rimmed, still had that glazed look.

"Yeah, I knew Joe. He talked about you all the time," Ryan lied.

"He ... did?" She started sobbing again, and he waited for her to compose herself. It was obvious she was grief-stricken, but her behavior seemed more peculiar. By her smell, she'd obviously been drinking. *Was she high on drugs too?*

Ryan sat down next to her on the sofa. "I'm sorry for your loss, Margo."

She nodded. "I ... don't ... know ... what I'm ... going to do ... without ... him ...."

"Listen, Margo, I'm one of his business partners, and I needed to square away some things. I'm hoping you can help me."

She gave him a vacant look, as if she didn't understand his statement. Standing up abruptly, she said, "I got ... to take ... some ... medicine ... I'll be ... right back ...."

Margo left the room, he heard the sound of running water, and minutes later she was back.

When she sat down on the couch, she appeared much more alert, and her eyes shone with a bright intensity. "You said your name was J.T? I don't remember him talking about you." She spoke very quickly, rushing her words together.

"That's right. I did business with him."

"What kind of business?" she asked rapidly.

"He sold me product."

"What kind of product?"

Ryan grinned. "Let's just say it wasn't legal."

"You a cop?"

"Of course not, Margo."

She gave him a hard look. "What do you want with me?"

Whatever medicine she had taken had eliminated her confusion and grief. She appeared much more intelligent than before. *Was Flash the 'medicine' she had taken?* The change in her personality might indicate that, he thought.

"Information," he said. "And I'm willing to pay for it."

"Just information? The men I meet come for sex. I'm expensive."

"So I've heard."

"I'm not some cheap hooker, giving blow jobs for twenty bucks, you know."

"I know that, Margo. Joe thought a lot of you."

"Bullshit. Joe had a frigid wife. He just needed me to get his rocks off."

Ryan nodded. "Listen, I'm not here for sex. I just need information. He sold me narcotics, a particular kind. Now that he's dead, I need to find the source."

"How much?" she asked.

"How much what?"

"How much are you willing to pay?"

"A lot, if the info is accurate."

She crossed her arms across her chest and studied him, as if trying to figure out if she could trust him. "Let's see the cash first."

He took out his wallet and he pulled out five hundred-dollar bills. H usually didn't carry that much on him, but he came prepared, knowing the woman was expensive.

"Not enough," she sniffed, "but it's a good start. She reached for the money, but he pulled it away.

"You saw the cash, Margo. I want the info before I hand it over."

"Okay. What do you want to know?"

"I was buying Skyflash from Joe. I want more of it."

Her eyes lit up at the name of the drug. "You know about Skyflash? I thought you wanted cocaine."

"Forget that stuff – that's crap. I need Flash."

"So do I," Margo said, licking her lips. "I need it too."

"You're hooked on it, aren't you?"

"Fuck yes!" she cried out. "Joe started me on it. God, I loved him for it. That shit is sweet – the best drug I've ever had ..." her eyes clouded over a moment. "Now that he's gone ...."

She shivered, and she hugged herself as if she was cold. "God, I need another fix ...."

"Is that what you took a little while ago?"

"Hell, yes! But I didn't take enough, shit I'm running out, I only have a little left, I've got to get more, God, I gotto find some more ...." She said this breathlessly, in one long rush, the words running together.

A look of desperation came over her face – the woman was showing signs of drug withdrawal. She was junkie who needed a fix. And fast.

"I can help you get more, Margo. But first you have to tell me what you know."

"Yeah, fuck yeah, I'll tell you what you want to know, God I need a fix, please help me, God damn it, please ...."

"Sure, Margo. Did Joe produce the Flash here in Atlanta?"

"What?"

"Did he make it in a lab somewhere locally?"

She seemed confused by the question – now that the effect of the drug was fading, he suspected she was reverting back to her normal personality – a woman lacking intelligence.

After a moment, Margo shook her head. "No. He told me ... he got it... from ... Tampa," her words came out slowly, haltingly. "The stuff ... comes ... from there ..."

"Who is his contact in Tampa?"

"Contact? What ... do you ... mean?"

"Who did he deal with, Margo? What's their name?"

"I don't ... know ... I don't know ... who it is ... please ... you ... have to help me ... I need more Flash ... please help me ...."

"I'm trying to, Margo."

She stood up suddenly, unfastened the sash of her robe and let the garment fall to the floor. "I'll do anything ... you want ... I don't care about ... your money ... just get me ... the drug ...."

Ryan stared at her voluptuous nude body with its pendulous breasts and well-rounded hips. The blonde was very good-looking, and he was aroused, in spite of the tense situation.

Pushing those thoughts aside, he said, "Tell me about the Tampa connection. Who is it?"

Ignoring his question, she reached out with her hand, grabbed desperately at the crotch of his pants. "Please ... I need Flash ..." She began stroking him over his pants, a look of desperation in her sunken eyes.

His arousal intensified, and it took every ounce of self-control to gently push her hand away.

She sank to her knees and began to cry.

Picking the robe off the floor, he wrapped it around her and, helping her to her feet, guided her back to the sofa. He sat next her, watched as her crying jag continued unabatedly for several minutes.

When she stopped, she looked at him, a confused look on her face. "Who ... are ... you?"

"I'm J.T., remember? Joe's friend."

She wiped her eyes with both hands, then she shivered. "Joe? Who's ... Joe?"

She's too far gone, thought Ryan. With a sinking feeling he realized he wouldn't get any more out of Margo, at least not today.

Chapter 19

Cartagena, Colombia

Jose Garcia stared out the windows of his study, located on the second floor of his hacienda. The study overlooked an expansive garden and beyond that he could make out the city skyline in the distance.

The phone on his mahogany desk rang and he walked over and picked up the receiver. He had been expecting the pre-arranged call, and was not looking forward to it.

Sitting behind the desk, Garcia said, "Hello Paul."

"Jose," Paul Shaw replied, "how are you?" The call was encrypted and scrambled, and Shaw's voice sounded tinny.

"I am fine, my friend. In your email you mentioned you had an urgent matter to discuss."

"That's right, Jose. It appears your product is somehow being distributed in Atlanta."

Garcia paused a moment, trying to decide on how to answer. "Really? I don't see how that's possible," the drug dealer lied. "You have exclusive rights to it."

"Yes. That's why I'm calling. This is a big problem for us. It puts our whole project in jeopardy."

"I understand, my friend," Garcia replied. "I don't see how it could have happened. One of my middle-men must have diverted a shipment by mistake."

"I see. That's what I thought. I hated to even bring this up, but you know Jessica – she's a worrier."

At the mention of Jessica, Paul's wife, Garcia's blood pressure spiked. He hated the American bitch and her domineering attitude. "Please tell her not to worry so much. I will call my people today, make sure the product is only delivered to you."

"That's what I wanted to hear, Jose. I'll let Jessica know you're taking care of the situation. By the way, how's the weather in Cartagena? I've been thinking of visiting you soon."

"You are welcome to come anytime, my friend. But it's hot and humid here, even in November. Not as nice as where you are."

Paul Shaw laughed. "You're right about that – the weather in St. Croix is beautiful today – 72 degrees, with a cooling breeze. Okay, Jose. It was good talking with you. See you soon."

Garcia said goodbye and hung up the phone.

Leaning forward in his chair, he selected a cigar from the humidor on his desk and lit it up. After taking a few puffs, he picked up the phone and made a call.

Two minutes later his trusted lieutenant, Manuel Ochado, came into the study and stood in front of the desk.

"Manuel," Garcia said, "remember the shipment of Skyflash we sold to our Tampa distributor?"

"Of course, *senor*."

"It's creating a bit of problem for the Shaw's."

Ochado nodded. "I see."

"Let's hold up on any more of that for the time being."

"*Si, senor*." The lieutenant turned to go, then faced Garcia once again. "Last week you told me to ship some of the product to our Los Angeles and Phoenix people. Should I cancel that?"

"Put a hold on that as well, Manuel," Garcia replied, mulling over the huge potential profit of expanding into those areas. "But it's only a temporary delay. As soon as this blows over, we'll start again."

"*Si, senor*."

As soon as Ochado left the room, Garcia stood and went to the windows, staring out at the bright, sunny day. A smile spread on his lips, as he thought about Skyflash, and its incredible money-making potential. It was more profitable than the other narcotics he sold, cocaine, meth and heroin. He found it humorous that Paul Shaw had come up with the formula for the drug and had bankrolled part of the factory in Colombia.

Garcia chuckled, realizing that he was in the driver's seat. Yes, he had a contract with the Shaw's for exclusivity. But what the hell was a contract, anyway? Only a piece of paper. He puffed on his large cigar, and continued staring out the windows.

Chapter 20

Washington, D.C.

"I've been reading the newspapers," General Robert Burke said, after taking a sip of his vodka. "What's happening in Atlanta has me worried."

Jessica Shaw placed her wine glass on the table and stared at Burke as she thought about what to say. She had dreaded this meeting, but knew it was unavoidable. The two people were in an out of the way, nondescript restaurant on the outskirts of the city, far from the corridors of power. They were sitting in a booth at the back, well away from the other diners.

Tonight Burke was wearing a suit and tie, but even without his Army uniform it was clear from his short cropped hair and precise bearing that he was military. Burke was a brigadier, a one-star general, but she knew he hungered for much more.

"We've contained the situation," Jessica replied, with a tone of confidence she didn't feel.

Burke gave her a hard look. "Have you?"

"Yes."

"You'd better have, Jessica." He took another long pull from his drink, draining it. He signaled the waiter for a refill.

Burke leaned forward in his chair. "When I gave you the contract for the project a year ago, you assured me I'd have an exclusive on your product."

"And you do, General. We've just run into a slight complication."

The waiter returned with fresh drinks for both of them and Burke waited for the man to leave, then said, "If I'm reading in the *Washington Post* about people dying in Atlanta from the product, I wouldn't classify that as a 'slight complication'."

"Don't worry. I told you we're handling it."

"Easy for you to say. I stand to lose everything I've worked for the last twenty years." He paused and held a thumb and forefinger in the air. "I'm this close from getting my second star."

Jessica was starting to despise the greedy man. *Fuck him*, she thought. Once this contract was done, she never wanted to set eyes on him again.

"But if this thing blows up in our face," he continued, "I'll be lucky to stay out of a military prison."

She took a sip of wine, but said nothing.

"I think, Jessica, since things aren't as rosy as you predicted a year ago, that we should renegotiate our contract."

A stab of fear surged up inside her. "What do you mean?"

Burke mentioned a monetary sum, an amount much different than what they had agreed to previously.

"That's unacceptable, General."

"Is it?" he replied, his voice cold. "I could cancel everything right now. How would that be?"

She knew her options were limited. She and Paul were counting on the original agreement. The higher kickback amount Burke was demanding would substantially decrease their own profit. And to make things worse, the Shaw's had already spent lavishly in anticipation of the payoff.

"What's you're answer, Jessica?"

She swallowed hard. "I accept your new terms."

"Smart girl," he said condescendingly.

Her anger welled up at hearing the bastard call her that. *I'm nobody's girl*, she thought, her hatred for Burke escalating. But she kept her resentment in check, instead plastered a fake smile on her face.

"Once we get the next installment payment from the Defense Department," she said, "I'll wire you the new kickback amount to your offshore account."

He returned the smile, and then downed his drink. He signaled the waiter for another.

Chapter 21

Atlanta, Georgia

Ryan was in his mid-town office reading a case file when he heard a knock at the door.

It opened and Erin Welch stepped in, a dejected expression on her face. She took off her Burberry raincoat and sat on one of the visitors chairs fronting his desk.

"Got any coffee, J.T.?"

He closed the file and laid it on the desk. "Things must be *really* bad," he replied with a grin, "when you'll drink my coffee."

She scowled. "I'm in no mood for jokes. It's been a terrible day." Today she was wearing an expensive looking navy jacket and matching skirt with a gray silk blouse. A cultured pearl necklace was draped on her neck; Ryan knew the woman only wore Hanadama grade pearls, the highest quality. Her long blonde hair was pulled into a ponytail and her eyes looked tired, as if she'd hadn't had much sleep.

Ryan got up, went to the coffee maker on top of the filing cabinet and poured two cups. Handing her one of the styrofoam cups, he sat back down.

Erin took a sip and grimaced. "This is crap." She placed the cup on his desk.

"Yeah, but it's hot," he replied, taking a sip from his. It didn't taste *that* bad to him, but he knew his culinary standards were low.

"It may be, but it's still swill."

He leaned back in his chair. "So. To what do I owe the honor of this visit? It's not everyday I get an ADIC gracing my sumptuous office. We usually meet at your building."

She glanced around the small area, as if noticing the sparse decor for the first time. The office contained his metal desk, three chairs, and metal filing cabinets. The floor was covered with industrial gray carpet and there were only three items hanging on the walls: his Private Investigator's License, his college diploma from Georgia State, and his U.S. Army Officers Commission certificate, all on inexpensive frames. Resting on his desk was a photo of Lauren, a black desk phone, and stacks of file folders.

"I wouldn't call it sumptuous, J.T."

He laughed. "It's adequate."

"You should have Lauren decorate it –" she blurted out, then caught herself in mid-sentence.

At the mention of his girlfriend's name, his heart sank.

"Sorry, J.T. How's she doing?"

Ryan shook his head slowly. "The same. No change."

She nodded and they were both quiet for a moment.

"So, did you come here for the coffee," he said, wanting to change the subject, "or to listen to my charming wit?"

"Actually, I had to get out of the FBI building for a while and clear my head. My boss is driving me crazy."

"He's still gunning for you?"

"Every day."

"Well, as soon as we solve the case, the pressure will come off."

She frowned. "Maybe. Maybe not. Regardless, I still have to solve it."

He smiled in an attempt to lighten her mood. "I've got your back, Erin. We'll solve it."

"I wish I were that confident," she replied. "I have some news about the case, and it's not good."

Ryan tensed. "What is it?"

"Remember the laptop you found at Joe Miller's house in Stone Mountain?"

"Yeah?"

"Well, as you know the files were encrypted. My tech guys have been trying to break the encryption. To make a long story short, during the process, the computer fried itself."

He leaned forward in the chair. "So – the drug dealer installed mal-ware – once your guys got close to breaking through, his security program kicked in, erasing the files and burning out the hard drive."

"Exactly, J.T."

"Christ – I was sure we'd get info from that."

"Me too," she replied. "Except I used a lot stronger language when I heard about it. I really lit into my tech guys. But after I calmed down, I realized it wasn't their fault."

Ryan shook his head. "We're back to square one. We got nothing on nothing."

"Not quite," she said. "I was able to find out some things."

He felt a glimmer of hope. "What?"

Erin tucked a loose strand of her hair behind her ear. "I personally questioned Joe Miller's mistress, Margo. I spent several hours with her, and I learned some things about the source of the Flash." She paused. "In between her crying jags, Margo was helpful."

"How so?"

Then Erin told him.

Chapter 22

Tampa, Florida

J.T. Ryan gazed out the jet's window at Tampa's urban sprawl down below. His Delta flight from Atlanta was circling over the airport, waiting to land.

The flight was packed with passengers. He'd been lucky to get an aisle seat, which gave him the most leg room. His tall, rugged build was a tight fit for the cramped coach-class seats. He would have preferred first-class, but his FBI contract didn't cover it. An elderly couple was sitting in the seats next to him, who luckily had been quiet the whole flight. *There's nothing worse*, he thought, *than screaming kids in a packed airplane.*

As he continued looking out at the window, his thoughts focused on the case. During her interrogation of Margo, Erin Welch had been successful in learning a few things about the source of the Flash. Unfortunately, it wasn't much. According to the mistress, the drug came from somewhere in the Tampa area, and it appeared that commercial flights were being used to transport the narcotic. The Tampa metro area spread out over four counties and had a population of over four million people. So his upcoming search was similar to looking for a needle in a haystack.

During his years in the Army, Ryan had been stationed for a time at MacDill Air Force Base, the operations center for the U.S. military's Special Forces Command (SOCOM). There he had worked with some very proficient Special Forces soldiers, in particular an NCO, a female sergeant named Ana Martinez. He hoped she could help him generate some leads. Before leaving for this trip, Ryan had called her and arranged to meet.

He heard the jet's flaps creaking as they were lowered, and a moment later he felt the plane decelerate as it went into final approach over the runway.

After deplaning, he grabbed his bag from baggage claim and headed for the Hertz counter, where he rented a car. He also called Sergeant Martinez to let her know he'd landed.

Locating the Chevy Impala in the rental lot, he climbed in and made the short drive from the airport to MacDill. The sprawling base had very tight security, and if he hadn't been cleared by Martinez, he would have had a more difficult time getting in. After driving through the front gate, he made his way to the Non-Commissioned Officers Club, which was located on the south side of the base.

He parked the Impala and entered the large NCO club, which was mostly empty – not surprising, he thought, since it was mid-morning. He spotted Martinez right away, sitting at a booth in the back.

Ryan walked over and she got up and they shook hands.

"Good to see you, Captain Ryan," she said. "It's been awhile, sir."

"Yes, it has," he said with a smile. "And you can drop the sir part. I'm not in the Army anymore. Call me J.T."

She smiled back. "Sure thing. Call me Ana, then."

They sat down on opposite sides of the booth, as he studied her. She was an attractive Hispanic woman in her mid-thirties. She was wearing her military fatigue uniform, its loose, baggy fit not flattering to her trim figure.

"I was surprised by your call, Captain ... I mean J.T."

"Sorry I haven't kept in touch," he replied. "After I left the service, I got my P.I. license and haven't been back to Tampa."

He noticed the added stripe on the rank insignia of her uniform. "I see you made Sergeant First Class – congrats on the promotion."

"Thanks."

"Still happy with Army life?"

"I can't complain," she replied with a shrug. "I'm so used to being in the military, I don't know what I'd do without it."

"You're a bright woman, Ana. I always figured you'd go into Officer Candidate School and make lieutenant."

She smiled. "I like being a sergeant. You know, work for a living."

Ryan laughed. It was a long running joke between officers and enlisted personnel, sergeants always pointing out how important a role they played in the military. "You're right about that."

He flagged down a waiter and they ordered coffee. When the server moved away, Ryan said, "As I told you on the phone, I'm working on a case and I'm hoping you can help."

"Sure thing. Anything I can do."

Ryan leaned forward in his seat and lowered his voice. "I'm working with the FBI on a drug case. A new, illegal narcotic has turned up in Atlanta. It's responsible for the deaths of several people. It appears this drug is coming from Tampa."

She nodded. "I see. I assume you'll be talking to local PD here?"

"My boss at the Bureau is handling that on her end. And frankly, I prefer it that way. I find that if I work directly with people I know personally and trust, I get better results."

The waiter returned with their coffees. He placed them on the table and moved away.

After taking a sip, he said, "You grew up in this area, didn't you, Ana?"

"That's right. It's funny that I've been stationed all over the world while in the service, but my longest duty has been right here. I live across the bay, in Clearwater."

"That's why I thought of you. I figured anyone who had spent so much time here would know the lay of the land."

She nodded and he drank more of his coffee.

"The name of this drug is Skyflash. Most people refer to it by its street name, Flash. Ever heard of it?"

"No, Captain. Most of the crime in Tampa is associated with cocaine and meth."

"You're attached to the Intelligence unit here at MacDill?"

"That's right. I work on information gathering for special operations in the Middle East. Satellite images, that type of thing."

He took another sip of the strong, savory coffee. *It's a lot better than the stuff I make*, he mused. "Do you have access to domestic intelligence? Drug running, in and out of the area?"

"I might be able to access that," she replied, a hesitant look on her face. "But I'd be breaking several Army regs ...."

Ryan lowered his voice so it was no more than a whisper. "Normally I wouldn't ask, but this is personal. My girlfriend is in a coma because of this drug, so solving this case is more than a job to me."

Martinez leaned back in the seat and was quiet for a few moments.

"You got me out of some tight jams when we were both in Afghanistan," she said, "so what the hell, I'll help you."

Ryan nodded. "Good. Let me give you some specifics that may narrow the search. The guy that was distributing Flash in Atlanta was named Joe Miller – he's dead now, along with his family – someone ordered a hit on him. Miller wasn't a low-life crack dealer – he was affluent and well-connected – so my guess is whoever is distributing the stuff in Tampa is a major player." Ryan continued, giving her a ten minute summary on the details of the case.

"Okay," she said. "That's useful. I'll start working on this right away. As soon as I have something, I'll call you. Where are you staying locally?"

"At the Marriott on West Shore Drive, not far from here."

She glanced around the NCO club, which was beginning to fill up from the lunch crowd. "Next time we meet, sir, we should do it off-base. I want to help you, but I've got a career to protect."

***

Sergeant Martinez lived in Clearwater Beach, a half-hour's drive from McDill. The non-descript high-rise building didn't overlook the beach, but rather was three blocks inland. No doubt it was a much less expensive apartment than the pricey units fronting the ocean.

After taking the elevator to the 8th floor, Ryan located the right apartment and knocked on the door.

Ana opened it a minute later, a smile on her face. "Come in, sir." Today she was dressed in civilian clothes, a blue polo shirt and tailored tan slacks, which showed off her trim figure much better than her fatigues. He noticed she had applied light makeup and a hint of perfume.

He smiled back and entered. "J.T., remember?"

"Sorry, sir – it's a hard habit to break."

"I know what you mean."

Ryan glanced around the small living room, which was furnished in simple, inexpensive furniture. But the place was spotless and very orderly, with everything in its place. A group of magazines was stacked neatly on the coffee table and the books in the bookcase were organized by size.

She pointed to the small balcony at the far end of the living room. "I thought we'd eat out there. I usually do."

"Sounds good."

"Can I get you something to drink, J.T.?"

"I'll have a beer, if you have it."

"Go on outside and I'll go get it."

Ryan stepped out on the terrace, which overlooked a traffic choked boulevard below. It was late November and the tourist season was in full swing, the snowbirds from Michigan, Wisconsin, and New York flocking to the area's beautiful weather. It was 73 degrees and a light breeze was blowing. He breathed in the scent of clean sea air.

He sat down at the small dining table, which had already been set out with silverware and covered dishes.

Ana came out moments later carrying two bottles of Budweiser. Handing him one, she sat across from him. "Cheers," she said, taking a sip from hers.

"Cheers," he replied, doing the same.

She pointed out toward the ocean, a sliver of which was visible in the distance, in between other high-rise buildings. "According to the realtor who sold me this condo, this unit has an ocean view."

He chuckled as he looked out. The sun was beginning to set on the horizon, casting a soft orange glow over the terrace. "It's nice here. Now I know why you like it so much."

"Once I retire from the military, I plan to stay in the Tampa area."

"Good for you, Ana."

"Sorry I didn't call sooner. But it took me a couple of days to track down the info." She frowned. "I had to be careful and cover my tracks."

"No problem."

Ana took a pull from her beer, then said, "I found out some interesting information. A local thug by the name of Robb Fornell has had a lot of contact with your Atlanta drug dealer, Joe Miller. I found records of phone calls and emails going back and forth. They were encrypted, so I couldn't see or hear everything they said, but our intel software was able to break through somewhat. There's enough contact to know they weren't casual acquaintances – they were doing business with each other."

"Good work, Sergeant."

"Fornell has a long rap sheet, mostly dealing narcotics and illegal firearms. He did time at Florida State Prison in Raiford." She glanced at the covered dishes. "Damn. The food's going to get cold. Let's eat while we talk."

"Sure. I'm starved."

Ana uncovered the platters and served the veal piccata and red potatoes on the dishes and handed him one. The food looked and smelled scrumptious.

He took a bite of the savory veal. "Didn't know you were a gourmet cook."

"It's a hobby. But I don't get to show it off much. Most nights I eat alone."

Ryan studied her dusky, attractive features. "You're a good looking woman. I'm surprised you're not married."

She shrugged. "It's not for lack of trying. I'm twice divorced. Now I'm resigned to single life."

He took a sip of the Budweiser. "Don't give up hope. The right guy is out there – you just haven't found him yet."

"I guess ...." She leaned back in the chair and looked pensive. After a long moment, her eyes narrowed. "Well, enough about that. Let me fill you in on the drug dealer, Fornell. From what I was able to piece together, this guy brings narcotics into the U.S. via drug mules. Mostly he uses young women who swallow prophylactics filled with the stuff. That's how they get it through security at Tampa Airport. The women fly in on commercial flights and after that the drugs get distributed by truck or vans to other parts of the U.S."

Ryan nodded. "What kind of drugs? Flash?"

She took a bite of the food, then wiped her lips with a paper napkin. "No way to know. Fornell's been busted for heroin and cocaine before. My guess is those are his main staples."

A gust of wind circulated into the balcony, the scent of sea air strong.

"That's good info, Ana. What else can you tell me about this guy?"

"I think he's a mid-level dealer – he doesn't run the show, from what I could tell."

"Yeah, but he could lead me to the bigger fish. Any idea where I can find him?"

"I found records of calls from his cell phone to a warehouse on Waters Avenue in Tampa." She told him the street number.

Ryan smiled. "Excellent. I'm going to have the FBI cut you a check."

Ana shook her head. "No need. Having you around is all the thanks I need."

There was an awkward silence for a minute as they studied each other. Deep down, he'd always known she had feelings for him, and he had been attracted to her in return. But back then he was her commanding officer and that was a line neither of them had wanted to cross.

"As I told you before," Ryan said, "I'm in a committed relationship."

Ana smiled sadly. "I know, J.T. I always hoped we'd eventually get together – but I know now it's never going to happen."

Ryan nodded, and they continued eating the meal while talking about the case.

When they were done he helped her take the empty plates back to the kitchen. They grabbed fresh beers and went back out to the terrace.

The sun had set and the temperature had cooled to the mid sixties.

As they sipped their drinks, they leaned over the railing and looked out toward the sliver of ocean view.

"So," she said, "what are your plans now?"

"I go find Fornell."

"Will you need any more of my help, J.T.?"

"No thanks. I like to work alone. And anyway, you've already done more than enough. I don't want you getting into trouble with the Army over this."

She turned toward him, smiled and placed a hand on his arm. "You're welcome to stay here. It's too late to start looking for Fornell tonight."

He glanced at his watch and realized she was right. *I'll start tomorrow morning.* Then he looked back at her. They were less than a foot apart and he breathed in the scent of her perfume. After three beers, he felt the sexual tension between them even more.

Then the image of Lauren in a coma filled his thoughts. "I think I better go now, Ana, and head back to the Marriott."

She gave him a sad smile and slowly pulled her hand away. "I understand."

They finished their Budweisers in silence, and after an awkward goodbye, he left the apartment.

Chapter 23

St. Croix, U.S. Virgin Islands
the Caribbean

Jessica Shaw parked her white Rolls-Royce Phantom Coupe in the semi-circular driveway that fronted her large estate. Climbing out of the car, she got her suitcase from the trunk and stormed into the house.

Dropping the bag in the marble floor foyer, she let out a long breath. Exhausted and still aggravated from her trip, she yelled out, "Paul, I'm home."

Not hearing a response, she went through the vacant, luxuriously-appointed living room, the spacious dining room, and finally the state-of-the-art kitchen. Not finding her husband, she checked the attached three-car garage and saw his Mercedes sedan parked there. "Where the hell is that man," she muttered, her irritation growing. She strode up the wide, marble step stairway to the second floor.

Hearing music coming from the den on that floor, she barged in, saw her husband reclining on the leather sofa, holding a hardback book.

"You're home," Paul Shaw said with a smile.

She marched over and crossed her arms. "Hell, yes, I'm home. I've been looking for you for ten minutes."

He closed the book and set it on the glass-topped coffee table. "How was your trip?"

"How do you think it went," she spat out.

Paul frowned. "That bad?"

"Worse."

Jessica realized the music coming from the speakers was jazz. "How can you listen to that crap, Paul?"

"Actually, I like it."

She crossed the room and turned off the stereo. Then she began pacing the den, her thoughts still churning about her trip.

"Can I get you a drink?" her husband asked calmly.

"No, damn it. That's not going to help."

"Tell me about your meeting with Burke."

Jessica stopped pacing and scowled at him. "It didn't go well. Not well at all. The newspapers in D.C. covered the deaths in Atlanta. He's worried and pissed." She continued pacing. "Not that I can blame him. We *did* guarantee exclusivity on Flash."

Paul got up from the sofa and, going to a side cabinet, poured himself a glass of white wine. After taking a sip, he turned back to her, "Don't worry, Jessica. It's all going to work out."

Her cold, black eyes bored into his. "How the hell can you be so calm about this?" *God, he's infuriating*, she thought. *Why in hell did I ever marry him?*

"Please don't worry," he repeated.

"God damn you! Don't tell me not to worry. Our plan is falling apart and I find you reading a book. I could *strangle* you right now!"

"Please. Settle down."

"Fuck you, Paul," she screeched.

Then she slumped down on a leather armchair, the aggravation and fatigue feeling like a thousand pound weight on her shoulders. She sat still for several minutes trying to calm herself.

She looked up at him. "I haven't told you the worse part."

He was standing in front of her, and a frown crossed his face. "What is it?"

"The fucking general renegotiated our contract. We'll be getting a lot less than we counted on."

"How much less?"

Jessica told him, and for the first time today, he looked worried.

He downed his drink and sat on the sofa across from her. "That's not good."

"That's all you can say?" Jessica spat out, venom in her voice. "That it's not good? It's a fucking disaster, Paul!"

She waved a hand in the air. "All this – this house, the furniture, my Rolls – we bought all of it on borrowed money. We were counting on *every* penny of that contract!"

Paul stood up, walked over to her and placed a hand on her shoulder. "Calm down. We can still make it work. We'll just have to cut back on a few things, sell some of our assets."

She pushed his hand away and stared up at him. "I like this lifestyle! I don't want to cut back!"

Paul sighed, as if realizing nothing he could say would make her feel better. He went back to the sofa and sat down.

A new thought struck her. "Tell me about your trip to Colombia."

He took off his bookish, wire-frame eyeglasses and began cleaning them with a handkerchief. "I didn't go yet."

"What?" she spat out, her rage boiling over. She stabbed a finger in the air at him. "You said you were going down there to see Garcia and straighten him out."

Paul put his eyeglasses back on. "I called him and talked with him."

"You *called* him?" she said acidly. "You fucking *called* him? You need to fucking get down there and take care of this. *Now!*"

"Don't worry, Jessica. I told Garcia we were concerned that we weren't the only ones getting Flash."

Her blood pressure spiked and she bolted up from the armchair. "Concerned? We're more than fucking *concerned*. I'm mad as hell! When we started this whole project I said I'd take care of the sales end and you were supposed to take care of the production end." She placed her hands on her hips. "But now I'm wondering if you have the balls to handle Garcia. Maybe I should go to Colombia and kick his ass myself."

"I don't think that's a good idea," Paul said, a sheepish look on his face. "He doesn't like you very much."

Jessica stabbed a finger in the air at him again. "How close are you to finding a replacement for Garcia? We need another supplier – one we can trust. Just find a new lab, give them the formula you developed and the key ingredient."

He rubbed his forehead. "I'm working on that."

"We've talked about this before – can't you find a lab locally?"

"That's too dangerous, Jessica. You know the key ingredient comes from the blue flower only grown here. There's too much risk a local lab in St. Croix could figure out the formula. We have to find a manufacturing operation away from here."

"Well? Get it done!"

"I'm working on it."

"That just means you failed. You've been telling me the same thing for weeks. And to make matters worse, I find you reading a book and listening to music, while I'm busting my ass trying to clean up the mess."

"I really am working on it, hon. Please understand. I just haven't found a suitable replacement. I'm sorry, Jessica."

"Sorry? Sorry doesn't cut it anymore." She paused, her body literally shaking in anger, her face bright red. "My father warned me about you. Before we got married, he told me he thought you weren't enough of a man to handle me. I *should* have listened to him."

A shocked expression crossed his face. "Please, Jessica. Don't say things like that. You know how much I love you."

"Love? What the fuck is that? We had an arrangement. You're the intelligent one. You're the genius at chemistry. I figured with your brains and my *chutzpa*, we'd make a fortune. But now? I'm not sure anymore. I still want that brass ring. I'm not settling for second best. I want to be fucking rich."

Paul's shoulders slumped as he continued sitting on the sofa. He seemed crestfallen at her tirade, but he remained quiet, saying nothing in reply.

She glared down at him, trying to control her rage. But it wasn't working. She knew there was only one thing that would calm her nerves.

"We need to fuck, Paul."

He stared at her, a blank look on his face, as if he didn't understand. "What?"

"Just what I said, damn it. We need to fuck. Right now."

He shook his head. "I can't. I'm too upset. We're both too upset. Later, maybe ...."

She slapped him hard across his face, his glasses flew off and he flinched away from her.

"I said now, Paul."

Her husband rubbed the bright red mark on his cheek. "I don't feel well ... I'm not sure I can even get it up right now ...."

She crossed her arms across her chest. "You don't need an erection for what I want. You just have to give me an orgasm. Several in fact. You know the drill by now. I spread my legs and you let your tongue do all the work."

"But ...."

"I need this, Paul. I want this. And I'm going to get this. The way I figure it," she continued, venom dripping from her voice, "if you're not man enough to handle our business problems, you might as well make yourself useful and service me."

Paul was quiet for several minutes, his face showing a succession of emotions – fear, sadness, and eventually resignation. Finally he nodded.

Jessica smiled, her anticipation of what was to come replacing her anger. "Let's go to the bedroom," she ordered.

Then she turned and left the room.

Chapter 24

Tampa, Florida

J.T Ryan drove slowly past the warehouse on Waters Avenue, looking for any activity. He spotted only three vehicles in the parking lot, a Honda Civic, a battered pickup truck, and a new Lincoln sedan. It was 2 a.m. and he'd picked the time on purpose, hoping for minimal activity. A good time to break in.

Ryan had spent the previous day doing surveillance on Robb Fornell's building, trying to ascertain the comings and goings. The warehouse was a busy place – small trucks and vans making deliveries and pickups throughout the day. He'd also identified the most expensive vehicle in the parking lot, the brand new Lincoln, figuring this was Fornell's car. Unfortunately that car never left the lot during the day, so he couldn't follow it and find out where the man lived.

He cruised on the mostly deserted four-lane road, looking for an inconspicuous place to park. This part of Tampa was mostly industrial: warehouses and factories. Two blocks away he found an empty lot, pulled in, and parked the rented Chevy Impala. Taking his wallet out of his pants pocket, he locked it in the glove box. Then after checking the load in his revolver, he replaced it in his hip holster and zipped up his windbreaker.

A lifetime user of semi-automatic handguns, Ryan had switched to his current weapon a year ago. Although he preferred the larger magazine capacity of his previous 9mm pistol, he'd made the switch after the gun jammed and nearly cost him his life. Now he liked the revolver, a weapon that literally could not jam. He carried a Smith & Wesson .357 Magnum with the two-inch barrel. Enough power to go through an engine block, but still compact enough to fit discretely under a jacket. True, it only held six rounds, but he knew most close-quarter conflicts were resolved with three, no matter what you saw in the movies, where dozens of bullets were exchanged. Erin Welch called him old-school for preferring a revolver, but he laughed that off – better to be alive than fashionable.

After glancing around the empty lot, he got out of the car, locked it, and started walking toward the warehouse. It was cool night, in the low sixties with an overcast sky. The area smelled of gasoline fumes and machine oil, no doubt from the industrial businesses.

He neared Fornell's building moments later and stopped short of it, watching closely for activity. Other than the dim lighting coming from one of the front windows, he spotted nothing. Outdoor floodlights illuminated the three vehicles in the lot. He figured two of them belonged to factory workers or guards, and the Lincoln to Fornell, signifying the man was inside now. Ryan had contacted Welch yesterday and asked her to find a home address for the drug dealer, but she had come up empty. It appeared Fornell covered his tracks well and was able to keep his address a secret.

The PI approached the warehouse, went around the side and towards the back, hugging the walls in order to avoid detection. He saw several closed loading bays and finally found what he was looking for – a regular-size door. He also spotted wall-mounted security cameras, one of them pointing down toward the back entrance. Praying the cameras weren't being monitored 24/7, he pulled his gun and sprinted toward the door, where he paused to inspect the entry mechanism. It was a keypad, the type you punch in a passcode. The door itself was heavy-duty metal, with no exterior lock mechanism. Ryan realized he wouldn't be able to pick the lock and knew entering the wrong password more than three times would likely set off an alarm. He'd brought along a small crowbar, in case he'd have to pry open a door – but here again an alarm would go off.

He checked the time: 2:32 a.m. *Should I wait out here*, he thought, *and hope someone comes out? Or should I pry open the door and barge in?*

Before he could decide, he heard the racking of a shotgun from behind him. "Freeze right there!" a man's voice yelled.

Ryan whirled around, found a heavy-set guy with a ponytail pointing a Mossberg shotgun at him. He was wearing a work shirt and dungarees.

"Don't even think about it," the heavy-set man said, "or I'll blow your head off."

The PI had been wrong, he knew now – the security cameras were being monitored at all times; he'd been spotted and the guard had come out the front and around to the back.

"Drop the gun," the guard ordered, "and put your hands up."

Knowing he had no choice, Ryan complied.

Then the back door opened and another man, armed with a handgun, stepped out. Tall and thin, this guy was well-dressed in a sport jacket and slacks.

"You must be Robb Fornell," Ryan said, guessing.

"Who the hell are you? A cop?" the tall man asked in a Southern drawl. Ponytail guy kept the shotgun aimed squarely at Ryan's chest.

"I'm a friend of Joe Miller's," the PI answered.

At the mention of Miller's name, Fornell frowned. "Miller? You know Joe Miller?"

"Yeah. I worked with him in Atlanta."

"Miller's dead."

"Yeah, I know that," Ryan said. "Did you kill him, Fornell?"

"Who the fuck are you? What the fuck do you want?"

"Like I said, I'm a friend of Miller's, and I'm looking to take over his business. Since you're his source for drugs, I figured we should meet."

"Listen Ryan, or whoever the hell you are," Fornell replied in his heavy Southern drawl, "you've got it all wrong. I'm not in the drug business. My company is strictly legit. All I know is you come to my place of business in the middle of the night and were about to break in."

"Okay. In that case, call the police. Let them arrest me."

"I don't trust cops." He leveled the Glock pistol at him and said to the guard, "Frisk him. Make sure he doesn't have any other weapons."

Ponytail guy leaned his shotgun against the wall, pocketed Ryan's revolver, then patted him down roughly. "He's clean, boss. No guns and no ID. All he had was a crowbar."

Once the guard was covering Ryan with the shotgun again, Fornell pointed to the back door. "We'll finish this inside."

Ryan was led into the large warehouse. After going down a long corridor, they entered a cluttered office that reeked of cigarettes and burnt coffee.

The PI was pushed down on to a chair and his arms and legs were tied.

Fornell sat behind his desk and lit a cigarette, while ponytail stood guard with his shotgun.

In between puffs, Fornell drawled, "Let's start at the beginning ... who the hell are you?"

"As I said before, my name's J.T. Ryan and I'm a friend of Miller's. I do business with him – or I did before he got wacked."

The drug dealer stubbed out the cigarette in an overflowing ashtray and his eyes narrowed. "I don't buy a word you're saying. You've got cop written all over you."

"If I was a cop, wouldn't I be carrying a badge?"

"Maybe, maybe not. Undercover narcs are pretty smart these days."

Ryan glanced at ponytail guy. "You got my piece. What kind of gun is it?"

"A revolver," the guard replied.

The PI stared back at Fornell. "See. How many cops carry those?"

The drug dealer was a quiet a moment, then nodded. "You got a point there. All the police I know carry automatics. Have been for a long time."

"I'm no cop."

"I'm still not convinced," Fornell drawled. "You say you know Miller. Where'd he live?"

"Stone Mountain. Just outside of Atlanta."

"Okay. That's right. If you're really a friend of his, tell me about his personal life. Was he married, have kids?"

Ryan nodded. "He had a wife and one son. They were wacked along with Miller. By the way, Miller's wife was frigid and he had a mistress by the name of Margo."

At the mention of Margo name, Fornell's face lit up with a smile. "Yeah, I know all about her. She's a sweet cunt. Joe and I would do her when we were scoring dope together." He leaned forward in his chair. "Okay, Ryan, sounds like you're who you say you are."

"In that case, could you untie me?"

Fornell's eyes narrowed again. "Not so fast. You may have known Joe, but I still don't know what your angle is."

"You're his drug source, Fornell. I'm taking over his business and I figured we should meet face to face."

"By breaking into my place?"

Ryan chuckled. "The drug trade is dog-eat-dog. It's not like I could invite you out for crumpets and tea."

The drug dealer barked out a harsh laugh. "You're a funny man, I'll grant you that. But you're right, this is a tough business." After a moment he said, "You're looking for a source of coke? Or heroin?"

"I can get that from anybody. I want the new stuff. Skyflash."

"You know about that?" Fornell drawled, a surprised look on his face. He glanced toward ponytail, then back at Ryan. "The supply of that is limited. I only gave Miller a small amount. And it's expensive. Very expensive."

Ryan nodded. "Quality always demands a premium price."

The drug dealer lit up another cigarette and blew out several puffs of smoke. The acrid smell permeated the office. After tapping the cig on the ashtray, he said, "The supply of Flash is very limited – it may be awhile before I get more."

"No problem. Just point me to your source – I'll deal with him directly."

"Bullshit," Fornell said angrily. "If ... and it's a big if ... I decide to sell you the stuff, you'll get it from me, and only from me." He stubbed out his cigarette. "And anyway, I'm not going to do business with you on your say-so alone. I need to check you out thoroughly first. If you're who you say you are, my contacts in Atlanta will know about you." He pushed his chair back and stood up abruptly. "Wilson," he said to the guard, "I'm going home – got to do some research on our friend here. Keep him tied up and keep a close eye on him. Don't let him out of your sight for a minute."

"You got it, boss," Wilson replied.

Ryan felt a sinking feeling in the pit of his stomach. Once Fornell started checking, his cover would evaporate.

The drug dealer lit up another cigarette, and after giving Ryan a long look, left the room.

Wilson, who'd been standing this whole time, plopped down on the chair behind the desk. Then, with a smirk on his face, held the shotgun pointed directly at Ryan's chest.

The PI stared at the man as he mulled over the situation. He needed to gain Wilson's confidence. *But how?* He studied the man closely. Wilson's work shirt and jeans were shabby and dirty. Crude prison tattoos covered his arms and neck. Clearly he was a low-life, so Ryan knew he had to appeal to his base instincts.

With a broad smile, Ryan said, "Since we've got time to kill, I might as well tell you some jokes."

Wilson said nothing, just gave him a hard stare.

The PI leaned forward in his chair. "So the wife tells her husband, 'Go out and get something that makes me look sexy'. The husband went out and came back drunk."

Wilson chuckled.

"What do a clitoris," Ryan continued, "an anniversary, and a toilet have in common? Men usually miss all three."

The guard laughed. "You're pretty funny."

"I got more. Here's another one – Guys are like bras: they hook-up behind your back. Women are like condoms: they spend more time in your wallet than on your dick."

Wilson guffawed. "You're killing me ...."

"A truck full of Viagra was stolen," Ryan said, "and police asked the public to be on the lookout for a group of hardened criminals."

The guard continued laughing and when he finished a minute later, the PI said, "Listen, I got plenty more jokes for you, but I got to take a piss first."

"The boss told me I gotto keep an eye on you. You'll have to piss in your pants."

"C'mon man, we're on the same team here. I'm going to be working for your boss, just like you. Untie me a moment and point me to the bathroom. You'll still be covering me with your shotgun."

Wilson thought about this a moment. "All right. You're an okay guy." He got up from the chair and untied him. Then he aimed the shotgun at a closed door in a corner of the office. "The johns in there. But leave the door open."

Ryan stood. "Thanks, man." He took a step toward the bathroom, then he whirled around and spun one leg in a roundhouse kick, which caught the guard in the gut. The shotgun clattered to the floor as the guard staggered back.

Ryan punched him with a right hook, followed that with hard uppercut that caught the man's nose. He heard the *crack* of cartilage breaking and watched as blood spurted from Wilson's nostrils. The man crumpled to the ground, howling in pain. Wasting no time, the PI picked up the shotgun and aimed it at the man.

"You broke ... my fucking nose," Wilson gasped, as he touched it gingerly with both hands.

"That's not the only thing I'm going to break. Now shut up and put your hands behind your back."

The man complied and Ryan tied him up. Recovering his handgun from the guard's pocket, he came around and faced him.

"Where does Fornell live," The PI demanded.

"You're a crazy fucker – you know that?"

"I know. Now, where's he live?"

"I can't tell you."

"You can and you will. The only question is how much of a beating you'll take before you talk."

Wilson stared at him, a defiant look in his eyes. "The morning shift crew will be here soon. Those guys will tear you apart."

Glancing at his watch, Ryan realized the man probably wasn't bluffing. "In that case, let's not waste any more time." He swung his revolver hard across the guard's face, striking his nose again. Wilson screamed and more blood spurted from his bent nose. The front of his shirt was covered in gore.

"Tell me his address, damn it!"

The guard shook his head, said nothing.

"Not talking, huh? We'll see about that." The PI went to the desk and rummaged thru the drawers. Finding what he was looking for, he went back to Wilson.

Ryan flicked the disposable lighter he'd found and held the flame close to the man's face. "You know what burning skin smells like, Wilson?"

The man's eyes went wide and he tried to evade the flame.

Grabbing Wilson's throat with one hand, Ryan held the lighter underneath the man's chin. "You're going to find out how it smells."

The guard struggled to move his head, but Ryan was too strong.

"Stop!" Wilson yelled. "Stop damn it!"

The stench of charred flesh filled the office.

"I'll talk!" the man screamed out. "Please stop. I'll talk!"

The PI turned off the lighter, but kept it close to Wilson's face. "Where's he live?"

"Lakewood Crown Estates."

"Where the hell's that?"

"North Tampa, about ten miles from here. It's one of those communities where rich people live."

"What's the address?"

Wilson told him. Then he said, "What happens now? You gonna kill me?"

"I want to, that's for sure. But I don't work that way." Then he swung the gun again, striking the guard in the back of his head. His eyes rolled white and he slumped, unconscious. After gagging him and tying up his feet, Ryan dragged him into a closet. Then he picked up the shotgun and left the room. A minute later he was out of the warehouse, headed for his car.

Chapter 25

Alaska

Jessica Shaw had always hated her father's house. More of an estate than a home, the three-story Victorian was over 20,000 square feet, on 100 plus acres, with countless bedrooms and bathrooms. Although it was decorated with priceless art and filled with classic 16th century Italian furniture, the place felt cold and soulless. But the feel of the home had less to do with it's location in frigid Alaska, and more to do with her father's icy personality. Jessica had never grown up there; her father shipped her off at an early age to expensive boarding schools and later, to even more expensive colleges.

As Jessica followed her father's female bodyguard down the wide main corridor of the house, her thoughts turned toward her upcoming meeting with him. It would not be pleasant. Still, she had little choice, considering everything that was happening.

The bodyguard, a nubile and athletic-looking twenty-something brunette stopped by an open door and pointed inside. "He'll be with you shortly, Ms Shaw."

Then the bodyguard, who was dressed in a tight-fitting blouse and a mini-skirt, walked briskly away. Holstered on her hip was a semi-automatic pistol.

Jessica entered the massive study, its walls lined with floor-to-ceiling bookcases. She knew her father despised reading and only owned the scores of rare books in order to impress his guests.

She approached the fire burning in the large, natural-stone fireplace and stood in front of it to warm her hands. She felt cold, in spite of the heavy coat, wool sweater, and wool pants she was wearing. *God, I hate this place*, she thought, as she rubbed her hands together.

Moments later she heard a familiar sound and she steeled herself. It was the squeaking of rubber wheels over marble floors coming from the hallway.

She turned around just as her father, sitting in his titanium wheelchair rolled himself into the study.

"Hello, father," she said, realizing for the thousandth time she had never once felt close enough to the man to call him dad, or daddy, or pop.

"Jessica – it's good to see you." He pointed to one of the gilt-edged, brocaded sofas at the center of the room. "Why don't you sit and we can talk."

"I think I'll stand by the fire," she said, "it's damn cold in here."

The old man chuckled. "It's not, really. Your blood's thinned, living in St. Croix."

"Maybe so. But it sure beats living in the frozen tundra like you do."

Standing there, she studied her father, a frail-looking seventy-year old with sunken eyes and long, hooked nose. What was left of his gray, thinning hair was plastered to his bony skull. The man was dressed in nightclothes and a royal blue bathrobe, which was odd, she thought, considering it was mid-day.

"Would you like something to eat or drink, Jessica?"

"I'm not hungry right now. Maybe later."

"Just say the word, and I'll have Heather fetch it." A smile crossed his lips. "You've met her already."

"Yeah. I noticed the change in your staff. Did you get rid of Thomas, you're previous bodyguard?"

"No. I've assigned him other duties. Heather and her sister Meagan are doing his old job now."

"I see. Not often you see a bodyguard in a mini-skirt."

"True." He pointed to his legs. "But I'm an old man. I have difficulty walking ... and doing other things. The girls are very helpful in all sorts of ways." He leered. "In fact, Meagan was giving me a bath when you arrived."

"Please, father, I don't need details of your pathetic sex life."

The man chuckled. "So. What brings you here? It's been over a year since your last visit."

Jessica wrapped her arms around herself, not sure where to begin. Finally she said, "You remember that project I told you about, the one that would make Paul and I wealthy?"

He rolled his wheelchair closer to her. "I remember. The government project."

"That's right. Well, things haven't gone exactly as planned."

"That fuck-up of a husband of yours screwed it up, I bet."

She held her palms in front of her. "I know you never liked Paul."

"Liked him? He's a worthless piece of shit. You're a strong, beautiful woman – I never understood what you saw in him."

"Please, father, let's not have this discussion again."

"All right. But take your coat off and have a seat, will you? You're making me nervous standing there."

"Fine." She went to the nearest sofa and sat, and he rolled his chair across from her.

"Tell me what's happening," he said.

"The government project we're working on isn't exactly legal."

"Although you never told me the details, I figured that. Not that I'm judging you." He waved his arms in the air as if to encompass the whole room. "Hell, I made my money the old-fashioned way." He smiled. "I stole it."

Jessica's face turned red from anger, remembering how her father had cut her out of his will. "Yeah. I know that. But you're a real bastard for not sharing any of it with me."

His voice turned cold. "I told you you're whole life: you need to stand on your own two feet. I paid for your fancy education. That was enough help. It's not my fault you married that loser."

She pointed a stern finger at him. "If mother were still alive, she'd make you share your wealth."

"Don't bring her into this, Jessica. She's been gone a long, long time. My money is my money!"

"You're a fucking, greedy bastard. You know that?"

The old man laughed. "Yeah. I know. And I'm glad to see you're still the spunky, brash daughter I remember."

Jessica's hands formed into fists, her anger boiling over. *I should slap him right now*, she thought, *and wipe that grin off his face.*

"Did you come here to fight," he said, "or to talk?"

She stood up suddenly, ready to walk out of the room and leave the house. But after a moment she sat back down on the sofa. "I came to talk."

Her father rolled his wheelchair closer and reaching out, covered one of her hands with his. "I know this is difficult for you, Jessica. Coming here and telling me your problems. We've never been close – hell, most times I'm sure you hated my guts. I know you're an independent woman, something I really admire; something I could never say about your mother. But I'm not *totally* a greedy bastard that you called me before. You're still my daughter, and I do care about you in my own way."

She pulled her hand away from his, crossed her arms, and stared into his cold black eyes. "You're damn right this isn't easy. If I could have avoided it, I would have."

"Tell me your problem. Maybe I can help."

"We're supplying an illegal narcotic to a government agency for one of their high-tech projects. There's kickbacks involved, and other criminal activity. Like I told you last year, Paul and I have made a lot of money from this, but unfortunately we've also spent quite a bit of it already ...."

He smiled. "You always did like the finer things in life."

"I had a very privileged childhood. What did you expect?"

He shrugged, said nothing.

"Anyway, Paul and I are in hock up to our eyeballs. And we've run into production problems with the narcotic, which caused the government agency to cut our fee."

"What kind of production problems?"

Jessica mulled this over. She didn't want to reveal too much to her father, never sure how much she could trust him. Eventually she said, "As you know, Paul is a chemist. A brilliant chemist. He came up with the formula for this new drug. Unfortunately the actual production of it is being done by some unsavory characters in South America."

"Drug dealers, I presume?"

"Yes."

"I see. What's the name of this new narcotic?"

"I'd rather not say, father."

"Where's the manufacturing location in South America."

"I'd rather not say."

"Jessica, you're being evasive."

"It's for your own good. No sense in putting you in danger. The less you know the better." *I'm not worried about your well-being*, she thought. She was only concerned the old man would learn too much and be tempted to steal her project.

"I'm not an angel, Jessica. Far from it. I've had to deal with criminal types my whole life. I can take of myself. But, that's okay, just tell me what you want to tell me."

She uncrossed her arms and placed them on her lap. "Good. We have en exclusive supply contract with the government – the problem is our drug source has been selling it to other people besides us. That's caused ... some problems ... serious problems ... problems that have pissed off my contact at the agency. If the problem gets worse, he'll probably cut our fee even further."

"I see. I assume you've tried rectifying the production problems?"

"Of course. My husband is handling that end of it."

"And he's failing miserably at it."

She was about to object, then simply said, "That's right."

Her father nodded.

"Paul handles the production end," she continued, "and I handle the sales end."

"Sounds to me like you're going to have to take over the whole thing."

"I'm giving Paul one more chance – if that fails, I'll do exactly that."

"That's good, Jessica. You have more balls than he'll ever have."

In spite of the tension she felt, she almost laughed at his comment, agreeing with the old man for one of the few times in her life. Suppressing a smile, she said nothing.

Her father rubbed his bony chin. "Okay. Now I know your problem. How do you expect me to help you?"

She knew they had arrived at the crux of the situation. She couldn't avoid it any longer. "I need a loan, father."

"A loan?"

"Yes. A short term loan, until I can sort this thing out."

"What do I look like? A bank?"

"I just need your help."

He was quiet a moment. "How much?"

She told him.

"That's a hell of lot of money, Jessica."

She waved a hand in the air. "You're rich."

"I am rich. And I intend to stay that way."

"Please, father."

His hands slid to the tops of the wheelchair rollers and he rolled his chair back and forth an inch or so as he mulled this over.

"What do I get out of this, Jessica?"

"What do you mean?"

"If I give you this money, and that's a big if, what do I get out of it?"

"You'd be helping out your one and only child."

His head snapped back in raucous laughter. When he finished laughing moments later, he gave her a cold stare. "I'll give you the loan. On one condition. I want a cut of the action."

"What do you mean?"

"If this project of yours is so profitable, I want a cut of any future earnings. Say 25%.

"That's outrageous. No bank charges that kind of interest."

His lips pressed into a thin line. "You came to me because I'm your last resort. No bank is going to finance the kind of illegal operation you're running."

She knew he was right. Then she calculated in her mind the share of the profits he wanted. *Can I make it work? Damn, I'll have to cut back on so much.*

"I'll give you 15%, father."

"Not good enough. 20%. That's my final offer." When she said nothing, he rolled his wheelchair backward and turned it toward the door.

Jessica ground her teeth. "Okay, damn it."

"You're sure? Don't you want to check with your husband first?"

"Fuck him."

He smiled. "That's my girl." He rolled the chair toward her again and extended a hand. "Let's shake on it."

Jessica shook his thin, frail hand. "I'm sure, father, that you'll want your lawyer to write up a formal agreement. I can stay at your home until it's ready and we can both sign it."

Her father shook his head and chuckled. "That won't be necessary. A handshake is enough. You *are* my daughter, after all."

She snatched her hand back and under her breath she murmured, "Bastard."

With a twinkle in his eye, he said, "I heard that. But no matter. You're the only family I have. I'll go write you a check for the full loan amount you wanted." He paused a moment. "You've traveled a long way. I hope you can spend the night here. I'd like to have dinner with you, catch up on your life."

Jessica thought about this. *Do I want to stay in this soulless house? A house I hate, with a man I hate even more?* Still, the loan was going to save her butt. No sense being rude.

"I'd love to, father."

"Excellent. I'll have Heather show you to one of the bedrooms. Dinner is at six. See you then." He turned the wheelchair and rolled quickly out of the room.

A minute later the miniskirted female bodyguard came into the room. "If you'll follow me, Ms Shaw, I'll show you to your room."

"Fine, Bambi," Jessica responded, already penning a nickname for her father's bodyguard/whore.

"My name's Heather," the young woman said, visibly miffed.

"Whatever." Then she stood and followed the bodyguard out of the room.

***

The massive bedroom suite was on the estate's third floor. Its tall windows overlooked a clearing, which led to a wooded area beyond. Wild deer were visible, scampering among the trees. In the far distance she could make out the jagged peaks of mountain ranges. She stood there looking out the windows, and from this vantage point the highly secluded location of her father's property appeared to be a vast wilderness. And it actually was, since there were no neighbors for many miles. Her father's plane had flown her here; it was the only fast way in, since the road that led to the home became impassible much of the year.

Although it was only late November, winter was already in full force here. The mountains were all snow-capped, and even the clearing was covered by deep snow drifts. She shivered, thinking about the bitter cold outside. *Father's right*, she thought, *my blood's thinned living in the Caribbean for so long.* Her thoughts turned to Paul, hoping he'd fixed the problems with Garcia, but deep down knowing he'd probably fucked it up. *I was weak – I should have never married him. I should have never let sex enter that equation.* She shook her head slowly, knowing that wallowing in self-pity was a waste of time. *Should have, could have, would have – those are excuses weak people make. And I hate excuses! No, I'm strong. I'll make this work.* Securing the loan from her father was the first part of getting the program back on track. With the money she was sure it would all work out in the end.

Jessica heard a knock at the bedroom door. Turning away from the windows' panoramic view, she went to the door and opened it.

It was Heather, the female bodyguard. "Ms Shaw, it's dinner time. Please follow me."

"Sure, Bambi," Jessica replied with a smug smile.

Chapter 26

Tampa, Florida

While driving north on I-75, J.T. Ryan made a call on his cell phone.

The call was answered by Erin Welch a moment later. "Hope you have good news for me," she said tersely.

"No hello, good to hear from you," Ryan replied with a laugh.

"Cut the crap, J.T. It's been a bad day already. There's been another death in Atlanta attributed to that wonder drug, Flash. On top of that, the director has already called me twice, ragging my ass."

"Okay. I do have good news. I got a lead on Fornell, the drug dealer. I have an address and I'm headed there now."

A pickup truck cut in front of him and Ryan jammed on his brakes and leaned on the horn.

"You want me to call Tampa PD," Erin said, "get you some backup?"

"How long has Fornell been in the drug business in this area?"

There was a pause from the other end and he heard the tapping of computer keys. "About ten years, from the info we have."

"If in all that time the local police haven't shut him down, I think I'll do it on my own."

"Always the cowboy," she said.

He chuckled. "Anyway, I've got somebody here that I trust. She can help me."

"Got to go, J.T. Keep me informed." The line went dead.

Easing into the right lane of the Interstate, he tapped in another number on his phone.

"Hello?" he heard Ana Martinez say.

"It's J.T., Ana."

"How you doing, Captain?"

"You can call me J.T."

"Hard habit to break."

"Yeah. You told me you were going to be off work for a couple of days. What are doing today?"

She sighed. "Absolutely nothing. I'm bored out of my skull. I'm sitting in my terrace, trying to read a book. But to tell you the truth, I can't concentrate on it ...."

"How'd you like to do some detective work?"

"Working with you?"

"Yeah."

"Sounds like fun," she replied, excitement in her voice. "It'll be like old times."

"Good. And don't worry, you won't be doing anything dangerous. All you need to do is sit in my car while I go into Fornell's house. If you see his reinforcements arrive at his home, you call me and the cops."

"Easy enough. What should I wear, J.T.?"

He laughed. "Why do women always ask that?"

"Wiseass. Because we're women, that's why."

"Wear casual clothes. I'll pick you up at your place in half and hour. How's that?"

"I'll be ready, J.T."

***

Ryan drove the rented Impala past Fornell's large home, reached the cul-de-sac of the exclusive neighborhood and, after circling around it, pulled the car to the curb. Several cars were parked on the street as well, so his vehicle didn't look out of place.

He turned to Ana, who was seated on the passenger seat. She was dressed sensibly in jeans, flats, and a light jacket. Pointing to Fornell's home, he said, "We're only half a block from his place, with a clear line of sight. You'll be able to see any incoming vehicles. If you spot anything, call me, okay?"

"Got it. Anything else?"

"No. That's it."

"What are going to do, J.T.?"

"What I do best. What the FBI can't do. Break in, kick ass, and take names."

She smiled briefly at his joke, but she looked tense.

"Don't worry, Ana. Nothing bad's going to happen. I do this for a living, remember?"

She placed a hand on his arm. "Be careful."

"Careful's my middle name," he said with a chuckle.

She nodded but didn't smile, her look of concern still etched on her face.

Ryan gazed out the car's windows at Fornell's house. It was morning and it was a bright sunny day. He would have preferred doing this in the middle of the night, but he couldn't take the chance the drug dealer would skip town. The guy was his best lead – his only lead.

He unzipped his windbreaker, pulled his revolver from its hip holster, and after checking the load, he took out his sound suppressor and screwed it unto the barrel of the gun. Replacing the pistol in the holster, he zipped up his jacket.

Opening the car door, he climbed out and began walking. He went past the home and at the end of the street, took a left at the corner. When he'd explored the area earlier today, he noticed there were alleyways behind each row of homes for garbage pickup and service deliveries, which was typical for this type of upscale neighborhood.

He marched around the corner and slipped into the alley until he came to the right home. It was a large, single-story ranch-style house. The extensive backyard was professionally landscaped. A manicured lawn was dotted with palm trees and bright, colorful plants. He could see a swimming pool, which was covered by those screened-in enclosures you often find in Florida. Seeing no one about, he entered the backyard and using the trees for cover, carefully made his way closer.

Crouching behind shrubbery just outside the screened porch, he listened closely for sounds from inside the home. He heard only the burbling of water from the pool's waterfall, the chirping of birds, and the rustling of palm fronds.

Taking out his pocketknife, he approached the enclosure and pried open the screen door. Pulling his weapon from his holster, he slipped inside the terrace area. Going past the waterfall and hot tub that bordered the large pool, he hugged the home's back wall by the floor-to-ceiling sliding glass door panels. *No doubt about it*, he thought, *there's a burglar alarm on the panels.*

Peering cautiously inside, he spotted one man sitting at a breakfast nook reading what appeared to be a porno magazine. Resting idly on the guy's lap was an MP 5 submachine gun. So he was clearly Fornell's bodyguard. *Were there more guards?* As if to answer that question, another man entered the kitchen. After leaning his own submachine gun against the wall, the second guy sat down across from the first. The two began talking, but the PI couldn't hear what they were saying.

What's my next move, Ryan wondered. Blast my way in, shoot the guards and find Fornell? The drug dealer, obviously at home because his bodyguards were here, might hear shouting or gunshots and either flee or call for reinforcements. *No. There's got to be a better way.* Still out of sight, he continued hugging the back wall, as he finalized his plan.

Once again taking out his pocketknife, he pitched it in the air and the knife clattered on the patio's tiled floor. Both guards, alerted by the noise, looked outside. One of them grabbed his weapon and after going to a keypad and turning off the alarm, slid open one of the glass doors and stepped outside.

Ryan lunged at him, striking him in the head with his pistol. The guard sagged to the floor. Then the PI spun around and pointed his weapon at the second guard who was still sitting at the breakfast nook, a shocked expression on his face.

"Freeze," Ryan said, "or I'll shoot."

The guard, a large, heavy-set guy, slowly raised his hands in the air.

Ryan went into the house, took the man's MP 5, and slung it over his own shoulder. "Where's Fornell?" he asked, his voice low.

The guard's head turned right, toward the interior of the large home. "In there, with his wife."

"Any other guards?"

The man hesitated, as if weighing his options. The PI pressed the barrel of his gun to the center of the man's forehead. "The truth, or you die now."

The guard swallowed hard. "There's another one with them."

Ryan swung the weapon quickly, striking the guy twice, once in the face and then on the back of his head. The man slumped to the floor. Pulling plastic flex-cuffs from his pocket, he bound both men's hands and feet.

Confident the two thugs were out of commission for awhile, he left the kitchen and holding his gun in front of him, went deeper into the house. He passed a couple of vacant rooms, one of which was full of clear plastic bags filled with a white powder, cocaine he assumed. Also in the room he saw a crate of high-powered assault rifles.

After following a long hallway, he heard animated conversation coming from the front part of the house. He crouched by an open doorway and peered in. Three people, two men and one woman, were seated around a table playing cards. He recognized Fornell immediately and guessed the other guy was the guard. Leaning against the wall nearby was another MP 5.

Holding his revolver with both hands, Ryan jumped out of the crouch and bolted into the room. "Nobody move!" he ordered.

The guard, whose back was to the PI, scrambled up from his chair and went for the submachine gun. Ryan fired one shot, the pistol making a low thudding sound, and the guard screamed and slumped to the floor.

From the corner of his eye, Ryan saw a blur of motion as Fornell reached inside his blazer and pulled a Glock.

Ryan fired again, aiming for the drug dealer's shoulder – the man dropped the gun on the table and with a moan clutched his now blood soaked jacket.

Sweeping the gun between Fornell and his wife, Ryan said, "Either of you move again and you both die. Understood?"

The wife's eyes were wide and she nodded furiously, while the drug dealer, in obvious pain, groaned. "I understand."

Ryan removed the pistol from the table and, still training the revolver on the two people, went to the fallen guard. Checking for a pulse, he found none. Then he pointed to the woman. "Get up and put your hands behind your back."

The wife, a plain-looking, middle-aged woman dressed in a print dress, complied and the PI tied her with the flexi-cuffs. After patting her down for weapons, he pointed to a corner of the room. "Sit there, lady. Shut up and don't move."

After she sat on the floor, he turned toward Fornell. "You know the drill. Get up, slowly, hands behind your back."

"I'm bleeding," Fornell said with a grunt.

"You should thank me," Ryan replied, "I could have killed you."

The PI cuffed him and frisked him, finding no more weapons. He did find a cell phone, which he pocketed. Sliding a chair away from the table, he pushed the drug dealer onto it.

"Now," Ryan said, "you and I are going to talk."

"You won't get away with this Ryan. My men will be here in a minute."

"You mean the two goons in the kitchen? I already took care of them."

Fornell frowned. "What the fuck do you want?" the man drawled in his Southern accent. "I did some checking on you. None of Miller's people ever heard of you. Whoever you are, you're not here to do business with me." He cocked his head. "You're a cop aren't you?"

Ryan rammed the muzzle of his gun into the drug dealer's wound, blood spurted, and the man flinched in pain.

"I'll ask the questions, Fornell."

"Please don't hurt him," the wife pleaded.

Ryan glanced at her. "Shut up, lady."

Pulling his weapon out of the wound, he wiped off the blood on Fornell's jacket, while the man groaned.

"I'm going to bleed to death ...." the drug dealer gasped.

"Yes you are."

"What do you want, Ryan?"

"Information."

"What do you ... want to know?"

"Who's your source of the Flash?"

Fornell shook his head. "I can't tell you ... he's a dangerous fucker ...."

"I'm a dangerous fucker. Now talk."

"If he finds out I ratted him out," Fornell said, in between groans, "he'll kill me and my family ...."

"If you don't talk now, I'll do the same thing," Ryan lied. He wouldn't kill the man and his wife in cold blood, but he had to convince him that he would.

Fornell shook his head forcefully. "You won't kill me – you're a cop, I'm sure of it."

The PI glanced at his watch – he needed to finish this quickly – more of the drug dealer's thugs could show up anytime. *I was lucky to subdue the three guards*, he thought. *The next batch won't be easy. I won't have the element of surprise anymore.* Ryan was big and strong and extremely well-trained, but he knew he wasn't bullet proof.

"Last chance, Fornell. Talk!"

"No."

Ryan rammed the barrel of his gun into the wounded shoulder again, and the man screamed in pain.

"Talk damn it, or I kill your wife. And it's going to be a slow and painful death."

The woman, still huddled on the floor, began crying.

The PI pulled out the gun and the wound bled profusely. Fornell's eyes lost focus and he momentarily lost conciosuness. When he came to, he groaned loudly. "I'll talk ... you bastard...."

"It's about time. Who's your source for the Flash?"

"His name's Garcia," Fornell blurted out.

"What's his first name?"

"I don't ... know."

"Where is he? Here in Tampa?"

"No."

"Where then?"

"Colombia."

"Colombia's a big country. Where in Colombia?"

"I don't know."

"You expect me to believe that? He's your source for probably the most profitable drug you sell."

"Garcia's secretive. I've never been down there. I've never even met him. I've only met his men, when they come here. But I know his reputation. He's supposed to be the craziest of the *narcotraficantes*. Even his own men are afraid of him. He took over after the Ochoa brothers were arrested."

Ryan had heard of the Ochoas – before they were locked up years ago, they were the most ruthless drug lords in South America.

"Okay, Fornell. What else can you tell me about Garcia?"

Just then the drug dealer groaned, his eyes closed and his head sagged on his bloody chest.

Ryan felt for a pulse – the man was alive, but barely. He'd lost a lot of blood and if he didn't get to a hospital soon, he wouldn't make it.

Pulling out his cell phone, he dialed Erin Welch's number. "It's Ryan," he said when the woman picked up.

"What's happening, J.T.?"

"I got Fornell."

"Alive, I hope."

"Of course alive. But he won't be for long." He gave her the man's address. "Call Tampa PD and the EMTs. Get them here ASAP. TPD can arrest him for narcotics possession and illegal firearms; there's plenty of that here. As soon as Fornell's stable you need to get him to Atlanta for interrogation."

"You got it, J.T."

"Did you find the source of the Flash?"

"Yes."

"Well, are you going to tell me?"

"No."

"I'm in no mood for games," she said icily. "Why the hell not?"

"Not over the phone. This isn't a secure line."

"Fine. When are you leaving Tampa?"

"The next flight out."

Chapter 27

U.S. Army Base
Aberdeen Proving Ground
Aberdeen, Maryland

Brigadier General Robert Burke drove up to the military base's highly-secure front entrance, and after clearing the two security checkpoints, made his way through the military installation. He eventually came to an unmarked four-story building in a remote part of the base. Pulling into the building's parking lot, he found an empty slot and turned off his government issue sedan.

Highly secret, the building housed Army scientists and contractors who specialized in new weapons development. It was referred to in Pentagon circles as the AWT facility, for Advanced Weapons & Tactics. General Burke was in charge of AWT and was responsible for allocating funds to the numerous research projects conducted there.

Getting out of the car, he strode to the entrance, where his ID was scanned and he was patted down by an armed security detail of three MPs. Although the guards obviously knew who he was, it was a procedure they carried out on every visitor, regardless of who it was. In fact, it was Burke himself who had instituted the protocol to insure the security of the highly-classified operation.

After entering the building, he made his way to an underground level, where after going through another checkpoint and a retinal scanner, he went into the large lab. The room was filled with very sophisticated computers, medical equipment, and an extensive array of other high-tech gear. The lab was staffed by a group of twenty scientists, medical doctors, and technical support staff. Called the 'Soldier 2.7' room, this particular lab was the nerve center of activity to enhance the physical and mental capability of military personnel. It was specifically tasked to augment the ability of soldiers fighting in war zones and doing under-cover work in world hot spots.

Of the myriad of projects that Burke managed, he felt 'Soldier 2.7' had the most promise. In fact, he was pinning his military career on its success. If the venture achieved its goal, he was sure to get a promotion to Major General, and maybe even, reach his ultimate goal of four stars. These were his thoughts as he glanced around the large room, looking for Colonel Deaver, who oversaw the day-to-day operation of the project.

Spotting him across the room conferring with two other men, he walked over and said, "Colonel, I need to see you in your office."

"Yes, sir," Deaver replied, and turning away from the two he'd been talking with, led Burke into a glass-walled office in a corner of the lab. Closing the door behind them, he said, "What can I do for you, General?"

"I want a status report."

"Sure."

The colonel sat behind his desk, while Burke took a chair in front of it. Unlike the general, who was dressed in his Army dark blue dress uniform, Deaver wore a white lab coat, the same as all the other personnel in the laboratory. Also unlike the general, who was tall and beefy, with short cropped hair and a precise military bearing, Deaver was the opposite – short, wiry, and mousy looking. Although Burke admired the colonel's high intellect, he frowned on the man's longish hair, slouched posture, and relaxed attitude toward military regulations. If the man hadn't been such an integral part of the project, the general would have replaced him years ago.

"How are things going, Colonel?"

"I think we've made progress since your last visit."

"You think?" Burke barked out. "Either you have or you haven't. Which is it?"

Deaver's cheeks reddened and he pushed his black frame eyeglasses up the bridge of his nose. "I meant to say that, yes, we have made progress."

"Well, it's about time, Colonel." He lowered his voice for emphasis. "You know how important this is to me."

"Yes."

Burke scowled, not pleased the man wasn't following military protocol. "Yes, what?"

Deaver's cheeks turned a brighter shade of crimson. "I meant to say, 'Yes, sir.'"

"That's better, Colonel. Now, don't just sit there, tell me."

Deaver adjusted his eyeglasses again. "As you know, sir, we've been adjusting the levels of the drug in order to more precisely control the test subject's physical and mental reactions."

"You've been doing that for six months."

"You're right ... General .... But it's a difficult process. We have to inject just the right amount into the bloodstream. And the accurate balance between Skyflash and the other additives we've developed here is crucial." Deaver then launched into a highly technical five minute dissertation on the chemical and medical science behind the process, most of which went over the general's head.

Finally Burke raised a palm. "All right. That's enough of the technical bullshit. I know you have multiple PhDs and an IQ of 150. You don't have to prove how smart you are. I just want results. That's all that matters. Do I make myself clear?"

"Of course. What I was trying to say is that if we inject too high of an amount, the test subjects could die. Too little and it's not effective."

Burke raised his palm again. "Another thing. Don't call them test subjects. Call them what they are. Soldiers. A select group of soldiers who have volunteered for this project."

Deaver nodded. "Yes. I mean, yes, General. As I was saying, it's extremely critical that we administer the proper dosage. Three soldiers have already died. We started with ten men in the test group and we're down to seven."

"I'm aware of that, Deaver. A tragic situation, the deaths. But we have to press on, in spite of the setbacks. I expected this project to be fully operational by now. It seems to me you're being way too cautious." The general paused a moment, as a new thought struck him. "I asked you last time if you were any closer to duplicating the Flash drug from scratch."

"No, sir; it's a very complex chemical compound. We haven't been able to duplicate it yet."

"That's too bad," Burke responded, realizing he'd have to continue dealing with that bitch, Jessica Shaw. "Keep trying. We need to have complete control over this operation. Depending on an outside source is unacceptable."

"Who *is* the source?"

"That's classified information, Colonel. Anyway, it's not your concern. You get the packages from me. That's all that matters." The general leaned forward in his chair. "Now, tell about the progress you've made."

"Of course, sir." Deaver swiveled the computer monitor on his desk so that Burke could see the screen. "I have video clips of the experiment we conducted this week. I think, general, that you'll find the results encouraging." Deaver tapped on his computer keypad and a video filled the screen. The scene showed an athletic-looking man wearing military fatigues and boots standing by an outdoor running track. Two other men wearing white lab coats and carrying clipboards and stopwatches were standing next to him.

"The soldier in the video is test subject 6," Deaver said, tapping on the screen. "The technicians administered the injection five minutes before this was filmed. You'll be able to see the result in a moment."

The soldier in the video kneeled at a starting block and when one of the techs yelled "Go!" the man literally leapt off the blocks and in a blur of speed, raced down the track as if he'd been shot out of a cannon, crossing the finish line in seconds. A third technician, who was posted at the finish line, called out the electronic measured time.

"Test subject 6," Deaver said, "ran the 100 yard dash in seven seconds, which is much faster than the world record."

"By God," Burke replied, "That is impressive."

"And there's more." The scientist tapped on his keyboard again, activating another video. This one showed the same soldier climbing the sheer face of a granite cliff with incredible speed, unaided by pitons or any other mechanical devices. Deaver then played several more videos depicting a variety of activities: swimming, lifting weights, firing a rifle, and others, where the soldier exceeded world records.

Burke sat back in his chair, feeling an incredible sense of accomplishment. "That's amazing, Colonel. These are the best results we've ever had. And the uncontrolled rage we saw in previous tests is absent here."

"I agree, sir. And there's more. We gave the same soldier a battery of tests to ascertain his mental acuity. His ability to comprehend advanced math, physics, and several other topics was impressive while the drug was in his system."

"How long did the enhanced capability last?"

"Three days, one day longer than we had been able to achieve before."

"That's excellent work," Burke said, beaming. "We've come a hell of long way."

Deaver frowned. "Unfortunately, after the drug wore off, we had a setback."

"What kind of a setback?"

"The soldier lost consciousness and when he came to minutes later, began convulsing and suffered a heart attack."

Burke's enthusiasm vanished, replaced by a wary apprehension. "He died?"

"Fortunately, no. We have him at the hospital here, in intensive care."

"I see."

"So, General, as you can tell, we have made progress. But we still have a long way to go. In light of this new development, I recommend we slow down the project. Do more tests using chimpanzees until we can fine tune the dosage."

Burke shook his head forcefully. "I disagree. We're too close now."

"But, sir, it's too dangerous."

"Fuck that. We can't give up now. The project continues, full speed ahead."

"Sir, as a scientist and a doctor, I can't condone further testing. It's totally irresponsible."

The general crossed his arms and leaned forward in his chair. "We've already had three deaths, deaths that we've covered up. You, Colonel, personally signed off on the death certificates. If an investigation were to take place now, you would be as guilty as I of falsifying information. Is that a risk you're willing to take? If all of this is exposed, we'd both end up at Leavenworth, for a long, long, time."

A shocked expression settled on Deaver's face. "I ... I ... don't know ... what to say ...." he mumbled out.

"The project continues on schedule. Don't you agree, Deaver?"

After a long moment, the colonel's shoulders sagged. "Yes, sir."

Chapter 28

Atlanta, Georgia

J.T Ryan paced the small hospital room, waiting for Dr. Archer to arrive.

As he walked, he glanced down apprehensively at Lauren Chase, who lay motionless on the hospital bed. She looked almost the same as when he'd last seen her over a week ago – her head was still heavily bandaged and a breathing tube was still inserted in her mouth, held in place by medical tape. The bruises that had covered her pretty face were mostly gone now, but she was still pale and frail looking. Wisps of her auburn hair showed from under the bandages.

As he sat down on the chair by the bed, he took one of her hands and gave her a gentle squeeze, but felt nothing in return.

"Lauren," he said, "it's me, J.T. Can you hear me?"

She said nothing, her eyes stayed closed and the only way he could tell she was alive was the soft rise of her chest as the breathing apparatus did its job.

His stomach churned seeing her like this. Fighting back tears, he said, "Lauren. Can you hear me?"

Once again there was no response. He continued sitting there, holding her hand, praying for her recovery.

An hour later Dr. Archer stepped into the room and Ryan stood.

"Hello, Doctor."

"Mr. Ryan. Sorry you had to wait so long, but it's been a hectic day."

"What's wrong with her, Doctor? Her condition hasn't improved."

Archer shook his head slowly. "Comas are like that – some patients snap out of them quickly – others take longer ...."

A stab of fear hit Ryan in the gut. "But she will recover, right?"

"I've consulted with several specialists, and they agree that the prognosis is that she will. Unfortunately, the fact she's been unresponsive for so long isn't a good sign. She may remain comatose for some time."

"How long, Doctor?"

Archer frowned. "I wish I could tell you."

"There must be *something* we could do."

The doctor thought about this for a long moment. "Emory Hospital has a trauma unit that specializes in these types of cases. You could transfer her there. But it's expensive."

"I'll do it. I don't care what it costs."

"Fine, Mr. Ryan. I'll get the paperwork started." The man glanced at his watch. "I've got rounds in a minute. I'll be in touch."

Archer turned and left the room just as Ryan's cell phone buzzed. Taking it out of his pocket, he answered it.

"It's Erin," he heard the FBI woman say. "Where are you?"

"Grady Hospital."

"How is she, J.T?"

"The same."

"Sorry to hear that. Listen, we need to meet. I've got something for you on the case."

"Okay. Where and when?"

"My office. ASAP."

"You got it, Erin."

He hung up and put the phone away. Turning to the bed, he reached down and softly caressed Lauren's face.

"I love you," he whispered.

Then he left the room.

***

Half an hour later Ryan stepped into Erin Welch's corner office at the FBI building.

Erin was at her desk, tapping on her computer keyboard. She pointed to one of the visitor chairs. "Grab a seat. I'll be with you in a moment."

Ryan sat and watched as the attractive woman finished what she was doing. She appeared tense, and she had dark rings under her eyes. Her long blonde hair was carelessly pulled back in a ponytail.

A moment later she closed the lid on the laptop and slid the computer aside.

"How are things, Erin? You look like hell."

She frowned. "I feel like hell. I'll be lucky to keep my job another week the way things are going."

"I'm sure it's not that bad."

"Don't count on it. You don't know the Director."

"That's true, Erin. But I know you. And you're the best FBI agent I've ever worked with. The Bureau would be crazy to get rid of you."

A surprised expression crossed her face. "Oh my God. You just gave me a compliment. Imagine that. A real compliment from John Taylor Ryan."

"I compliment you all the time," he said.

"Yeah. But it's always a wiseacre remark about my cute ass."

"I guess you're right."

"I *know* I'm right."

Ryan leaned back a moment in his chair, his thoughts on Lauren. Seeing her in a protracted comatose state had put him in a morose mood. Trying to lighten the moment for both Erin and himself, he said, "How much money do you make as an FBI Assistant Director in Charge?"

She told him and he said, "Look at the bright side of it, Erin. If you do get fired, you could make more money as a fashion model. You certainly have the looks for it."

She pointed a stern finger at him and clearly was going to respond angrily, but she stopped herself and instead chuckled.

"Damn it, J.T. Get serious, will you?"

"I made you laugh, didn't I?"

"Yeah, you did. How's Lauren, by the way?"

"Still in a coma. I'm transferring her from Grady to Emory. The doctor said they have a special trauma center there."

"Good." She pulled a thick file from one of her drawers and placed it on her desk. "Let me get you up to speed on Fornell, the Tampa drug dealer. After we brought him here, I personally interrogated him. Unfortunately, he didn't have any more info about the source of the Flash than what you got out of him. Just that his name was Garcia and that he was from Colombia."

"Damn."

"That's what I said too, J.T. Except I used stronger language."

"Any luck on tracking down this Garcia?"

Erin shook her head. "Garcia is a very common name in Colombia. In fact, Garcia is probably the most common surname in South America."

"So we still got nothing on nothing."

"We did get a bit of a break," she said with a brief smile. "Remember the cell phone Fornell had on him?"

"Sure."

"My tech guys have been working on it. Most of the calls Fornell made were to Florida numbers. But there were several calls to Marinilla, Colombia. That's a small town in the mountainous part of the country, and close to Medellin."

"Medellin," Ryan said. "Isn't that the Colombian city known for drug smuggling?"

"That's right. Pablo Escobar, one of the world's most infamous *narcotraficantes* was from there. He's dead now, but the city's reputation lives on."

Ryan nodded. "It makes sense. Maybe this Garcia has his drug operation in Marinilla."

"That's what I'm thinking too. Ever been to Colombia, J.T.?"

"Once."

"How's your Spanish?"

"I'm fluent. When I was in Delta Force I did several covert ops in Latin countries."

"That's good. Because I need you to go to Colombia."

"You don't have to ask me twice, Erin. I'm ready to go. The sooner I can get Garcia, the closer I am to getting payback for what those bastards did to Lauren."

Erin raised a palm. "We're still working on that cell phone. Before you go I want to see if we can get more info about Garcia."

"Okay. I've got you two questions. First, are you assigning agents to go with me on this trip?"

She shook her head. "No. The politics in this office are toxic. I don't know who I can trust."

"Good. I like to work alone. Second question. Who in the FBI knows about the Colombian connection?"

"A couple of my techs. I haven't told anyone else."

"Let's keep it that way, Erin. If things are as bad as you say, I don't want to get blindsided."

"I agree. I don't want a repeat of what happened recently, when one of my agents was tailing you without my knowledge."

Ryan stood. "Unless there's something else, I'll get going. I need to take care of some things before I go on that trip."

Erin nodded. "Plan on going within a few days. By then we'll have extracted as much data as possible from that phone."

***

Ryan was in his office in midtown Atlanta, taking care of paperwork on several of his other pending cases. He didn't know how long he'd be in Colombia and he had spent most of the day wrapping up as much as possible.

He'd also been on the phone with Grady Hospital, finalizing the transfer of Lauren to Emory. Luckily that process had been smooth, thanks to Dr. Archer, who had turned out to be a godsend. Although the physician was an ER doctor, he had taken a special interest in Lauren's case and had gone out of his way to help facilitate her care at Grady and then help with her transfer to Emory. Although Ryan was still worried about her condition, he was relieved knowing his girlfriend would be getting the best care possible at the new hospital.

Finishing up at nine in the evening, the PI left his office. After picking up take-out food from a corner deli, he went to his apartment. He'd wanted to stop at the martial-arts dojo he frequented, but he was dead tired from his recent trip and realized he needed a good nights rest before the next phase of his next assignment.

He ate the take-out Italian food in his living room while watching a college basketball game on TV. His alma mater, Georgia State, was being crushed by a much superior Georgia Tech team. After finishing his second Coors, he turned off the TV in disgust.

He went to bed at eleven and was asleep as soon as his head hit the pillow.

Ryan slept fitfully, at first having nightmares about Lauren going into convulsions and dying, but eventually his dreams turned peaceful, recalling times from a vacation the two of them had taken years before in the Bahamas. They had made love on a white sand beach at midnight in an isolated part of the island. Both of them had treasured that trip and recalled it often.

As the dream vividly continued, he visualized a bikini-clad Lauren, lying on her back next to him on the beach as the waves crashed nearby. The moonlight illuminated her beautiful face, her curves, and her long auburn hair, partially wet from the salty ocean spray. The dream was so realistic that he could clearly see the freckles on her face, even smell the perfume she was using. Ryan, his sexual desire at a fever pitch, leaned over and began unfastening her bikini top as Lauren, her hazel eyes sparkling, whispered, "I want you now."

Suddenly Ryan was startled awake by a loud buzzing noise.

Grabbing his pistol from the nightstand, he glanced around the dark bedroom, and realized it was the front door buzzer. The alarm clock glowed the time: 2:13 a.m. "Who the hell could it be at this time of night?" he groused out loud, as the pleasurable dream of love making faded away into nothingness.

The buzzing noise at the door gave way to loud knocking and he got up from the bed, put on a bathrobe and padded on bare feet to the door. Looking through the security peephole, he spotted two crew-cut men dressed in dark suits, white shirts and dark ties on the other side. One of them was holding up a badge.

"It's the FBI, Mr. Ryan," the man said. "Open up."

After placing his gun in the bathrobe pocket, he unlocked the door and opened it.

"What's this about," Ryan demanded.

"We're with the FBI, Mr. Ryan," one of the suits said. He held up a badge with one hand and a piece of paper with the other. "And we have a warrant for your arrest."

Chapter 29

Cartagena, Colombia

Jose Garcia stared out the floor-to-ceiling windows of his study, mulling over his upcoming meeting with Paul Shaw. He had to finesse it and keep the flow of the key ingredient coming. Without it the production of Skyflash would come to a grinding halt. *I won't let that happen,* he thought. *I can't let that happen. It's too profitable.* Garcia made more money selling one ounce of Flash than 100 pounds of cocaine. *No, I definitely can't let that happen.*

There was a knock at the door and Manuel Ochado, Garcia's lieutenant, opened it and showed Paul Shaw into the room. Ochado left and closed the door behind him.

"Paul, it's so good to see you," Garcia said effusively, walking over to Shaw and giving him a manly hug. "It's been too long, *amigo.*"

"Yes, it has, Jose."

"Let's sit over here," Garcia said, "and I'll pour us some drinks."

Shaw sat at one of the plush sofas while the drug lord went to a cabinet and poured out large tumblers of Chivas. After handing the other man his drink, Garcia sat down across from him.

"*Salud,*" Garcia said, hoisting his glass in the air. Before taking a sip, he scrutinized the mousy-looking chemist, who appeared nervous. *Maybe I can use that to my advantage*, Garcia thought.

"How is production going, Jose?"

"Fine, *amigo*. The factory is running smoothly. Our processing of coca is nearing full capacity. I'm going to hire more workers."

Shaw fidgeted with his bookish, wire-frame eyeglasses. "How about the Skyflash production?"

Garcia gave him a wide smile. "It's going extremely well."

"That's good to hear ...." Shaw paused, a worried expression on his face. It was clear the man didn't want to broach the reason he had made this trip. "You remember ... the conversation ... we had ... several weeks ago."

"Which one, Paul?"

"About ... the distribution problem ...."

"I don't recall that." Garcia remembered that conversation word for word, but he wanted to downplay that issue as much as possible.

Shaw fidgeted with his eyeglasses again. "It was ... in regards to Flash ... the product was being distributed ... in Atlanta ... people died from it ...."

"Oh, I remember now. One of my middle-men accidentally shipped a small amount of it to Atlanta. But don't worry, I've taken care of it. I've put strict controls in place. That will never happen again."

"That's good, Jose ... but you know Jessica ... you know how she is ... she keeps badgering me to make sure ...."

The mention of the woman's name instantly put Garcia on edge. It was one thing dealing with the soft-spoken, pliable Paul, but she was just the opposite. He took a sip of his scotch to calm himself.

"I'm giving you my word, Paul. I've handled it."

Shaw shrugged. "I believe you. But Jessica ... she wants me to find another manufacturer ...."

"What? What are you saying?" Garcia blurted out, alarmed by the news. "How long have we known each other?"

"A long, long time, Jose. Since we were in college together."

"That's right, *amigo*. Remember it was me who supplied you with whores because you were too shy to ask out any of the coeds."

Shaw's eyes stared toward the floor. "I remember."

"And it was me who got you out of that jam with the University of Miami police when you got drunk and crashed your car."

"I remember that too, Jose."

"You owe me, *amigo*."

Shaw looked up at him and nodded. "I know I do."

"So. All you have to do is convince that arrogant wife of yours that I've taken care of the situation."

"Yes ... you're right ... I'll convince her."

"That's the spirit!" Garcia downed the rest of his drink.

"Now that we've got that out of the way, Paul, let's turn to more pleasant matters. I want you to spend a few days here in Colombia. Recently I flew in a new group of coke whores from Bogotá. They're very young – prime meat, *amigo*. I want you to sample all of them."

"I don't know, Jose ... if Jessica were to find out ...."

"C'mon, Paul. Grow some *cojones*. It's not like you haven't cheated on her before. Remember the last time you visited me? Anyway, these new *senoritas* are pretty, willing, and more than able. They'll ride you all night. And you can have your pick – have two or three of them at the same time. How's that sound, *amigo*?"

Garcia could tell the man was considering the proposal, since a wistful look was on his face. No doubt Jessica, being the bitch that she was, was probably withholding sex from him.

A moment later the chemist nodded. "It sounds good, Jose."

"Excellent! Now let me get us some cigars and more drinks."

Chapter 30

Atlanta, Georgia

Erin Welch tapped on her car's brakes and stopped at the intersection's red light. She and J.T. Ryan had just left the Fulton County Jail and were headed north on Piedmont Avenue.

She turned to Ryan, who was in the passenger seat of her Lexus. "Sorry about what happened, J.T."

Ryan nodded, but didn't answer. He hadn't said a word since she'd finally succeeded in getting him out of jail. He'd been locked up for two days and his unshaven face and unkempt hair marred his rugged good looks.

"What the hell *did* happen?" he finally blurted out angrily. "At first I thought it was a prank. Some clowns with fake badges posing as FBI agents, pulling a crazy stunt in the middle of the night. But I inspected the ID and the arrest warrant and saw they were real."

The red light turned green and Erin stepped on the gas pedal. "Yeah, they were real Bureau agents."

"Who were they? Some of your guys?"

"Hell, no. They were agents from D.C."

"Washington D.C.? What does that mean?"

"It means, J.T., that there's a spy in my office informing on me to FBI Director Stevens. One or more of my guys has sold me out. Stevens got that warrant issued and he sent those guys from D.C. to lock you up."

"They told me I was obstructing a criminal investigation," he groused. "They said it was the Flash case – the one you hired me to investigate."

"I know, I know. Look, I feel lousy about the whole thing. But it happened without my knowledge."

Ryan shot her an angry look, then rubbed his two-day-old stubble. After an awkward silence, he said, "All right. You were blindsided just like I was. Now I know why you hate Stevens so much. What's his agenda anyway? I thought he wanted to solve this case."

Erin accelerated the Lexus as she weaved around the slower moving cars; it was midday and traffic was heavy on Piedmont. "He does. But he also wants to get rid of me. From what I've heard, he's already picked out a 'yes man' to replace me as head of the Atlanta office. But he needs to discredit me first. He figures arresting my contractor, you, helps make his case. It's a good thing I know the judge who issued the warrant. I was able to convince him the whole thing was a big mistake."

"Okay, Erin. I get the picture. So what's next?"

"I've got some information on the drug dealer in Colombia, and I want to give you some things for the trip."

"We're going to your office?"

Erin shook her head. "No. It's not safe for you to be seen there. The walls have ears. Let's go to your apartment. What's the address?"

He told her and she continued north until they reached his apartment building in midtown. She parked the Lexus in the underground lot, and after getting a large metallic suitcase from the trunk, she followed him to the elevators.

***

Ryan unlocked the door and let them in.

Erin had never been to his apartment before and she glanced around the sparsely furnished living room.

"Typical bachelor pad," she said, amused by the look of the place.

"What do you mean?"

She pointed to the unadorned walls. "No paintings on the walls, not even posters." Then she pointed to the simple furnishings. "IKEA furniture, which I'm sure you assembled yourself. A big, flat-screen TV for watching sports. I bet you even have dinner right here in the living room, at that coffee table."

Ryan smiled. "You're quite the detective. Guess I'm guilty as charged."

"I bet, J.T., that you have beer in your refrigerator, and not much else."

He laughed at her remark. It was good to see him smile – it showed he wasn't holding a grudge from the arrest.

"I need to shower and shave," he said. "After being in lockup I look and smell like crap."

"You do."

"Make yourself at home, Erin. I'll be back in a few." He turned and left the room and a moment later she heard the shower running. She sat on the only couch in the room and leafed through a *Sports Illustrated* magazine that was on the coffee table.

Ryan came back ten minutes later, clean shaven and wearing fresh clothes.

When he sat down across from her on the metal folding chair, she said, "Let's get down to business."

Erin picked up the large suitcase she had brought and placed it flat on the coffee table. After unlocking the case, she opened the lid. Taking out a thick envelope, she handed it to Ryan. "In there is what we were able to find out about Garcia. It's not much, but it's all we've got. Also in there is an FBI issued ID saying you're our contractor. It may help you if you get into a tight jam. There's also a plane ticket to Medellin and cash in U.S. dollars and Colombian pesos."

Then she pulled a bullet-proof vest out of the case and gave it to him.

He took the vest, said nothing.

There was also a Glock 9 mm semi-automatic in the suitcase and she grasped it and offered it to him.

Ryan held a palm up. "No thanks. I already have a weapon."

"You're still using the revolver, right?"

"Yes."

"Then you better take the Glock, J.T."

"Thanks, but no thanks."

"Suit yourself." Putting the pistol back in the case, she took out the last item, a small, flat device the size and shape of a dime. "You'll need this."

He took the gray-color disk and looked at it closely. "What is it?"

"A tracking device. Slip it in your shoe, or tape it to the inside of your belt. It's already activated. We'll be able to monitor where you are at all times."

Ryan chuckled. "Big Brother, or in this case, Big Sister is watching."

Erin pursed her lips, irritated by his flippancy. "This isn't a joke, J.T. It's for your own good. There's a tiny button on the device – you can switch it on if you get into trouble. I may be able to get you help in time."

He laughed. "The operative word is 'maybe'."

"Damn it, J.T. Quit kidding around."

"Okay. But don't be so uptight, all right? Life is short. We deal with a lot of crap in our jobs. It's good to have a little levity every once in a while."

Erin shook her head, still angry at his cavalier attitude. Then realizing she wasn't going to change his personality, regardless of what she said, she shrugged. "Any questions, J.T.? This will probably be the last time we meet before you leave."

Ryan's face turned serious. "No questions. But I do have one request."

"What is it?"

"I've transferred Lauren to Emory. She'll get the best care at that hospital. But I need to make sure she's settled there. So I'm staying in Atlanta for a few more days before I go on this trip. My request is, would you look in on her when I'm gone? She doesn't have any family."

"All right, J.T."

"One last thing. If God forbid, I don't make it back alive, would you help her until she's better? She's the beneficiary of my life insurance, so it wouldn't be a financial burden for you. I know it's asking a lot, but this is very important to me."

Erin thought about this for a long time before answering. The last thing she wanted was to be responsible for a woman she didn't even like. But Ryan, while doing contract work for her over the years, had been a tremendous asset, even helping her get her current position as Atlanta ADIC. And the man had put his life on the line numerous times on assignments. Still, it was a huge responsibility.

"You're being melodramatic, J.T. Of course you'll make it back. You always have before. Aren't you the one who's always saying you can leap over tall buildings in a single bounce? Isn't that right?"

He didn't crack a smile as she'd expected, his face staying grim. "Please, Erin."

For once the man wasn't making jokes; worse than that, she realized he seemed to be genuinely worried about his chances of success. *Is he feeling his own mortality?* It was a side of him she'd never seen.

Against her better judgment, she finally said, "Yes, I'll do it."

Chapter 31

Alaska

Nicholas Drago stared intently at the blazing fireplace, his thoughts alternating between his various business ventures, and concern over his enigmatic daughter. She was a handful, that one. Deep down he knew he loved her. And he admired her spunky spirit. Yet, she had made big mistakes in her life – the main one was marrying Paul. And this illegal venture of hers worried him too – on several levels. Drago knew that once you went into a life of crime, it was difficult to get out. Now that Jessica was involved in criminal activity, it would be hard for her to return to a normal life. It was a quicksand that he himself had stepped into many, many years ago. Now it was too late for him to get out. Sure, he had all the wealth he ever wanted, but at a high price. Drago was always looking over his shoulder, always wondering when one of his rivals or the police would come for him. *That's why I live here,* he thought, *in the middle of nowhere. If they come for me, I'll be ready. I won't go down without a fight.*

And he also had an additional worry regarding Jessica. He had lent her a very large amount of money, with little guarantee he would get it back. *Damn. Why did I agree to that? I'm getting soft in my old age.*

Drago heard a knock from behind him and he swiveled his titanium wheelchair around and faced the open doorway of the massive study.

Thomas Carpenter was standing there and Drago waved him into the room. "Come in, Thomas."

Carpenter, a big, bulky man in a light gray suit walked in and stood at ramrod attention in front of him. "Heather said you needed to see me, Mr. Drago?"

"That's right." Drago placed his frail, bony hands on the tops of the wheelchair rollers and idly rubbed the metal. "I want you to work on a new project for me."

"Yes, sir."

"You know my daughter, Jessica Shaw."

"Of course, Mr. Drago. She's visited you here over the years."

"That's right. This new assignment I'm giving you is about her." Drago rolled the wheelchair an inch closer to the other man. "She's involved in a criminal narcotics scheme and it involves some unsavory characters."

"Yes, sir. What do you want me to do?"

Drago filled him in on what little he knew about it, then said, "Find out everything you can about this scheme – who the South American drug connection is, who in the U.S. government she's peddling the stuff to, what the narcotic is – everything. Then report back to me."

"Yes, sir. From what you're saying, Jessica has put herself in a dangerous situation. I assume you want me to protect her also?"

Drago waved a dismissive hand in the air. "Of course. But just as important is the money I've lent her. It's a large amount and I want to make sure I get it back."

"Yes, Mr. Drago. I'll probably need to hire additional staff to complete this assignment."

"Whatever it takes, Thomas. Whatever it takes."

Chapter 32

St. Croix, U.S. Virgin Islands
the Caribbean

Jessica Shaw strolled through her estate's extensive garden, breathing in the scent of the assorted flora which mingled with the fresh, salty aroma of the nearby Caribbean. The estate was located in a remote part of the island and had its own private beach. She could hear the crashing of waves near by.

It was early December, but here on the island it was a beautiful, sunny day with no clouds, and a perfect temperature of 72 degrees.

Jessica stopped at her favorite area of the garden, which was populated with a bed of blue flowers. Paul always referred to them by their Latin name, *cichorium intybus ex*. The blue plants were a hybrid variation of chicory flowers. She remembered Paul telling her one time that the soil makeup of the area was such that the special blue flowers could only be grown here.

Jessica never referred to them as *cichorium intybus ex*. To her they were just the special flowers. Bending down, she picked off one of the blue petals and held it to her nose. Unlike many types of flowers which have a pleasant scent, the blue flowers smelled rancid. She was used to its acrid scent, liked it even. To her it smelled of money – lots of money.

Cichorium intybus ex was a harmless flower, safe to touch, inhale, or even swallow it its natural state. It was only when it was ground into powder and prepared chemically with various additives that Paul had devised that it became Flash, the shortened name people used for Skyflash.

Jessica glanced at her watch, irritated that her husband wasn't home yet. His flight had landed an hour ago and the man should have been here by now.

She heard the crunching of gravel from the front of the house, and the whine of the garage door opening. "Well, it's about fucking time," she said, dropping the flower petal and racing into the house.

She found Paul in the first floor hallway, a suitcase in one hand.

"Hi, hon," he said with a smile. "I just got in."

"I can see that," she replied curtly, crossing her arms in front of her. "Tell me about your trip to Colombia."

Paul leaned over and attempted to give her a hug and kiss, but she took a step back.

He frowned. "I'm tired from the trip – I'll go upstairs and take a nap, then we can talk."

"No, Paul. Now."

"I'm tired, hon."

"I said now."

He set the suitcase on the marble floor. "All right. But let's at least sit down."

"Fine," she replied, leading the way into their sumptuous living room, where he sat in one of the ornate, leather wingback chairs. She remained standing, her arms crossed in front of her.

"Okay, Paul, let's have it."

Her husband took off his wire-frame eyeglasses and cleaned them with a handkerchief, then put them back on. It was obvious to her the man was stalling for time.

Finally he looked up at her, and said, "I've handled the problem, Jessica. Garcia and I are on the same page. Everything is fine now."

"I want details," she replied, her voice hard.

"Like I said, everything is fine. I had a long talk with Jose and he's assured me that we have exclusive distribution of Flash."

"He *assured* you? What proof do you have he'll keep his word this time?"

"I told him how important this is to us. He assured me he's put in strict controls to insure the mistake that happened before won't occur again."

Jessica frowned. "Did you go to the factory? Did you verify yourself that these 'controls' were really in place?"

A nervous look crossed his face. "No. I didn't think that was necessary."

"So, basically we're supposed to take his word for it."

"That's true, Jessica. But I've known Jose a long time. Since college."

She shook her head slowly. "Yeah. I know all about your shenanigans in college. It was before we met, but I did a thorough background search on you before we got married. I know about the shit you pulled. But we're adults now, and we have a *hell of a lot* to lose if Garcia fucks up again."

"He won't."

"Don't be sure about that, Paul. I saw a news report yesterday. Two people died in Los Angeles recently. From a drug overdose with symptoms very, very similar to those of Flash. And I also heard about another suspicious death in Phoenix. So it's not just an Atlanta problem anymore. It's more widespread. The news said the FBI is now involved. If General Burke finds out about these latest problems, we're screwed."

"Let's not panic, Jessica."

Her face flushed red as her blood pressure rose. "Don't panic? Fuck yes, we need to panic. Our whole project could go down the drain. Our whole financial future is at stake."

"Please, Jessica. It's not that bad."

"Yes, it is *that* bad," she barked, her voice cold. "I don't trust Garcia. We have to make a change. We need a new supplier. Now."

Paul looked nervous and he fidgeted with his eyeglasses again. "What do you mean?"

"I mean we fire Garcia and manufacture the narcotic at a new factory."

"I haven't found a suitable replacement."

Jessica hands formed into fists. "You've been saying that for months."

"It hasn't been a simple process."

"Show me."

"Show you? Show you what?"

Her cold black eyes bored into his. "I want to see the work you've done trying to find a new supplier."

"What?"

"It's a simple request, Paul. I want to see your records – your notes and findings on locating a new factory."

Paul glanced up at her – his eyes had the look of a scared rabbit. "It's ... it's ... I mean ...," he stammered, "I don't ... really ... have ... any notes ...."

"You *fucking* asshole," she yelled out, seething now. "I bet you haven't done a fucking thing to locate a new supplier."

She stabbed a finger at him. "You fucking *lied* to me."

"I'm sorry ... Jessica ... you know ... I've known Jose ... a long time ... I didn't think ... it was ... really necessary ...."

"God damn you, Paul!" She was so angry she almost couldn't get the words out. She jammed her hands on her hips. "As of this moment, I'm running this whole operation myself. Sales *and* production. I don't want you fucking things up anymore, understood?"

A shocked expression crossed his face, but he said nothing. After a long moment he nodded.

"First thing," she said, "you're going to show me all of your files for Skyflash. I want to know the specifics of how it's manufactured, the chemical formula, the additives, all of it. I may not be a brilliant chemist like you, but I'm smart enough to understand the basics. Then we're going to spend the next several days researching alternate labs – places that can make the narcotic. I'm going to find a new source, and find it fast."

"Okay, Jessica."

She pointed a stern finger at him. "Let's go to your office. I want to start now."

"Now?"

"Yes."

"I'm tired, hon. I need to rest first, okay?"

She gave him a long look, becoming suspicious of his weariness. The man did look tired – much more tired than he should have been from a business trip.

"You were in Colombia for four days," she said, acid in her voice. "After you talked with Garcia, what did you do?"

"Do? What do you mean?"

Jessica crossed her arms in front of her. "Your 'talk' couldn't have lasted more than a couple of hours. What did you do for the rest of the time?"

His eyes had the look of a deer caught by headlights. "We ... we had some drinks ...."

"You drank for four days?"

"Well ... yes ...."

"What else?"

"Nothing else, Jessica ...."

A sudden realization dawned on her and her anger boiled over. "You went *whoring*, didn't you?"

"No, Jessica ... of course not ...."

"You fucking bastard! Not only did you lie to me about the project, you screwed whores, too!"

"No ... I didn't," he replied sheepishly, but the man was a poor liar and she could clearly see through his attempt at deception.

"I know Garcia supplied you with whores in college," she spat out, "but now I'm getting the whole picture. He's been doing the same thing since the project started, to keep you in line. No wonder you didn't want to find another manufacturer."

Paul held his palms in front of him. "It's not like that ... you have it all wrong ... I would never cheat on you ...."

"You *betrayed* me!" she shouted. "You're *never* going to touch me again, Paul. I don't want your hands, or cock, or tongue near me *ever* again. You've been fishing in a filthy, scum-infested pond. From now on, we're having a strictly business relationship. Understood?"

"But I love you," he pleaded.

She took a deep breath, feeling weary from the tense conversation. "You should have thought of that before you betrayed me. Now let's go to your office. We need to get started right now."

A resigned look settled on his face. He shrugged, stood up, and followed her out of the room.

***

Jessica Shaw felt confident.

After spending a week with Paul learning the chemistry of the drug and the manufacturing process, she was sure she could take over the production end of the project. They had even identified two labs that could produce the narcotic in large enough quantities.

But their relationship had stayed icy during the whole week, although her husband had apologized repeatedly for his infidelity. She had accepted his apology, but would never forget his betrayal.

These were her thoughts as she worked in her home's state-of-the-art kitchen. Jessica had given the cook a night off, preferring to prepare tonight's dinner herself. She was making filet mignon with béarnaise sauce, Paul's favorite dish. It was a peace offering on her part, a temporary thaw in their relationship as a way of showing her thanks for his cooperation during the past week. She had even dressed up for the occasion, wearing a low-cut Versace dress, her best pearl necklace, and high heels.

When she finished making the filet and the other dishes, she set out the fine china in their sumptuous formal dining room. After using the house's intercom to let him know dinner was ready, she served the food and opened a bottle of Dom Perignon champagne. Then she took off her apron and waited for him to arrive.

"I'm surprised we're having dinner in here," Paul said as he came into the large dining room. "We always eat at the dinette by the kitchen."

She turned to him and smiled. "We've worked hard all week. I thought we could use a pleasant evening for a change."

He beamed as he sat down at the table. It was the first time she'd smiled at him in a long time and clearly it made him happy.

"Dom Perignon?" he said, glancing at the bottle of champagne. "This *is* a special occasion."

Jessica sat across from him and poured the champagne into two flutes. After handing him one of the glasses, she raised the other one in the air. "To a bright future, Paul."

"To a bright future," he repeated, taking a sip from his drink. "I'm sorry ... for everything ...." His face looked genuinely contrite and for a moment she felt a pang of regret.

"Let's not talk about that anymore," she responded, "let's just enjoy our meal and our time together. Okay?"

"Sure, hon. I'm just glad to see you're in a better mood."

Jessica smiled and took a sip of the Don Perignon. *It tastes good*, she thought. *Considering the price, it'd better. But then, it is a special occasion.*

They spent the next hour having a leisurely dinner. She steered the conversation away from their current problems, and instead, reminisced about the early days of their marriage, when their future together looked bright and limitless.

After he finished his dessert, Paul pushed his plate aside and yawned. "That dinner was excellent, Jessica. But I'm so sleepy. It must be the champagne."

She grinned. "Why don't you head upstairs. I'll join you in the bedroom after I clean up the kitchen a bit."

Paul slid his hand over one of hers, an eager look on his face. "Maybe tonight ... you know ... we could ...."

Jessica caressed his cheek gently and smiled mischievously. Then she leaned forward, giving the man a chance to look down her low-cut dress and her cleavage. "Anything's possible. Now run along and make yourself comfortable in bed. I'll be up in a few minutes."

***

After finishing in the kitchen, glanced at her watch and knew it was time.

She made her way to Paul's home office on the first floor. Going through the office, she unlocked a door at the far end that led to her husband's small laboratory. It was here that he spent much of his time, tinkering with chemical formulas. Although he had developed Flash in this lab, it wasn't large enough to produce the narcotic in the quantities General Burke needed.

Jessica slipped on a pair of latex gloves. Then she dialed the combination of the free standing safe in a corner of the lab and opened it. The safe was full of pint sized glass bottles filled with blue powder. Although the powerful narcotic was effective in many forms – ingested as a pill, injected in liquid form, or snorted as a dry powder, the fastest and most efficient method was injection into the bloodstream.

She removed one of the bottles from the safe, unscrewed the lid, and placed it on the lab's counter. Taking a beaker from one of the cabinets, she poured one third of the contents of the bottle into the beaker. On second thought, she poured another third of the blue powder into the beaker. Then she went back to the safe and removed another glass bottle, this one filled with a clear liquid. She added the liquid into the beaker and stirred the contents until the powder had dissolved.

Reaching into a drawer, Jessica removed a hypodermic needle and filled it with the bluish liquid. Satisfied the injection was ready, she replaced the bottles into the safe, relocked it, and left the room.

She climbed the marble staircase and strode into the master bedroom. As she expected, Paul was sound asleep, laying on his back nude on the king size bed. She approached and sat next to him on the bed and listened to his loud snores.

"Paul," she said, "can you hear me?"

There was no response, and she reached over with her gloved hand and slapped his face hard. The man kept snoring and she knew the sedative she had mixed into his dinner had done its job.

She hesitated before proceeding, as guilt for what she was about to do washed over her. It was the same guilt that had prodded her to make his favorite food tonight, to serve the Don Perignon, to make pleasant conversation, and to hint that she would give him a night of sexual pleasure. After all, even death row inmates received a good meal before they died.

Then images of the man's whoring flooded her thoughts and the remorse evaporated.

"You bastard!" she spat out. "You betrayed me! You will never betray me again."

Wasting no more time, she pried open his mouth and lifted up his tongue with one of her gloved hands. She held the hypodermic with her other hand and she positioned the needle over his open mouth. Carefully, she stabbed the tip of the needle into the area under Paul's tongue and pressed the plunger until all of the blue liquid was gone. If an autopsy were done, which she doubted since the local coroner was an acquaintance of hers, the tiny needle mark under the tongue would be difficult to spot.

Pulling out the needle, she watched Paul's reaction. She knew she had injected a massive dose of Flash, a dose so large that a heart attack should be instantaneous.

Nothing happened for a minute and a tinge of fear ran down her spine. *Did I do it right? Did I give him enough?*

Paul's chest began heaving, his closed eyes snapped open and almost bulged out of their sockets. His mouth opened wide and she heard a croaking sound. Then his nude body convulsed on the bed, and an instant later it sagged and went still.

The lifeless eyes stared up at the ceiling and spittle oozed out of his gaping mouth.

"Ironic, isn't it, Paul," she said with a cold smile. "You invented Skyflash, and you died from Skyflash."

She laughed. "I hope you burn in hell, you bastard."

Chapter 33

Medellin, Colombia

The Avianca Airlines jet landed at Medellin airport mid-afternoon, after a two-hour layover in Bogota's El Dorado International.

J.T. Ryan collected his bag and made his way through the terminal. Finding the Hertz counter, he rented a 4-wheel drive Jeep and, after locating the vehicle in the airport lot, drove off. Ryan had been to Colombia before, but had never been to Medellin, so he used the Jeep's nav system find his way out of the large metropolitan area.

Wedged in the narrow Aburra Valley and surrounded by the Andes mountains, Medellin was located in the country's western highlands and was a modern city of over two million people. Since Ryan knew the city's reputation as a center for the *narcotraficantes*, he was surprised by the area's stunning architecture – sleek skyscrapers blended with colonial era buildings, all connected by a modern monorail system. In the 1980's Medellin had been the planet's cocaine capital, with the highest murder rate in the world. Since the year 2000, many of the area's drug lords had moved to Mexico, but there were still plenty of cocaine operations nestled among the extensive coffee plantations.

Ryan drove through the downtown's Zona Centro and made his way north, passing an industrial area and several gritty, impoverished barrios, then headed east toward his destination, the village of Marinilla. If Erin Welch's information was correct, that's where he'd find Garcia's drug operation.

Once he left the urban sprawl, the rugged countryside turned isolated, the two-lane road snaking its way through pine forests up the mountain ranges that overlooked Medellin. By the time he reached a ridge top, he felt slightly lightheaded and out of breath. He knew this part of Colombia was at an altitude of over 8,000 feet and it would take him time to adjust to the lower oxygen levels of the Andes mountains. Rolling down the Jeep's window, he breathed in the hot, moist air. Although it was December, it was warm here, typical for the area.

The secluded, rugged area was dotted with villages among the dark green coffee fields. After another twenty miles he reached the small, dusty town of Marinilla. As he drove through the main street, he passed shops selling rustic furniture, crafts, foodstuffs, and flowers. There was a town square, dominated by a colonial era *iglesia*, its tall spire jutting into the sky. The white-washed church was the only tall edifice in the village, which was composed of unassuming, single-story homes and buildings. The structures were all painted white, with colorful blue, red, and green accents, the only bright spots in their otherwise drab appearance.

From what Ryan could tell, there wasn't much wealth in the town. The people he saw were dressed simply and appeared to be shopkeepers or *campesinos*, farmers from the surrounding coffee plantations. The vehicles he saw were worn, older cars, mopeds, and plenty of bicycles. He did spot several late-model Mercedes-Benz trucks as they rumbled through the main street, and he made mental note to check on that later.

Close to the town square he found a small motel with an attached cafe. Parking, he checked in the place, and after unpacking, went to the cafe for dinner. After scanning the sparse menu, he ordered the house platter of *bandeja paisa.* This was a traditional Colombian dish which consisted of grilled steak, fried pork rinds, chorizo sausages, on a bed of rice and beans, topped with a fried egg. He sipped a Tequendama Negra, a local beer, as he waited for his food.

The waitress, a short, plump woman wearing a floral print dress, came back ten minutes later, laden with several large plates which she placed on the table. She also served him a bowl of *ajaico*, a typical Andean soup of corn, chicken, and potatoes.

She was dark-complexioned and appeared to be of Andes mountains indigenous heritage. He had noticed most of the people in the town appeared to be of the same indigenous heritage.

"*Muchas gracias, senora,*" Ryan said.

"*De nada,*" she replied. The woman seemed shy or at least uncomfortable with strangers. It was clear the town of Marinilla didn't get many out-of-towners.

"*La comida aperece deliciosa,*" he continued in Spanish, which meant: *The food looks delicious.*

The waitress smiled. "*Gracias. Quieres algo mas?*" *Do you want anything else?*

"*Otra cervesa, por favor,*" he replied.

The woman walked away to get him another beer and Ryan plowed into the flavorful meal. Other than crappy airline food, he'd had nothing to eat all day.

As he ate, he observed the other patrons in the cafe. Most looked like *campesinos*, wearing long sleeve white shirts and white pants, typical garb for farmers in hot countries. In a corner of the restaurant was a small Christmas tree decorated with a few lights and ornaments, the only colorful thing in the otherwise drab environment of the dusty, faded cafe. The tree reminded him of the upcoming holiday. He hoped to be home by then, so he could spend time with Lauren, even if it was just to sit by her bedside watching her sleep.

The waitress came back with the beer and set the bottle in front of him.

"*Gracias, senora,*" he said.

She placed the check on the table and after giving it a glance, Ryan took out cash for the amount of the bill plus a very large tip and handed it to her.

"*Estoy buscando al Senor Garcia. Lo conoces?*" he said. *I'm looking for Mr. Garcia. Do you know him?*

At the mention of Garcia's name, the woman's eyes grew wide. She shook her head forcefully. "*No.*"

Ryan took several more large bills from his wallet and held them up to her. "Are you sure?" he continued in Spanish. "He's a wealthy man, has a ranch nearby," he added, guessing.

The waitress shook her head again, ignored the offered cash, and quickly walked away and into the kitchen.

By her reaction it was clear to Ryan that Garcia's operation was in the area. Her scared demeanor told him something else – Garcia was a man to be feared. No doubt anyone who crossed him met an unpleasant end. *Narcotraficantes* had an expression: '*Plata o plomo*', which meant 'silver or lead'. If they couldn't buy your cooperation with bribes, they shot you dead instead. The waitress, and he was sure now the rest of the people in the small town, were very familiar with the expression.

Ryan sipped the last of his beer and mulled over his next move.

He considered going to the local police station. But that could be risky. Like the waitress, the local cops probably feared Garcia and may even be on his payroll. No, he had to find the drug kingpin on his own.

Glancing at his watch, he decided it was too late to start looking tonight. He'd start in the morning, after getting a good night's rest. There was no telling what he was going to encounter.

Chapter 34

Alaska

Nicholas Drago rolled his wheelchair across the large study and stopped in front of Thomas Carpenter, who had just come into the room.

"What do you have for me?" Drago asked as he stared up at the bulky man in the gray suit.

"I've been working on the assignment you gave me, sir. The one regarding your daughter, Jessica."

"Good." Drago leaned forward in his chair, eager for the information. "What did you find out?"

"I have a friend who knows someone at the FBI. I've been able to obtain good intel on what's going on."

"How reliable is the source?"

"The FBI guy is not high up in the Bureau," Carpenter continued. "The man's a tech guy based in D.C., but he has access to lots of data."

Drago rubbed the tops of the wheelchair rollers. "How did you get this FBI guy to talk?"

"Money. Bribes were paid."

Drago nodded. "Yes. It's always about money. Tell me what you found out."

"Yes, sir. You told me Ms Shaw was involved with a new illegal drug. So the tech guy searched the FBI data bases for narcotic cases in the U.S. What he found was interesting. The Bureau has an open investigation into a new drug called Skyflash. Several deaths have been attributed to the narcotic in Atlanta, Phoenix, and Los Angeles. Apparently this Skyflash is some type of super drug – gives you a better high than heroin. But it's deadly, too. If causes violent behavior and is fatal if you overdose."

"I see. Were you able to find out which government agency Jessica is selling it to?"

"No, sir. I found nothing on that."

"Jessica mentioned the drug was being made in a factory in South America. What about that?"

"I haven't been able to track that down. I'm still working on that angle."

Drago ground his teeth. "Damn it, Thomas. I need more!"

The big man took a step back, clearly not expecting the outburst. "I understand, sir. I did find the specifics of the Bureau's investigation."

"Well, that's something at least. Let's hear it."

"The investigation," Carpenter continued, "is being conducted primarily out the FBI's Atlanta office. The person in charge is Erin Welch. She's runs that office."

"What else did you find out?"

"Erin Welch hired a private investigator to work on the case. A man named John Taylor Ryan."

"Interesting. I didn't know the Bureau hired PIs."

"According to my source, it's not that uncommon. The FBI employs contractors to assist in cases, especially when they involve overseas assignments."

Drago nodded. "That makes sense here, since there's a foreign connection. Anything else?"

"No, sir. That's about it. But I've hired some contractors of our own – that'll widen our search."

"Good thinking, Thomas."

Drago went quiet for a minute, as he thought through what the man had told him. Then he said, "Find out everything there is to know about this FBI woman Erin Welch and the PI, John Ryan."

"Yes, sir. Anything else?"

Drago smiled as a pleasant thought crossed his mind. "Go fetch Heather and Meagan for me. Tell them I'm ready for my bath now."

Chapter 35

Marinilla, Colombia

J.T. Ryan got up before dawn, showered, and began dressing in the motel's small room. He felt apprehensive, an unusual feeling for him. Ryan had worked on dozens of dangerous operations in his life, but for some reason this assignment in Colombia had spooked him. *Is it because the woman I love is in a coma?* Seeing Lauren so vulnerable had caused him to consider his own mortality.

After putting on his black pants and socks, he picked up his left shoe and inspected the inside. Still taped to the bottom, by the heel area was the dime-sized tracker Erin had given him. The tiny light was green, signifying the device was working and she knew his location. But considering he was in the middle of nowhere Colombia, it wasn't all that reassuring.

"At least," Ryan joked to himself, "she'll know where to find my body if things go bad."

Pushing the morbid gallows humor out of his mind, he checked the load in his revolver, stuck the gun in the holster, and clipped it to his belt. Next he strapped on the bullet proof vest over his bare chest. The vest was uncomfortable and chafed against his skin, but it was too hot to wear another garment underneath it. Then he put on a loose-fitting black shirt, which he didn't tuck into his pants. Lastly he checked himself in the mirror, satisfied his gun wasn't noticeable under the shirt.

He pushed aside one of the curtains and peered out of the room's only window – the sun was not up yet and it was dark outside.

Going out of the room, he strode to the rented Jeep in the parking lot and got in. Beads of sweat formed on his forehead and he wiped them away. Although it was before dawn, it was already hot and humid.

He leaned down, located the vehicle's circuit box under the dash, and disconnected the tail lights and interior lights. Then he started up the Jeep and drove east on the town's main street, the same direction he'd seen the Mercedes trucks take yesterday. When he reached the outskirts of the village, he pulled off the road and found a sheltered area under a stand of trees.

Turning off the vehicle and its headlights, he settled in to wait in the darkness. He rolled down the window and the moist scent of vegetation filled his nostrils. The chatter of crickets was the only sound he heard.

For the next hour traffic on the two-lane road was sparse – a few rusted-out pickup trucks, several motorbikes, and a horse-drawn buggy. After the sun peeked over the mountainous horizon, he spotted what he was looking for: A late-model Mercedes-Benz truck painted a gunmetal color.

Quickly firing up the Jeep, he drove out of the wooded area and back on the road, his headlights off. The truck was heading east and he memorized the look of its taillights, then dropped back several more car lengths as he continued to follow.

Ryan kept an eye out for other cars and trucks in his rear-view mirror as he drove, but saw nothing suspicious.

About five miles later the truck tapped on its brakes, slowed, and pulled off the road. Ryan slowed also and watched as the truck went up an incline on an unpaved road.

After waiting a minute he followed, driving up the rocky, muddy path bordered on both sides by woods. It was still twilight and the trucks taillights were visible up ahead. After another mile the incline on the road leveled off and they came to a mesa covered with coffee crops. He saw the taillights stop in front of a gated entrance. The truck's headlights illuminated a guard shack with two men armed with assault rifles.

The gate swung open and the truck drove through.

Realizing he'd have to continue on foot, and that once the sun came out fully his Jeep would be visible among the low-lying coffee shrubs, he doubled back and hid his vehicle in a wooded area by the unpaved road.

Then he crept back to the gated entrance, and kneeled behind a row of crops as he observed the activity at the guard shack. Deciding on his next move, he crouched and began moving left for several hundred yards to an area not visible from the entrance. After glancing around to make sure no one was nearby, he approached the 8 foot high chin-link fence, which was topped with razor wire.

Taking out his pocket knife, he pitched it at the fence. Sparks flew on impact and the knife dropped to the ground.

Damn, he thought. *The fence's electrified. This is going to be a lot harder.*

Crouching, he went over his options, which were all bad. Without the proper equipment, getting over the electrified fence was difficult, if not next to impossible. But finding the right supplies in a small village like Marinilla was unlikely. He'd have to improvise.

Ryan turned away from the fence and trekked through the rows and rows of coffee bushes until he came to a wooded area. He spent the next half hour scouring the woods for fallen trees. Finding three pine trees of adequate length, he lashed them together with vines and began pulling them toward the fence. It was slow, torturous work, made worse by the high altitude, the heat, and the humidity. By the time Ryan had pulled the trio of heavy trees to the fence he was exhausted, out of breath, and drenched in sweat.

After dropping the trees, he slumped to the ground, gasping for air. Once he recovered a few minutes later, he glanced around again to insure no one was around.

Standing, he grabbed the end of the trees that were furthest from the fence and lifted them. The combined weight of the wood was significant and his muscles strained from the effort.

Eventually he was able to right the logs until they were perpendicular to the ground. With another huge tug, he pushed the upright trees toward the fence, where they crashed a moment later. The logs now made a crude half-bridge he had to cross. Once he got to the highpoint, he'd have to leap to the other side of the fence. Since wood was a non-conductor, he'd be safe from the electrified shock. The tricky part, he knew, was walking on the trees without falling over. One slip and it was game over.

Ryan took a step on the trees where they met the ground and cautiously walked up the incline. He crouched as he did so and held himself steady with his hands. He reached the crest safely and he bent down for a moment to look over to the other side of the fence. It was a drop of about ten feet.

He knew he'd have to leap and roll when he made contact with the ground, otherwise he might break a bone or sprain an ankle. Guards would find him eventually and he'd be a dead man. Luckily there were more coffee bushes on the other side of the fence and hopefully they would break his fall.

Taking a deep breath, he launched himself forward and crashed into the bushes a second later. He rolled off and hit the ground and fortunately felt no intense pain. Standing, he brushed himself off. Other than minor cuts from the branches, he was fine.

Pulling his gun out, Ryan strode forward through the rows and rows of crops. Like on the other side of the fence, the mesa here was cultivated land, acres and acres of coffee plants. In the distance he could make out several structures – Garcia's compound he hoped.

Keeping a watchful eye, he continued walking and noticed something interesting. The coffee bushes gave way to another crop, one he recognized – coca plants. It made sense. Garcia not only processed cocaine, but grew it too.

He slowed his stride as he approached the large compound, which was comprised of three buildings. Off to one side was a large hacienda, and in the center, two industrial-looking buildings – a warehouse and the factory, he guessed. It was full daylight now and he spotted heavily armed guards posted along the buildings. To his surprise, there was only one guard by the hacienda. *Does that mean Garcia isn't there?* he thought. He needed to get into the home, but first he had to confirm what was going on at the factory. But that wouldn't be easy to do without being seen.

Ryan also observed several trucks and pickups driving in and out of the complex.

Using the coca plants for cover, he advanced until he was no more than twenty feet from the industrial-looking building he assumed was the factory. Even from this distance, the strong scent of chemical fumes was in the air. He got a good look at the guards – all where armed with Kalashnikov assault rifles, more commonly called AK-47s.

Just then a Mercedes-Benz truck pulled up and stopped in front of the building. One of the guards walked over to the back of it and opened the door.

One by one, a group of about twenty women hopped out of the truck and stood in a line. Like the waitress at the cafe, the women were all short and dark-complexioned. They were dressed in peasant clothes and carried paper sacks. Nothing happened for several minutes and Ryan couldn't figure out what was going on.

Then the front door of the building opened and a group of women streamed out, all of them naked except for the white aprons covering their torso. Under the watchful eye of the guards, the women who had just emerged from the factory took off their aprons and were handed a paper sack. That's when Ryan figured out it was shift change. A new group of women was beginning their shift and the last shift was leaving. He'd heard of this before although he'd never seen it first hand. Illegal drug operations many times forced their workers, mostly women, to work nude, wearing only aprons. That way, the workers couldn't conceal drugs to take for themselves.

After the group of women got dressed they piled into the truck, the incoming shift reversed the process, taking off their clothes and stuffing them into the paper sacks they were carrying. As the new group was led into the building, they were handed surgical masks, which they placed over their mouths and nose. To some degree the masks would protect them from the strong chemical smells inside.

The front door to the building closed and the truck rumbled away in the direction of the compound's front entrance. After the shift change, the guards took positions around the complex, bored looks on their faces. It would be many hours before the next shift change, many hours of standing in the heat, doing nothing. Seeing the naked women, Ryan figured, was the highpoint of their day. But the boring nature of their work played into the PIs hands. He'd experienced numerous occasions in the past where sleepy, disinterested guards napped, or simply gazed off into the distance and he'd been able to slip in and do his recon unseen.

He gazed at the building and planned his next step. He needed to get much closer to see what was going on inside. Luckily the structure had numerous industrial-size windows. The window glass was painted black but they were tilted open, probably to allow the chemical fumes to escape and let fresh air in for ventilation.

To the right of the building was a stand of trees and he slowly made his way there, careful not to attract attention. When he was close enough, he peered into the structure through the open windows. It was a hive of activity. He spotted an assembly line of sorts, with the apron-clad women doing a variety of chores – operating machinery which processed or filled white powder into brick sized plastic bags. Other equipment grouped the bags, which were placed into boxes, labeled, and sealed. A fork-lift scurried about, lifting full pallets and carrying them to a bay door at the other side of the room. Armed guards walked around the large, open room, keeping an eye on the women workers. The caustic smell of chemicals was oppressive, and Ryan pulled out a handkerchief and covered his nose. He wasn't close enough to read the labels on the boxes but he was sure the white powder was cocaine.

Hugging the exterior wall, Ryan moved toward the back of the long building, periodically peeking into the windows. The process he had seen was repeated in the next room, although here they were processing a brown powder. *Heroin? Probably*, he thought. But it wasn't until he reached the third room at the very end of the structure that he spotted what he was looking for – women processing a blue powder. *Skyflash?* Unlike the two previous rooms, this one was very different in one big respect. Only two women worked in it, while four armed men stood guard, a dramatic reversal of the guard to worker ratio he'd observed before. This could only mean one thing. The blue powder was a lot more valuable. It had to be Flash, he was certain now.

Elated at his find, he knelt down and considered his next steps. He needed to get into the hacienda, figuring that even if Garcia wasn't there, he'd be able to get a lead on his whereabouts. Then he needed to destroy the manufacturing facility, or at least cripple it.

Since he didn't trust the local cops and the FBI was nowhere around, he'd have to rely on himself. The problem was he had no explosives. The only solution he came up with was to wait until nightfall and start a fire in the factory and the nearby warehouse. There were so many chemicals in these places that the buildings would go up in flames in minutes.

Putting that thought aside, he focused on his top priority – getting into the hacienda. He needed to do that first, hopefully find Garcia, subdue him and somehow get him out of the complex. Considering how many guards were about, that appeared doubtful. His next best option was to interrogate him, then kill him if necessary. *But what if he's not here at all?* he thought. Then he'd have to learn all he could from files or computers in the hacienda.

Ryan looked up at the bright blue sky above – it was midday, a long time before nightfall. Still, it was too risky to try anything now. There was too much activity going on in the compound, too many armed guards, too many workers walking around. He remembered the words of Sun Tzu, the famous Chinese army general of the 6th century B.C., who said, *All war is deception.* Ryan knew the only way he could win the upcoming conflict was to keep surprise on his side. He'd have to wait until midnight to make his move.

Getting up, he cautiously made his way into the nearby woods and found a sheltered spot to wait.

Chapter 36

Christiansted, St. Croix, U.S. Virgin Islands
the Caribbean

Jessica Shaw walked out of the coroner's office with a bright smile on her face.

As she'd hoped, her husband's death had been ruled a natural death, the result of a heart attack. All it had taken were a few crocodile tears on her part, and the incompetence and lust of the medical examiner.

To spare the grieving widow any more discomfort, the coroner had decided not to conduct an autopsy. Also helpful was what Jessica intimated – that once her time of mourning was over, she'd entertain the idea of dating the man. In fact, she would never consider that, finding the short, fat man repulsive. *Men are such fools*, she thought. *All it took was a wink, a suggestive smile, and a flip of her hair.*

Jessica had parked her Rolls-Royce in the building's lot, but instead of heading to the car, she strode toward the town's waterfront, a couple of blocks away. It had been such a productive morning that she decided to splurge on herself. She knew she had to deal with a multitude of issues; but today, she decided, was going to be her day off. Her problems would wait.

She had a leisurely lunch at St. Croix's best restaurant, Tivoli Gardens. Located on Queen Cross & Strand Streets, the Tivoli was her favorite bistro. She had been there many times in the past, and she ordered her usual: lobster bisque soup, followed by a main course of lobster, accompanied by several glasses of chardonnay wine.

After lunch she took a stroll on the boardwalk, which overlooked the Caribbean. As usual it was a beautiful December day. A perfect 71 degrees, with azure blue skies. A gentle breeze caused ripples on the crystal-clear aquamarine water.

Stopping at several boutiques, she purchased items for her afternoon. Then, before heading back to her car, she made one last stop, a liquor store on Company Street. Going to the champagne aisle, she picked out a bottle of Cristal. Cristal was the most expensive champagne in the world, even pricier than Dom Perignon, but today she wanted only the very best. *Thank you father,* she mused, *for the generous loan you gave me. I'm already putting it to good use.*

Soon after she started up her Rolls-Royce and drove out of Christiansted, reaching her estate in a remote part of the island thirty minutes later. After parking in the three car garage, Jessica took her parcels from the car's trunk and entered the home, passing by a row of boxes stacked in a corner of the garage. Yesterday she had packed all of Paul's personal items – his clothes, memorabilia, photos, anything and everything that reminded her of her husband. She kept only his notes and files related to his chemistry work. When she had more time she planned to burn all of the boxes and their contents in a fire pit in the backyard.

Going upstairs, she went into the master bathroom and began filling the large Jacuzzi tub. She poured in the lavender bath oil she had obtained in town and lit the scented candles she'd also bought.

Opening the Cristal champagne, she took a long sip, drinking straight from the bottle. She already had a slight buzz from the wine at lunch but she wanted to be fully relaxed for what she had planned.

Sitting on the edge of the Jacuzzi, she watched as the swirling, soapy water slowly filled the tub. Her thoughts turned to Paul and her anger boiled over, the man's betrayal still fresh in her thoughts. With remorse, she realized now she had killed him way too quickly, way too painlessly. *I should have done it slowly,* she thought. *Excruciatingly slowly. I should have tied him down, flayed his skin, and burned him alive. That would have been much, much better.*

But it was too late for that.

He was dead and she needed to move on. Gritting her teeth, she made a vow to herself. Never again would she dwell on that weak, despicable man.

She had to focus on the future.

Jessica took another long swallow of the Cristal, savoring the exquisite champagne flavor she loved so much: a perfect blend of citrus, vanilla and nutmeg. As she drank, she forced herself to relax. This was *her* day and *nothing* was going to ruin it. She inhaled a deep breath, filled her lungs with the bath oil's lavender aroma as it mingled with the scent of the lit candles.

The tub was full now and she turned on the Jacuzzi jets, the soapy water instantly frothing into foam. Using both hands, she tilted up the bottle of champagne and guzzled the rest of the contents. Setting the empty bottle on the marble floor, she turned off the bathroom's lights, then slowly removed her clothes.

She stepped into the tub and slowly lowered her body into the hot, silky water until only her head was exposed. Resting her back against the side of the tub, she luxuriated as the water jets gently massaged her nude body.

Jessica closed her eyes a moment, as the effect of the alcohol hit her full force and her cares and worries finally drifted away.

Opening her eyes again, she took in the twinkling candlelight, the perfumed scent of the foamy water, the luxury of the bathroom's marble walls, the 18-carat gold fixtures, the ornate, gilt-edged mirrors, and most of all, the sensuous feeling of the Jacuzzi jets on her bare skin.

This is heaven, she mused.

Feeling fully relaxed now, she spread her legs and began touching herself – at first caressing her breasts, and then slowly, ever so slowly, sliding her hands down her torso and to her clitoris.

Jessica inserted one finger and gasped at the pleasure of it.

"Never again," she said out loud. "Never again will I depend on a man. It's just me now. I control everything. Just the way it should be."

Spreading her legs wider, she inserted several more fingers and began to massage herself, slowly at first, then picking up the tempo, the pleasure and pain increasing with every stroke. Her breathing was labored, coming in short, sharp gasps.

She brought herself to the very edge of orgasm, then forced herself to slow down, wanting to extend the exquisite pleasure awaiting her. Pulling her fingers out, she grasped the edges of the tub and breathed in the aromatic air.

After several minutes she began again, rubbing herself lightly, playing, teasing, stroking the pink folds until she couldn't fight it anymore and it all came in one long rush of pleasure.

Squeezing her legs together, she felt several more orgasms in quick succession.

***

It was an incredibly satisfying afternoon. When Jessica climbed out of the tub an hour later, she was physically drained and totally satiated.

Chapter 37

Marinilla, Colombia

J.T. Ryan crept over the hacienda's flagstone patio and, reaching the back entrance, hugged the wall to peer inside. Through the French doors he could see into the dimly lit interior.

It was midnight and he had spent the last couple of hours observing Garcia's home from a distance; he'd spotted almost no activity, just a faint light from inside the home. No lights had come on or gone off in the residence, and he'd only seen one man, a guard patrolling the grounds outside. It was fairly obvious that Garcia wasn't home.

Ryan tried the door knob, and as he expected, it was locked. *Is there a house alarm?* He hoped not. Taking out his pocket knife, he inserted the blade into the jam and pried out a chunk of wood. He continued until the deadbolt gave way and he was able to open the door. Putting away the knife, he pulled his gun and went inside.

He was in a large, unoccupied kitchen. Listening for sounds, he heard only the hum of an air conditioner. Faint light came into the room from a hallway that led into another part of the hacienda. Making his way there, he peered around the wall into the corridor. He saw several doors along the hallway, which led to a staircase by the front entrance.

Entering the corridor, he looked into the open doorways and found no one in the dining room, den, or the living room. There was a closed door adjacent to the living room and he tried the knob. This room, unlike the others, was locked. *A good sign*, he thought. *Whatever's in there must be important.*

Pulling his knife out again, he pried open the lock and went inside. As he'd hoped, the dimly lit room was an office. After shutting the door behind him, he closed the curtains and took out his miniature flashlight. Using the pinpoint light to illuminate the room, he went to the desktop computer on the large wooden desk. Turning on the device, he ran into a problem right away. The computer was password protected. He guessed at several possibilities before he gave up.

Next he began going through the desk drawers looking for any clues to Garcia's whereabouts or any details of his drug operation. He found several files which confirmed to Ryan he had found the right place – there were references to a Jose Garcia, listed as the owner of the hacienda and the surrounding property, which in the paperwork was described as a coffee plantation.

In a locked bottom drawer Ryan found a stack of notebooks. Each was labeled by a type of drug – cocaine, heroin, meth, and a last one which was marked *azul*, the word for blue in Spanish.

Opening the *azul* notebook, he scanned the contents. The booklet was filled with dates and quantities in grams. At the back of the book he found a notation in the margins: a P.O. Box number and the name Christiansted.

Suddenly he heard a muffled noise from somewhere outside of the room and he quickly turned off the flashlight. Stuffing the notebooks back in the drawer, he couched behind the desk, his weapon at the ready.

Hearing footfalls from the corridor, he tensed. The guard he'd seen patrolling the grounds outside must have come in to check the house. And once the man realized the office door had been broken into, he'd alert the other guards and all hell would break loose.

Ryan heard the door creak open and the room's overhead lights flicked on.

"*Cono, que es esto!*" he heard the guard yell out. *Damn, what's going on!*

Knowing he had no choice, Ryan peeked over the desk and fired off two rounds. The silenced pistol made muffled thudding noises and the guard dropped to the floor, but not before firing off a wild three shot burst with his AK-47.

"Hell," Ryan said, knowing the loud report from the assault rifle would alert the rest of the guards.

Sprinting to the door, he picked up the dead man's AK-47 and re-holstered his revolver. He ran down the corridor toward the back entrance. Reaching the door he crouched by the interior wall and peered outside. Unlike before, the patio area was now brightly lit by floodlights.

He spotted three guards taking positions in the back yard, their rifle barrels pointed toward the house. He also heard loud shouting, no doubt from the guards at the front of the home.

With his pulse racing, he broke one of the windows and fired off a quick burst. One guard fell to the ground, while the two others returned fire, bullets thudding into the wooden door. Glass shards flew everywhere as windows imploded.

Ryan sprayed the patio with rounds and the remaining two guards fell, clutching their chests.

Out of the corner of his eye he saw more men, more than he could count, run into the back yard and lay prone, their AK's pointed in his direction. Their assault rifles fired off a blaze of gunfire, the bullets ripping into what was left of the shattered door and kitchen walls. The roar of gunfire was deafening.

He began crawling his way out of the kitchen and, he hoped, to the relative safety of the corridor. But he heard loud voices coming from that direction and he stopped.

Then, as if in slow motion, he saw a projectile fly into the kitchen and clatter to the floor a few feet away from him. He knew what it was as soon as a plume of smoke billowed from the canister. A tear gas grenade. Acrid smoke filled his lungs and he began coughing uncontrollably.

***

When Ryan recovered, he was flat on his back with a group of men standing over him, pointing their AK-47s at his head. His lungs, eyes and throat still ached from the tear gas.

One of the guards kicked him savagely several times in the kidneys, and he almost blacked out from the blinding pain. Then another guard searched him thoroughly, taking his revolver and all of his other possessions, even removing Ryan's belt and shoes. The man inspected every item closely. Finding the tracking device in his shoe, the guard took it out and stomped it with his boot.

Then they threw Ryan on one of the kitchen chairs and tied his hands behind his back.

The guard who appeared to be the leader stood in front of Ryan. "*Quien eres?*" the man asked in Spanish. "*No tienes identificacion en tu cartera, nadames tienes dinero.*" *Who are you? You don't have identification in your wallet, only money.*

Ryan said nothing. He had left his ID in the motel room in case he ran into this kind of situation.

The leader swung his assault rifle by the barrel, so that the wooden stock hit the PI in the face. Ryan's head snapped to one side, the pain from the blow so intense he blacked out. When he came to blood trickled from his nose and lips.

"*Quien eres?*" the leader shouted.

"*Estoy buscando a Garcia,*" Ryan responded. *I'm looking for Garcia.*

At the mention of Garcia's name the man took a step back. "What do you want with my boss?"

Ryan shook his head. "That's none of your business."

"If you know what's good for you, you'll talk to me. I'm an angel compared to Jose Garcia." The guard went into a detailed description of the drug lord's ruthlessness, while the other armed men in the room nodded their heads, as if Garcia's reputation for cruelty was well-deserved. Afterward the lead guard said, "Sure you don't want to talk to me?"

"You're wasting my time," Ryan said. "I don't talk to lackeys. Take me to Garcia."

The lead guard snorted. "He's not here. He lives in Cartagena."

One of the other guards spoke up. "You want me to beat him some more? I'll make him talk."

"Not yet," the leader said, pulling out his cell phone. "I'll call Jose first, find out what he wants to do." The man turned away and left the room. He came back to the kitchen a few minutes later, a cold grin on his face. "I have good news and bad news for you," the man said. "The good news is you'll get to meet Jose Garcia. The bad news is we beat the hell out of you first."

Then the man lifted his assault rifle and swung it toward Ryan.

Chapter 38

Atlanta, Georgia

Erin Welch was worried.

J.T. Ryan's tracking device had stopped transmitting yesterday, and ever since she'd been calling his cell phone with no success. She paced her office, trying to determine her next move.

The last transmission placed Ryan near the village of Marinilla, Colombia.

Normally she'd dispatch a team from her office to assist. But things were far from normal. Her job was on the line. Her boss, Director Stevens, was looking for any excuse to fire her. And she didn't trust any of her agents.

Still, she knew she had to do something. She continued pacing, knowing none of her options were good.

Finally, Erin went back to her desk and made another call.

Chapter 39

Cartagena, Colombia

J.T. Ryan was certain he would die today.

Ryan stared down the barrel of a gun, his heart pounding. He was strapped to a chair and his hands were tied behind his back.

"How the hell did you find out about me?" the swarthy man standing in front of him spit out, as he shoved the muzzle of the large handgun to Ryan's forehead. The metal felt cold and stank of gunpowder. "Tell me, or by God, I will blow your head off!"

A trickle of sweat rolled down Ryan's face. He had to pick his words carefully – they could be his last. The man holding the gun, Jose Garcia, was a Colombian drug-lord with a reputation for brutality. Garcia had murdered his own son when he suspected the younger man cheated him out of drug profits. Before he killed him, Garcia had cut off his tongue and stuffed it down the man's throat. And to emphasize the point, he had his son's wife and three children murdered as well.

His mind racing, Ryan desperately tried to sort through his options. He was being held in the basement of Garcia's estate, and besides the drug-kingpin, there were four other men in the room, guards armed with AK-47 assault rifles. Although Ryan was big and rugged, he was securely bound to the chair. His body was racked with pain from the savage beatings he'd taken over the last week. The odds of escape were dim.

"Answer me, damn it!" Garcia shouted.

"Does it matter how I found out?" Ryan responded. "The thing you should worry about is I'm here, and I know all about your plan."

Garcia's face showed contempt, then he barked out a harsh laugh. "I should worry? You're the one with a gun to your head."

"You think I'm the only one who knows what you're up to?" Ryan said. "I work for the FBI. They know I'm here."

"You're lying!" Garcia yelled. "You know nothing." To prove his point, he struck the gun across Ryan's face.

When Ryan came to seconds later, he felt a burning, white-hot pain all over his face. Blood trickled from his nose and lips. The coppery taste of blood filled his mouth.

Garcia was still standing in front of him, now holding the large handgun at his side. "I don't believe you. You don't work for the FBI. You're from one of the other drug cartels. Which one? It's probably one of them in Mexico. Which one?"

"I know all about Skyflash."

Garcia stepped back, a surprised expression crossing his face.

"I know about Skyflash," Ryan repeated. "The FBI knows about it, and that you're behind the whole operation." The searing pain in his face intensified and he gulped in a deep breath. When the ache subsided, he tried his bluff, "Teams of agents are on their way here. They'll be arriving soon." This part was a lie. The FBI knew about Garcia, but they had no idea where Ryan was. There were no teams of agents nearby.

Garcia stood stock still, glanced at his men, then back at Ryan. It was obvious he was brooding over what the FBI operative had said. The drug-lord was a dark-complexioned man, with jet-black hair and a short beard. A long, wide scar ran down the whole left side of his face. He was built like a fireplug – short, stocky, and heavily muscled. His piercing black eyes were hooded and he had a cruel, menacing look that spoke volumes.

Ryan felt more blood trickle from his nose. He took a breath, smelled the blood's distinctive scent, plus the other rancid odors in the basement – urine and feces and vomit. No doubt Garcia used the place to interrogate and torture his enemies.

Suddenly Garcia laughed, the harsh sound reverberating in the concrete-walled room. "You lie. The FBI isn't coming. And you're no FBI agent – I've dealt with them in the past, and they broke after a third of the beating you got." He chortled, and his men joined in the laughter. "No – you're no FBI. You're a worthless piece of shit. Shit I scrape off my boots. Now tell me the truth. Which of the other drug cartels are you with?"

Ryan swallowed hard. His ruse hadn't worked.

A cold grin settled on the drug-lord's face. "I'm tired of this game. It doesn't matter to me if you talk or not. You're a dead man either way."

"Want me to kill him?" one of Garcia's lieutenants asked.

Garcia shook his head. "No. I want the pleasure to be all mine." He raised his pistol and pointed it at Ryan's head. "Do you know what kind of gun this is?"

The FBI operative stared at the large handgun. It was a Smith & Wesson .44 caliber Magnum with the eight-inch barrel, the same type of weapon made famous in the Dirty Harry movies. Clearly, Garcia used it as a way to further intimidate his enemies.

Ryan nodded.

The drug-kingpin laughed. "Then you know one bullet from this will blow your head clean off." He slowly pulled back on the gun's hammer and the weapon cocked on the double-action notch.

Garcia paused, the cold grin spreading on his face. It was clear he wanted to savor the moment, wanted Ryan to know he was about to die. "Say a prayer, because it will be your last."

It all happened in a split-second. Ryan heard an earsplitting roar and felt a blinding pain.

Then everything went black.

Chapter 40

Cartagena, Colombia

The MH60L Blackhawk helicopters dropped their second round of concussion grenades over the hacienda's property, then swooped low and landed in the massive back yard.

"Go, go, go!" Rachel West shouted into her head-set mike and watched as her CIA team piled out of the choppers.

Gripping her Heckler & Koch 416 assault rifle tightly, she jumped out of the Blackhawk and hit the ground running, joining her men as the group moved toward the large home. As she sprinted, she passed four prone bodies, Garcia's guards made unconscious from the barrage of concussion grenades.

All ten in her team were outfitted the same: H&K 416s, Glock semi-automatic handguns, black helmets with night-vision goggles, and black fatigues worn over Crye tactical bullet-proof vests. Considering she'd gotten the assignment from her CIA boss only days ago, she felt lucky to have put together the black ops team and the equipment on such short notice.

It was past midnight and the night-vision goggles gave the nighttime scene a ghostly green cast. Rachel checked her watch, her adrenaline flowing. They had begun the assault four minutes ago. Timing was crucial. They had to complete the mission before Colombian police or military showed up. Her boss at Central Intelligence figured the drug kingpin probably had the local authorities on his payroll.

As she and her team approached the home, she quickly thought through the objectives of her assignment. Her boss had given her sketchy details about what was going on, only told her what had to happen: Capture Jose Garcia; find and rescue an FBI contractor named John Ryan; and most importantly, from her viewpoint, stay alive during the whole process.

Suddenly a blaze of gunfire erupted from the rear of the house and Rachel and her team dropped to the ground as a hail of bullets whizzed over their heads.

One of the rounds had thudded against her chest, the sharp pain from the high-velocity impact feeling like a hammer blow. She took in several deep breaths and waited for the ache to subside, thankful for the high-tech Kevlar she wore.

"Light it up, guys!" Rachel ordered, speaking into her mike. "Let 'em have it with everything you've got."

The CIA assault team responded, firing a barrage of gunfire into the rear of the hacienda, the blaze of tracer rounds lighting up the nighttime sky.

Chapter 41

Cartagena, Colombia

Every part of J.T. Ryan's body ached.

Ever since he awakened an hour ago in the small, sparsely furnished room, he had tried, with no success, to get comfortable on the narrow cot. The brutal beatings he'd received from Garcia and his men had taken their toll. Although he didn't think he'd suffered any broken bones, the severe cuts and bruises would take weeks to fully heal.

Still, Ryan felt lucky to be alive. The last thing he remembered was Garcia holding the handgun to his head and then blacking out. He had no clue where he was now. The room's glass window was painted black, so he couldn't see outside. What was clear was that he was a prisoner. He was lying on his back, with his hands handcuffed in front of him, the cuffs chained to the metal cot.

Not that he could have made it far if he escaped – his bandaged arms, torso, and legs hurt like hell. No way he could run, let alone walk.

Ryan had seen only one person since waking – a Hispanic man wearing a sidearm who had fed him a plate of rice and beans. Ryan had tried talking to him, but the man had remained mute.

Hearing the door locks click, Ryan tensed. Was it Garcia, coming back to finish him off?

The metal door creaked open and instead of the drug lord, Ryan saw a stunning-looking woman enter the room. After closing the door and locking it behind her, she pulled up a chair and sat near the cot.

Slender and curvaceous, the woman was in her mid-thirties and had long, blonde hair. She was wearing a long-sleeve denim shirt, faded dungarees, and work boots, but the simple attire didn't disguise her natural beauty. Like the man Ryan had seen earlier, she was armed, a Glock pistol in her hip holster.

She didn't say a word, but rather sat there for a long moment as if studying him.

"Who the fuck are you?" Ryan said, thinking the woman was probably one of Garcia's people, there to interrogate him some more.

The blonde grimaced. "That's a hell of a thing to say to the person who saved your life."

Confused, he said, "What?"

"My name's Rachel West. I'm an operative with Central Intelligence. My team and I saved your ass."

"You're CIA?"

"Yes."

"You don't look like a CIA agent."

She smiled briefly. "I get that a lot."

"I bet." He raised his shackled hands and shook the chain, the metal links clanging. "I work for the FBI. If we're on the same side, why am I being held prisoner?"

"The cuffs are for your protection," she replied. "We didn't want you running off before you had a chance to heal a bit. Colombia can be a dangerous place."

"Tell me about it." He tried to smile, but the motion hurt too much.

The blonde took a key out of her jeans pocket and unlocked the cuffs.

It felt good to have his hands and arms unrestrained. "Thanks. What's your name again?"

"Rachel West. I'm based out of Langley. But I'm usually overseas on covert assignments."

Ryan waved a hand in the air. "What is this place?"

"You're in a CIA safe house on the outskirts of Cartagena."

"And the guy I saw earlier?"

"He's an Agency contractor. He and his wife are locals; they run this place. They'll make sure you're safe here. The wife used to be a nurse. She cleaned and dressed your wounds."

Ryan gingerly felt the bandages on his face and neck. "What happened to me? The last thing I remember was Garcia putting a gun to my head and cocking the trigger."

Rachel nodded. "After the firefight, we found you in the hacienda's basement. You were probably knocked out by our concussion grenades."

"Where's Garcia?"

"Dead. We killed him in the shootout along with his men. We wanted to capture him, but ... you know how it goes sometimes."

"Yeah, I do. I've been there before." Ryan was quiet a moment as a new thought struck him. "How did you find me in Cartagena? Garcia's men in Marinilla destroyed my tracking device. And another thing – how did the CIA get involved?"

"It's a long story, Ryan. I don't have much time, so I'll give you the Cliff Notes version. My boss at Langley, Alex Miller, got a call from Erin Welch. Apparently those two know each other and he owed her a favor. Miller called me and told me about you and that you'd gone missing. Lucky for you I was in South America at the time on something else. My team and I went to your last known location – the drug factory in the middle of nowhere, Colombia. We got into a pretty intense firefight – I lost two of my men."

"Sorry to hear that, West."

She nodded, a grim look on her face. "We killed all of Garcia's guards in Marinilla except one. From him we got the story about you – that you'd been taken to Garcia's home in Cartagena."

"What happened to the drug factory?"

"It blew up – during the firefight, bullets must have struck the chemical tanks and – whoosh!"

"Were you able to recover anything, West?"

"Yes. The main house caught fire too, but before it went up, we recovered some drug samples – coke, heroin, and a blue powder I didn't recognize. We sent all of that to Welch at the FBI."

"The blue powder is Skyflash," he said.

"Never heard of it."

"It's a new drug, that –"

She checked her watch as if in a hurry. "I have to go soon. Another assignment."

Ryan nodded. "Were you able to recover anything from Garcia's hacienda in Cartagena? Computers or files? I'm trying to track down all I can about Flash."

"Sorry, Ryan. Once we found you and killed the drug kingpin's men, we had to get the hell out of there. We heard police sirens in the distance. My operation ... wasn't sanctioned by Colombian authorities."

"I understand."

Rachel West stood. "I've got to go. I've got a flight to catch. The people here at the safe house will look after you until you're well enough to go home."

He extended his hand. "Thanks, Rachel, for saving my life."

They shook hands and she said, "Don't mention it. Just doing my job." She turned toward the door, then faced him again. "One other thing, Ryan. I have a message from my boss for Erin Welch: Consider the debt paid."

He smiled. "I guess I won't be seeing you again."

"That's right." She turned and left the room.

Chapter 42

U.S. Army Base
Aberdeen Proving Ground
Aberdeen, Maryland

General Robert Burke was in the Advanced Weapons & Tactics building when he heard his cell phone ring. Stepping away from the scientist he was speaking with, Burke answered the call.

"It's Jessica Shaw," Burke heard the woman say. The telephone connection was encrypted, and her voice sounded tinny.

"Shaw," Burke replied. "Glad you called. I've made a decision and wanted to notify you."

"Yes, General?"

"After some ... complications on our end ... we've achieved success on the Soldier 2.7 project. I'm ramping up the rollout."

"I see, General. Does that mean you'll need larger quantities of the product?"

"That's right, Shaw. I need more Flash and I need it now."

There was a pause from the other end. "You still there, Jessica?"

"Yes, General. I'll need a little time to set it up."

Burke gripped the phone tightly. "Unacceptable. I don't care what the fuck you have to do, but I want more product. Now. Do you fucking understand what I'm saying?"

"Yes, General."

Burke hung up the phone.

Chapter 43

St. Croix, U.S. Virgin Islands
the Caribbean

Jessica Shaw rested her cell phone on the granite countertop, unnerved by the call with General Burke. She was in the kitchen of her estate.

Jessica hadn't foreseen his new demand, at least not so quickly. From what she knew of the Soldier 2.7 project, they'd had multiple fatalities from test subjects overdosing on Flash. She had expected Burke to continue ordering the product at his usual quantities, with a ramp-up not occurring until next year.

Still, the general had been crystal clear. He needed more product.

"Shit," she said out loud to no one but herself. "The timing sucks."

Just this morning she'd seen an alarming TV news report on CNN. There had been a shootout at the home of a Colombian drug lord that left twenty people dead. The authorities identified the drug dealer as Jose Garcia, and suspected the shootout was the result of an attack by a rival drug gang.

Jessica had called Cartagena and confirmed the bad news – Garcia was dead, and his manufacturing facility in Marinilla had been burned to the ground.

Her thoughts churned, mulling over her next steps. Fortunately she had already identified a new lab that could produce the product.

Knowing she had to put that plan into high gear, she quickly left the kitchen and went to the master bedroom on the second floor. She needed to pack some clothes, go to the airport, and fly out as soon as possible.

Chapter 44

Atlanta, Georgia

"Thanks for getting me out of Colombia," Ryan said as he entered Erin Welch's office in the FBI building.

Erin, sitting at her desk, glanced up from her computer. "You look terrible, J.T."

Ryan gingerly touched the bruises on his face. His body still ached from the beatings, but he was feeling a lot better than a week ago.

He laughed. "Yeah, I guess I do. But I'm alive and that's all that counts." He took a chair across from her.

She closed the lid on her laptop. "Actually you ought to thank the CIA – they did all the heavy lifting."

Ryan nodded. "I've got a message for you from Alex Miller at the Agency. He said not to call him again."

"I figured as much," Erin replied.

"The woman agent, Rachel West, told me she sent you the drug samples from Garcia's house. Have they been analyzed?"

"Yeah, J.T. They were heroin and cocaine. And the blue powder matches the stuff we found here in Atlanta – it's Flash."

Ryan leaned forward in his chair. "So it all tracks – Garcia was the drug source. Since he's dead and his factory has been destroyed, I guess that concludes the case." He paused a moment. "How soon can you cut me the final check? I'm going to need it for Lauren's medical expenses."

Erin looked pensive and didn't respond.

He studied the woman. "Okay. What gives? That look tells me something's not right. Didn't we solve the case?"

"Maybe," she said, shrugging. "Maybe not. I have a friend at the DEA. I've been sharing info about this case with him – he doesn't think Garcia is the end of it. This Drug Enforcement guy thinks Flash is too sophisticated a drug for him to have developed on his own. He believes there's someone else involved, someone else who's pulling the strings."

"I see. And you trust this DEA guy?"

"As much as I trust anybody these days."

"Things with the FBI Director still bad, Erin?"

"We're in a stalemate right now. He still wants to fire me, but I was able to dig up some dirt from his past. I'm leveraging that and he hasn't been ragging me lately."

Ryan nodded. "Okay. Listen, when I was searching Garcia's house in Marinilla, I found notebooks with details of drug shipments. One of the books was labeled 'blue' and there was a notation inside about a P.O. box number and the name Christiansted."

"Could be a good lead, J.T. Maybe this Christiansted is the person pulling the strings."

"He may be."

Erin tucked her long hair behind her ears. "Okay. I'll start checking on that. You're still pretty beat up. How long before I can send you back out to the field?"

Ryan grinned. "I'm ready now."

"Bullshit."

"Yeah, you're right – I need a few days. Plus I want to see Lauren, check on her condition at the hospital."

"I'll call you, J.T., as soon as I track down more information."

He stood, a jolt of pain shooting through him. "Then I'll be on my way."

***

Ryan was in his midtown apartment, exercising in the extra bedroom he'd converted into a home gym. Earlier he'd tried punching and kicking the heavy bag in the corner of the room, but gave up, the pain in his legs and arms too intense.

He had just completed fifty push-ups and fifty sit-ups, half his usual amount, before collapsing on his back on the rubber mat. He stared up at the ceiling, gulping in long breaths, contemplating how much more pain he could endure before ending his exercise routine. He'd been at it an hour and his sweat shirt and pants were drenched in perspiration.

Ryan's front door buzzer rang, and after picking up his weapon from the floor, he got up from the mat and went to the front entrance. He verified who it was through the peephole and opened the door.

"ADIC Welch," he said with a chuckle. "What a welcome surprise. It's not every day I get a pretty lady visiting my humble abode."

"Cut the crap," Erin said. "I'm in no mood."

Ryan laughed as he let her in the apartment and closed the door behind her.

She pointed to the pistol in his hand. "You can put the gun away. I'm on your side, remember?"

He nodded, rested the pistol on the living room coffee table. "Force of habit. I've been kind of jumpy lately. Probably comes from people trying to kill me. Have a seat, Erin."

She sat on the sofa, and placed the leather briefcase she was carrying on the floor. Erin was dressed in her typical office attire: a Christian Dior suit, a gray blouse, and high heels. Louboutins, he noticed.

"Want a drink?" he offered. "I'm having a beer myself."

Erin glanced at her watch. "It's after seven p.m. and I'm off the clock. Yeah, I could use one. What do you have?"

"Coors beer and white wine."

"What kind of wine is it? Chardonnay? Pinot gricio?"

"They have different kinds?"

Erin shook her head slowly at his lame joke. "Yeah, they do."

Ryan laughed. "It's a chardonnay."

"I'll take it."

Ryan went to his bedroom and changed into fresh clothes, then went into the kitchen and got the drinks. He came back to the living room and, after handing her the glass of wine, sat across from her on the metal folding chair, the only seat in the room other than the sofa.

She took a sip of the wine and grimaced. "Before I leave today, tell me the name brand of this stuff. I want to make sure to avoid it."

Ryan drank from his bottle of Coors. "I don't make the big money like you do."

"Bullshit. You get paid plenty. You're just cheap, J.T." She pointed to the living room's sparse furnishings. "You're like most men – never want to spend money on your home. The only expensive thing you own is your car."

"That's what Lauren always tells me." Mentioning her name flooded his mind with images of her at the hospital and his mood soured.

"How's she doing?" Erin asked.

"The same. Still in a coma. I've spent a lot of time with her, but ...." His voice trailed off.

"Sorry to hear that."

He nodded. To change the subject, he said, "So – what brings you here?"

"I've been working the lead you gave me three days ago. The name Christiansted. So far, we've come up with a big fat zero. There are no drug dealers with that name, in Colombia or in the U.S. for that matter."

Ryan shook his head. "Not what I wanted to hear. I was sure that would be a good lead. What about your friend at the DEA – has he been able to come up with anything?"

"No – unfortunately not."

"So where are we, Erin?"

She took a swallow of the wine. "At a dead end."

Ryan mulled that over for a long moment. "Maybe we're looking at this from the wrong angle. Along with the name Christiansted, there was P.O. box number, remember?"

"Sure."

"What if Christiansted isn't a person, but a place. This P.O. box could be located someplace named Christiansted."

"You may have something there, J.T. I know there's a city in New Zealand with a similar name, it's Christchurch. Wait a minute, there's a Christiansted in one of the Virgin Islands, in the Caribbean."

"You're right. There's a Christiansted in St. Croix. Which makes sense, Erin, since the country of Colombia faces the Caribbean Sea."

The FBI woman shook her head slowly. "Damn it. I hate to admit it, but you figured out the city connection before I did."

"See," he replied with a chuckle, "you didn't just hire me for my brawn, witty repartee, charm, and good looks. I've got a brain too."

She suppressed a smile. "The jury's still out on that. Now let's find out if this post office box even exists." She pulled out her cell phone, spoke into it for several minutes and hung up. "I'm having my office check it out. They'll call me back."

Ryan stood. "I'm having another beer. Want more wine?"

"No thanks. That stuff is vile."

"How about a Coors, Erin?"

"I don't drink beer."

"Figures."

"What the hell does *that* mean, J.T.?"

"Anybody who wears Christian Dior and Louboutins doesn't drink beer."

Erin's face reddened. "Are you making fun of me?"

He raised his palms. "No. But I *am* a detective. I deduce things for a living."

"Fair enough."

He went to the kitchen and pulled another beer out of the refrigerator. When he came back into the living room, Erin was on her cell phone.

She hung up a moment later. "Bad news. There is a post office box in Christiansted, St. Croix with that number."

"But?"

"There's no person or business listed that rents it. The listing just says that it's rented out."

"How's that possible, Erin? You need two forms of identification, including a photo I.D. to get a post office box in any U.S. state or territory. And St. Croix is a territory."

"True. Someone was paid off, I'm sure. Money talks."

"You're right about that."

"J.T., I need you to go down there and find whoever is using that box. It may not lead to anything, but it's the only clue we have."

"Okay. I'll leave tomorrow."

"And this time, try not to get killed."

Ryan smiled. "See. You *do* have a heart after all. You do care about me."

Erin laughed. "It's not that. It's just that I've run out of people to come help you. And I do need help solving this damn case."

Chapter 45

Alaska

Nicholas Drago watched appreciatively as his bodyguard Heather walked out of the study, her hips swaying, her high heels clicking on the marble floor of the room. As usual the nubile young woman was dressed in a tight-fitting blouse and a mini-skirt, with a semi-automatic holstered on her hip.

Even though Drago was frail and in his seventies, being around Heather and her sister Meagan always peaked his libido. A session with both of them at the same time made him feel twenty years old again. *Once I'm done with this next meeting,* he thought, a smile crossing his lips, *I know what I'll be doing. And who I'll be doing.*

Drago turned his wheelchair around and faced Thomas Carpenter, who was standing in front of the study's blazing fireplace.

"I hope you have good news for me," Drago said, looking up at the big man in the dark gray suit.

"I do," Carpenter replied.

"That's what I wanted to hear."

"As I told you last time we met, sir, I hired several contractors, private investigators, to look into your daughter's drug scheme. I gave them Ms Shaw's address and other pertinent information. They've spent the last week in St. Croix investigating. Luckily for them, Jessica Shaw was traveling off the island and they were able to access her house and records. It's a small island and they knew your daughter's housekeeper – they threatened the old woman and she gave them the key and the password to the house alarm."

"Excellent, Thomas. What did they learn?"

"Quite a bit, sir. For one thing, her husband, Paul Shaw, is dead."

"What was the cause of death? Not that it matters. I'm glad that fool is dead."

"Heart attack."

"I see," Drago said, hoping Jessica had murdered the bastard. "What else did they find out?"

"As I said, my contractors accessed her records – notes and files. This new narcotic the Shaw's created, Skyflash, is some kind of wonder drug. It gives people vastly increased strength, agility, and intelligence, for a period of time. The Shaw's are selling it to the U.S. Defense Department. A general by the name of Burke is involved. The DoD is apparently using this new drug for a secret program."

Drago idly rubbed his bony chin with his frail hand. "This Skyflash increases strength and agility – I like the sound of that. Does it have a down side?"

"Unfortunately, sir, in the wrong quantity it makes you uncontrollably violent. Several murders have been attributed to it. An overdose of it also causes a heart attack."

"That's too bad," Drago replied, disappointed. Being old and infirm, he himself could benefit from such a drug. "So the Defense Department is testing it on soldiers?"

"Yes, sir. They've had several fatalities in the program. According to Shaw's notes, these deaths have been kept secret. And there's more. People have died in several cities – Atlanta, Phoenix, and Los Angeles – from Flash. The drug made its way to those places and that's why the FBI is investigating."

"I remember Jessica telling me about that problem. The supplier that was manufacturing the narcotic was also selling it to other middlemen. What else did you find out, Thomas?"

Carpenter continued, giving Drago more details of what he'd learned.

Afterward Drago said, "Good work. By the way, where is my daughter now?"

"Ms Shaw is not in St. Croix right now. Her previous narcotic manufacturer, Jose Garcia, is dead and his factory blew up. I suspect Ms Shaw is at the location of a new supplier."

"Any idea where that could be?"

"No, sir."

Drago rubbed his chin again. "All right. Keep digging."

"Yes, sir."

"And on your way out," Drago said with a leer, "find Heather and Meagan for me. Tell them I need to see them now."

Chapter 46

St. Croix, U.S. Virgin Islands the Caribbean

Jessica Shaw unlocked the front door of her home, stepped inside, and turned off the alarm system. She immediately knew something was wrong.

Dropping the suitcase she was carrying on the foyer's marble floor, she ran to the side cabinet and pulled out the pistol she kept there for protection. Gun in hand, she went still, listened for sounds.

All Jessica heard was the chime of her grandfather clock and the quiet hum of the central air conditioner. She sensed something wasn't right. *Did someone break in when I was traveling?* she thought, her heart racing. *Should I call the police?*

She almost pulled out her cell phone, then thought better of it. *I don't need the police snooping around. Not until I'm sure I need their help. It's not like I'm a school teacher or a librarian. The cops are bound to find out something about Flash.*

Turning around, she inspected the front door lock, saw nothing unusual.

With the pistol in front of her, she went through all of the rooms on both floors of the house, and checked every door and window, but found no signs of a break-in.

Still, something felt wrong, as if someone had invaded her space.

And it couldn't have been her longtime housekeeper. She'd told the matronly woman not to come to her house during her trip.

I'm getting paranoid, Jessica mused. *There's no sign of forced entry and my house alarm was on.* Shaking her head at her stupid paranoia, she went to the kitchen to get some wine. She needed something to calm her nerves.

But before she poured herself a glass, another thought struck her.

Gun in hand she sprinted out of the kitchen and raced to the home office on the first floor. She unlocked the door, flicked on the lights, and went inside.

She studied the office carefully, saw no signs of disturbance. Everything looked the same as she remembered from before her trip. Then she went into the adjoining laboratory, unlocked and opened the steel safe and counted the glass bottles filled with blue powder. Realizing none had been taken, she breathed a sigh or relief. Relocking the safe, she left the lab and went back to the home office.

Going behind the desk, she unlocked the drawers and inspected the files. Noticing some of the folders had been riffled through, her heart began to pound.

Damn, someone was here!

And worse, it dawned on her, who ever came in was a professional, someone who knew how to cover their tracks well.

Quickly closing the drawers and relocking them, she picked up the gun and left the room, her mind racing.

She had to figure out what the hell was going on. And do it fast, before the rest of her plans were compromised.

Chapter 47

St. Croix, U.S. Virgin Islands
the Caribbean

The American Airlines jet landed at St. Croix's Henry Rholsen Airport, and after deplaning and collecting his bag, J.T. Ryan rented a car at the terminal.

Ryan had been to the island a few times before and was familiar with the layout of the place. He drove the Chevy Impala to the Buccaneer Hotel, which was just a few miles from Christiansted, and checked in.

It was past six p.m. so he decided to wait until morning to start his search. After a meal at the hotel's Brass Parrot's restaurant, he went to the beach bar by the pool and idly watched, along with a group of sunburned tourists, the sun set on the horizon.

***

Ryan parked the Impala in the Christiansted post office parking lot and turned off the engine.

It was early morning and the place hadn't opened yet. He raked back his seat and settled in to wait. It was the drill he followed religiously when doing surveillance work. Get there early and observe the activity before jumping in. Sometimes it made for long, tedious hours doing nothing but sipping coffee; but he knew that in many cases, waiting and watching was the backbone of investigative work. *It's not as sexy as you see in movies*, Ryan mused. *Most times it's boring as hell.*

But he had so little information on his current assignment that he didn't have much choice. His only other option was to confront the local post office authorities and find out why the P.O. box regulations had been violated. But Christiansted only had a population of around 3,000 people. In a small city like that, everyone probably knew everyone else. Connections between people in power and those with money, he suspected, were probably tight. It was human nature, and he'd seen that scenario played out many times before. If he started asking tough questions too soon, it was bound to get back to the guilty party, who would likely get spooked and disappear. Something he couldn't afford. No, he'd have to do this the slow, boring way.

Ryan glanced around the mostly empty parking lot, then back at the post office building. It was a small, one-story structure of Dutch colonial era architecture, painted in the pastel yellow and pink so common in Caribbean islands. Graceful palm trees dotted the area.

The U.S. Virgin Islands, Ryan knew, were composed of four isles: St. Croix, St. John, St. Thomas, and Water Island. Luckily for him, St. Thomas was the hub of tourist activity, while St. Croix was much more relaxed. It was mostly a quiet island, with a population of only 50,000 people. *That's going to make my job easier*, he thought.

As the early morning progressed, activity picked up, with post office vans and Jeeps coming out of the gated area to the right of the building, and exiting the parking lot, no doubt on their way to make the day's deliveries.

There were large windows on the front of the building and he noticed lights flick on inside. At 10 a.m. sharp the front doors were unlocked and Ryan stepped out of the car and walked toward the entrance. By this time the lot was half-full and other postal customers began getting out of their vehicles to go inside.

Ryan entered through the glass front door and quickly scanned the place. Just ahead was the counter, where two postal employees were taking care of customers. To his left was an area with supplies for sale and directly to his right was a wall composed of post office boxes.

Going toward the wall of boxes, he found the right one, then turned around and gazed out the large windows of the building toward the parking lot. Luckily for him, the line of sight was good.

Turning back to the post office boxes, he counted the row and column of the correct one, memorized the location, and after watching for another minute as a few people opened boxes and got their mail, he left the building. It would look suspicious if he'd stayed inside, observing others. The last thing he needed was to have customers report a stranger to the cops.

He walked back to the car, got in and checked the vantage point. Realizing he could do better, he started up the Impala and re-parked the car in a different part of the lot with a better angle, but not so close to the building that it would be suspicious.

After taking a sip from his coffee, he propped the *Virgin Islands Daily News*, the island's newspaper, on the steering wheel and pretended to read as he kept a close eye on the place.

He'd brought along a small binocular but now knew he wouldn't need it much. After the morning 'rush' of a few customers, the activity at the post office dropped off. The locals who did go in headed for the counter.

The hours passed slowly.

Ryan moved his car a few times to avoid parking in one spot too long. He ate a bagged lunch in the vehicle, sipped coffee from a thermos, all while doing surveillance. It was a good thing he had a strong bladder and didn't have to leave the car.

During the day he noticed several people go into the building to check P.O. boxes, but none of them were close to the box he watched.

At closing time a postal employee approached the front door from the inside and locked it. Soon after the building's interior lights dimmed.

"Damn," Ryan muttered to himself. The day had been a total bust. He started up the Impala and drove off.

***

Ryan's second day of surveillance at the post office began much like the first. Sitting in the car, sipping coffee, he watched as a small group of customers went inside as soon as the place opened, did their business, and left. After that, activity dropped off, with just a few patrons going to the counter to mail packages. It felt like the movie Groundhog Day, and by one p.m. he was tired and irritable.

But an hour later he noticed something out of the ordinary. A late model white Rolls-Royce drove into the lot and parked. The car was the most expensive vehicle he'd seen since his arrival on the island, and he sat up straighter, eyed the Rolls closely.

A good-looking woman wearing a charcoal gray business suit stepped out of the car and began walking toward the building's entrance. She was a petite, athletic woman in her thirties with shoulder-length black hair. She went inside and instead of going to the counter, headed directly toward the wall of boxes. Ryan grabbed the binos and peered, and his pulse quickened when he saw she was opening the right one. She removed the contents of the box, and placed them in the leather briefcase she was carrying. Closing the box, she turned and left the building.

He watched as she marched back to her Rolls-Royce and noticed the certainty of her stride, and the hardness of her gaze. It was a look that said, don't get in my way.

As the car drove away he memorized the license plate number.

Instead of starting up the Impala and following, he pulled out his cell phone and punched in a number.

When Erin Welch picked up on the line, he said, "It's Ryan."

"Hi, J.T."

"I need you to run a plate for me. It's for a white Rolls-Royce Phantom Coupe with St. Croix plates." He gave her the number. "A woman was driving it. In her thirties, black hair, a little over five feet tall."

"Okay, J.T. Give me a couple of minutes. I'll call you back." She hung up and he placed the phone on the dash and took a sip of his now cold coffee.

Ryan's cell phone buzzed ten minutes later and he took the call.

"Okay," Erin said, "The Rolls is registered to a Jessica Shaw, and she has a St. Croix address. I also pulled her driver's license info. She's 37, shoulder-length black hair, black eyes, 5'2"."

"That fits her description. I'm sure it's her. Does she have a rap sheet, Erin?"

"No. No record of arrests. Only a few traffic tickets over the last five years, for speeding. Other than that, she's clean."

"What's her occupation?"

"It's listed as housewife, J.T."

"How does a 'housewife' afford a Rolls?"

Erin chuckled. "Good question. She's married to a chemist, or she was – from what the records show, he died recently of natural causes."

"A chemist, huh? That may be the drug angle here. What was his name?"

"Paul Shaw. Like Jessica, he had no record of arrests either. He didn't work for a company – it appears he had his own business but nothing is showing up on it. The Shaw's own a home there in St. Croix – an expensive place, more of an estate. The couple have no children."

"Okay, Erin. Did you find any connection to Jose Garcia or anyone else on the case?"

"No. But I'm still checking. What's your next move?"

Ryan thought about that a moment. "What I always do. Stake out her house. When the timing's right, I make my move."

"Don't get killed," she said in a serious tone. "I need your help solving this case."

"You're a sweetheart, you know that?" he replied with a chuckle. Then he hung up.

Ryan fired up the car and drove out of the lot. He input the address Erin had given him into the Impala's nav system. The island wasn't that large and it came up right away.

He took the coastal highway going east, noticing traffic was light.

It was a bright, sunny day in the mid-seventies, and he tabbed down the windows and breathed in the fresh, salty air. To his left lay the Caribbean, the water sparkling aquamarine blue. White sandy beaches dotted with palm trees stretched for miles. He spotted people swimming or lounging by the water's edge.

He passed several large resorts, some smaller hotels, and then the signs of development gave way to dense vegetation on one side of the road and vacant stretches of beach on the other.

Seeing a fork in the highway up ahead, he slowed and scanned the signs, noticed the turnoff was the right one. He followed the side road as it wound around dense vegetation of sea grape and mangroves. Five minutes later he spotted a very large, two-story home to his left and slowed the Impala. It was built in the graceful Dutch colonial style with lush landscaping. The home had a wide, semicircular gravel driveway. Parked in front of the place was the white Rolls he'd seen earlier. He could hear the pounding of the surf nearby, and he realized the back of the home faced the ocean.

Ryan didn't stop in front of the home, but instead kept driving well past it. Pulling his car off the road, he hid it in a sheltered area under some coconut palms.

After checking the load in his revolver, he replaced it in his hip holster, grabbed the binos, climbed out of the car and locked it.

Then he began walking.

Chapter 48

Alaska

Nicholas Drago was in his home office doing paperwork and heard a knock at the door.

"Come in," Drago said, putting his pen down on his desk, and turning his wheelchair so it faced the door.

His bodyguard Heather stepped inside. "Sir, there's a call for you on line two."

"Who is it?"

"The investigator you hired. He's calling from St. Croix."

"Thank you, Heather." He waited for the young woman to leave the room before he picked up the receiver.

"You have something for me," Drago said into the phone.

"Yes, sir," the man on the other line replied. "Per your instructions we've been keeping a close eye on your daughter, Ms Shaw."

"And?"

"We spotted a man watching her house. He's been at it for a couple of hours, so it's not a casual thing."

"I see. Is it a police officer?"

"No. We don't believe so. He's driving a car with rental plates. But by the precautions he takes and the stealthy way he moves, he's a professional, probably a PI. We would have never seen him except we've been watching her house 24/7. What do you want us to do, sir?"

Drago said nothing as he processed this information. He idly rubbed the top of the wheelchair roller with his bony hand.

"What do you want us to do?" the man asked again.

"Kill him," Drago replied.

"That wasn't in our original contract, sir. That costs more."

"I don't care what the hell it costs!" Drago yelled into the phone. "Just do it!" Then he slammed down the receiver.

Chapter 49

St. Croix, U.S. Virgin Islands
the Caribbean

Ryan was hiding in a thicket across the road from the Shaw house, his binoculars trained on the front of the place.

It was well past nine p.m., but the moonlight and the home's portico lights provided ample light. The Rolls was still parked in the semicircular driveway; it hadn't moved since he'd arrived. The only activity he'd seen was an hour ago, when one of the garage doors had rolled up and a small Honda Civic had emerged. From the dents in the bodywork of the Honda, he figured the driver, an older woman, was probably a housekeeper or cook.

The Honda had driven off, the garage door had rolled closed, and a short while later one of the second story lights came on.

Ryan glanced at his watch. *As good a time as any*, he thought.

Leaving the binos in the thicket, he crossed the road and walked onto the property, his shoes crunching over the gravel driveway. Pulling out the FBI contractor ID Erin had given him, he strode up the steps and pressed the door buzzer.

After a few moments he saw interior lights turn on in the first floor and he heard muffled footfalls from the other side of the door.

"Who is it?" a woman's voice called out.

"My name's John Ryan. I work for the FBI. I need to ask you a few questions."

"It's ten o'clock at night, damn it," the angry voice replied. "Come back some other time."

"I'm sorry, ma'am. But this is a murder investigation. This can't wait."

"A murder? Slide your ID under the door. I want to check it out."

Ryan did as instructed and a moment later the door opened partway. Standing there was the attractive woman he'd seen earlier at the post office, this time wearing a stylish white silk robe over white silk pajamas.

"Your ID looks real enough, Ryan. What's this about a murder, and what's the FBI want with me?"

"If I can come in, Ms Shaw, I'll explain everything."

"I don't like strangers coming to my home at night. I should call the police."

"If you'd like to do that, Ms Shaw," Ryan said, calling her bluff, "go ahead. I'll just wait out here until they get here."

Jessica Shaw had a sour, angry look on her face, but underneath that he sensed a hint of fear. He'd sensed that before when dealing with criminals. They were always wary of being found out. The last thing they wanted was more police involvement.

After another moment, the woman opened the door fully. "Fine. You can come in for a minute. But be warned. I have a gun and I'm not afraid to use it."

She stepped aside and he walked into the high-ceiling foyer. She closed the door behind him and he noticed she wasn't lying about the gun. She was holding a semi-automatic pistol at her side.

"Let's go in here," she said, pointing to a sitting room right off the foyer. By the elegant furnishings, the ornate, gilt-edged paintings on the walls, and cut-glass chandeliers hanging from the ceiling, the place looked and smelled of money. Big money.

They sat on opposite overstuffed couches and she placed the gun on her lap. She was still holding his ID and she tapped on it. "This says you work for the FBI and that you're out of Atlanta. What's all this about?" Her eyes, a coal-black color, flashed. By her icy tone and imperious manner, it was clear the woman was a tough customer, used to getting her way.

"I'm working on a murder investigation," Ryan began. "The murders took place in Atlanta and illegal narcotics are involved. We found a connection to you from a Colombian drug lord by the name of Jose Garcia."

At the mention of Garcia's name, her eyes grew wary. "There must be some mistake. I'm not involved with anything illegal."

He held up a palm. "I'm not accusing you of anything. I just need you to clear up some things for us."

She frowned. "Such as?"

"You rent a post office box in Christiansted."

"I do not," she replied icily.

"Yes you do. I saw you pick up your mail there earlier today."

Jessica Shaw's hand gripped the pistol in her lap.

"I wouldn't do anything rash, Ms Shaw. I'm armed and very well trained. You point that gun at me and you'll be dead a second later."

She relaxed the grip on the pistol and her hand went to her forehead, where she wiped away the beads of perspiration that had formed there. "Maybe I do rent a P.O. box, Ryan. So what? There's no law against that."

"When you rent a post office box in a U.S. state or a territory like St. Croix, you have to present identification, and your legal name has to be public. There's no record of that ever happening. So you've already broken the law." He paused, his eyes boring into hers. "But let's leave that aside for now. Let's talk about your connection to Jose Garcia, the Colombian drug kingpin."

"There's absolutely no connection between us!" she shouted angrily.

"Before Garcia was killed in Colombia, I searched his house in Marinilla – your P.O. box number was listed in his illegal narcotics records."

"I'm sure that's a mistake," she said, but by the look on her face it was clear she was afraid.

"There's no mistake, Ms Shaw."

The woman stood up abruptly. "I need to call my lawyer now."

In a split-second, Ryan drew his revolver from its holster and pointed it at the woman's chest. "Sit back down. You're not calling anybody."

She stared at the gun and froze, then slowly sat back down on the sofa.

Ryan reached over, took her pistol and pocketed it. "Now, Ms Shaw, it's time to tell the truth."

"I'm not saying another word. I know my rights. You work for the FBI, so you do too." She folded her arms across her chest, a smug look on her face.

"I do work for the FBI. But I'm a contractor. I'm a free agent, you might say. I make up my own rules."

Her smugness vanished. "What do you mean?"

"I mean I want answers and I want them now."

"Bullshit! You look tough and you sound tough, but what are you going to do? Shoot me? I don't think so."

"You're right, Ms Shaw. I won't shoot you. I wouldn't get answers that way, would I? But I can do the next best thing."

"What's that?"

Ryan re-holstered his pistol, stood up, and began rolling up the cuffs of his long-sleeve shirt.

"What are you doing, Ryan?"

"I'm going to beat the hell out of you," he stated, his voice hard.

"You'd beat up a woman? You fucking asshole!"

Ryan had no intention of beating her up, but he had to make it look convincing, otherwise she'd call his bluff.

He reached out with one of his large, rugged hands and gripped her by the throat.

Her eyes went wide, obviously shocked by his action.

"You're 5'2" and petite, Ms Shaw. I'm very strong, well over six feet tall and 200 pounds of muscle. How much pressure do you think it'll take for me to break you neck?" To make his point, he squeezed her throat hard and her face began turning red. She tried kneeing him in the groin, but he swatted her leg away.

He kept up the pressure on her throat and a second later she held up both hands.

Ryan let go of her and she began coughing and massaging her neck with one hand.

"You'll talk now, Ms Shaw?"

"Yes, damn it. I'll talk."

"Good." He sat back down across from her. "You and Garcia are connected."

"Yes."

"How?"

"I believe he did some work for my husband."

"Paul Shaw."

"That's right, Ryan. Paul was my husband."

"He's dead."

"Yes, the poor man died of a heart attack recently. I loved him so much," she said, trying to sound as if she was grieving, but Ryan could tell it was an act. From her arrogant attitude it was obvious the woman had a heart of stone.

"You're husband was a chemist."

"That's right."

"Did he develop chemical drug formulas for Garcia?"

She massaged the red marks on her neck some more. "I wouldn't know. Paul had business dealings with this Garcia character, but I wasn't involved."

"So you expect me to believe you don't know anything about illegal narcotics?"

"That's right!"

"You drive a Rolls-Royce. How'd you afford that?"

"I have – I had – a very generous, loving husband."

"I'm sure you did. But you don't strike me as a loving, adoring wife. You're no Tammy Wynnette, standing by her man. No. You strike me as a hard, callous, take-charge kind of woman. A woman who knows exactly what's going on."

"You're insulting me! You're wrong about me ...."

"I'm not buying it, Ms Shaw. Your husband was involved with Garcia and so were you."

"Look, Ryan, I'm telling the truth. I always suspected Paul was involved with something shady, but I'm just a housewife. I don't have a head for business."

Ryan laughed. "That's total bullshit."

"No, it's not."

He leaned forward and stared directly into her eyes. "You and your husband are part of this new drug operation."

"What new drug?"

"Skyflash, Ms Shaw."

Her mouth gaped open. She tried to say something but no words came out.

"Yes, I know all about Flash," Ryan continued. "I believe Paul Shaw, a chemist, developed this new narcotic and had Garcia manufacture it at his factory in Colombia."

The woman's mouth closed and she said nothing.

"You know about Flash, Ms Shaw. I'm going to search your house later. I'd be surprised not to find that drug here."

Jessica Shaw gave him a thin smile. "That's where you're wrong. Search all you like. You won't find anything here."

"Maybe not," he replied. "But I bet you know where it is. If it's not at your house, you have it stashed at some other location. And you'll tell me where that is. You're also tell me where you keep your files about Flash. That'll prove you're knee deep in criminal activity."

She shook her head forcefully. "I won't."

Ryan grabbed her face with one hand and held it tightly. Then he closed his other hand into a fist and pressed it hard against her cheek. "You're a pretty woman. Very pretty. But you won't be when I'm through with you."

Her eyes grew wide again and she flinched away from him.

It had been a good sales job on his part and she bought it.

"Don't do it, Ryan! I'll talk."

He lowered his fist. "Okay. Start talking."

Just then he heard the front door buzzer ring. Startled by the noise, he stood, pulled his gun and pointed it at the woman. "Who are you expecting?"

"Nobody."

"Maybe it's your housekeeper. I saw her leave earlier."

"She's left for the day. She doesn't live here full time. She only works for me a few days a week."

"Okay. Go answer the door." He motioned with the pistol. "I'll be out of sight, listening to everything you say. One wrong move and ...." He didn't finish the sentence.

Jessica got up from the sofa and slowly walked out of the room and into the foyer.

Ryan followed and hugged the wall to the right of the door, his gun in his hand.

The woman opened the door partway. "Yes?" she said.

"We're employed by your father, Ms Shaw," Ryan heard a man say.

"My father?"

"Yes, Ms Shaw. We saw a stranger casing your house earlier – he went inside a short while ago. We think you're in danger and we're here to help."

Jessica must have given them some type of signal because suddenly she jumped away from the entrance and the door slammed open as if someone had kicked it in.

In a blur of motion, Ryan went into a crouch and pointed his gun with both hands toward the entrance. At the same time he caught a glimpse of two large men holding pistols as they barged into the foyer. He heard the blast of a shot and saw a muzzle flash.

He fired off two quick rounds, spun away and went back into the sitting room, where he took cover behind the arched entry of the room. Pointing his gun forward, he peered into the foyer, saw a limp body crumpled on the floor, red splotches staining the white marble.

His adrenaline pumping, Ryan glanced around, didn't see Jessica Shaw anywhere. *Where the hell is she?* he thought. But that was secondary – first he had to deal with the second gunman who was out there, somewhere in the darkness outside the home.

Seconds ticked by as he planned his next move.

He heard a car door opening and closing, a car engine start and then the crunching of tires on the gravel driveway. *Had the second gunman fled?*

As if to answer him, Ryan saw a muzzle flash and heard the crack of a shot from the front doorway. Plaster chunks flew off the wall above his head.

He fired off two more rounds in the direction of the entryway. He caught a glimpse of a man's shoulder and he fired again, heard a strangled scream of pain.

Ryan rushed toward the open doorway, hugged the wall to the right of it. Peering around the door jam, he almost ran into the barrel of a large pistol.

He fired another two rounds and heard a loud thud, and then the clatter of metal on marble.

Cautiously, he peeked around the doorjamb again, saw a man's body lying inert on the stoop, a gun next to him. Rushing outside, he kicked the man's gun away, crouched next to the body and felt for a pulse. There was none.

Ryan stood and glanced around the front yard of the home. The Rolls-Royce that had been parked on the driveway was gone.

Chapter 50

Atlanta, Georgia

Erin Welch was startled awake by the ringing of her cell phone.

Sitting up on her bed, she groggily picked up the phone, which was resting on the night stand.

"It's Ryan," she heard the man say as she took the call. She glanced at the clock on the wall.

"It's past midnight, J.T. This better be good."

"Listen, Erin. I need you to do something, and fast."

Erin yawned. "What?"

"I found Jessica Shaw. She's definitely part of the Skyflash drug ring. She didn't confess to it, but she's guilty as hell."

Hearing this, Erin became wide awake. "You have her in custody?"

"No. That's where I need your help. Two goons with guns blazing barged in her house while I was questioning her and she fled. I tried following her, but she was long gone. St. Croix is not a big island and has only one airport. You need to contact the authorities here and have them stop her if she tries to fly out."

"You got it, J.T."

"One more thing. Put out a BOLO for her Rolls-Royce. You have the plate number. We may be able to pick her up that way."

"I'm on it. Where are you now?"

"I'm at her house; I want to search the place, see if I can find any records or evidence of Flash."

"Okay, J.T. What about the two gunmen you mentioned?"

"Both dead. I shot them."

"And you expect me to explain all of this to the cops in St. Croix, I suppose."

"I shot them in self-defense, Erin."

Erin shook her head slowly, a thin smile crossing her lips. "I always have to clean up your messes, don't I?"

She heard Ryan chuckle.

"Well," he said, "you did tell me not to get killed."

"All right. I'll call the police down there and explain the situation. By the way, who were the two men you shot?"

"They had no ID on them. I figure they were local guns for hire."

"Okay. I'll get busy on my end."

"Thanks, Erin."

She hung up the phone and got out of bed.

Quickly throwing on some clothes, she went to her condo's home office to make the calls.

Chapter 51

St. Croix, U.S. Virgin Islands
the Caribbean

Jessica Shaw drove the Rolls-Royce over the rutted dirt road, the large coupe's pristine white paint now covered with mud. She was in a remote, desolate part of the island and she saw less and less signs of life the deeper she drove into the densely wooded area. It was the middle of the night and the only lights visible were the headlights of her car.

Jessica stepped on the gas and the vehicle shot forward, bouncing over rocks and puddles of muddy water. She'd driven at high speed the whole way here, anxious to get away from the FBI guy Ryan and the two mysterious gunmen, who, she was certain, had saved her from certain arrest. *Who the hell were they?* She'd worry about that later. Now her priority was getting off the island.

In her race to escape, she'd only managed to grab her cell phone, passport, cash, and her credit cards. The only clothes she had were those she was wearing.

Jessica guided the car around a couple of curves and the road straightened, emerging from the dense woods on to a flat, low-lying area covered with wild grasses. Her headlights lit up her destination, directly ahead. A small house built of natural stone, and next to it, a landing strip. At one end of the strip was parked a single-engine, turbo-prop Cessna.

Driving to the front of the home, she stopped and turned off the Rolls. The house, like the airstrip, was dark, as she'd expected at this time of night. A Ford pickup truck was parked in front of the home which told her the man was here.

Getting out of the car, she went to the front door and knocked loudly.

She waited a minute, and hearing nothing, began banging loudly on the wooden door. Moments later the porch light came on and the door opened. A tall, unshaven man wearing a wife-beater T-shirt and dirty dungarees stood there.

"Oh, it's you," the man said in a Southern drawl. "Where's Paul?"

Jessica grimaced. "Guess you haven't heard, Scott. My husband died recently."

Scott belched. "Sorry ... to hear that. Come in ... come in ...."

She went into the small, shabby living room, which was littered with empty beer cans, pizza boxes, and fast food wrappers.

He pushed some of the liter off a faded, lumpy sofa, and said, "Have a seat ...."

She wrinkled her nose. "No thanks. Think I'll stand."

"Suit yourself, Jessica. What ... brings you here?"

"I need to charter your plane."

Scott rubbed his unshaven face. "Sure ... no problem ... flying's what I do ...." He belched then laughed. "That's ... my slogan."

"Yeah, I bet." She stared into his bloodshot eyes. "Are you drunk?"

"Hell, no ...."

The man stank of booze, but she knew her options were limited. The airport was probably crawling with cops by now.

"Listen, Scott. I need to go to Miami."

"No problem. I don't ... have any charters ... scheduled for tomorrow ... we can take off ... first thing in the morning."

"I need to go tonight."

He rubbed his stubbled face again. "Tonight? You're ... kidding, right?"

"No."

"What's your hurry?" He grinned. "You're not ... doing anything illegal are you?"

"That's none of your fucking business."

He laughed and belched again. "Yeah. That's okay. I'm ... no saint either. All right. We'll go out ... tonight ... but it'll cost you more ...."

"How much?"

"Since I did charter work ... for your husband ... I'll give you the corporate rate ...."

"How much, Scott?"

The man stated a large amount.

"You're crazy. That's too much."

Scott shrugged. "Hey ... I'm the one ... doing you a favor, remember?" Then he gave her a sly look. "But ... now that your husband's gone ... maybe we could work out ... another arrangement ...."

"Like what?"

He rubbed his crotch suggestively. "You're ... a good-looking woman ... Jessica ... you take care of me, and I'll charge you half price ...."

She leaned in close to him, her eyes blazing with anger. "How about I kick you in the balls instead?"

He shrugged, but he had a disappointed look on his face. "I'll take that ... as a no ...."

"You're a perceptive man, Scott." Reaching into her pocket, she took out one of the credit cards she had there. "You take American Express?"

"Yes ... I do."

"Good. Now, you got any coffee in this dump you call a home?"

"Sure ... why?"

"You need to sober up before we take off."

Chapter 52

St. Croix, U.S. Virgin Islands
the Caribbean

J.T. Ryan started his search of the Shaw's home on the second floor, carefully inspecting the bedrooms, sitting rooms, and even the bathrooms. Finding no evidence of criminal activity, he went downstairs and repeated the process in the rooms there.

Ryan found nothing suspicious until he came to the home office, located toward the front of the house. But here, it was what he didn't find that was suspicious. First off, there was no computer or printer in the room, as he expected, nor any rolodex of phone numbers. More importantly, as he went through the desk drawers, he found no files or folders of any kind. He checked the metal filing cabinets in the room and likewise noticed they also had been cleaned out.

Finishing in the office, he stepped into the adjacent room, which was a laboratory.

Here again, he located no files or records, not even any trace of chemicals. The cabinets were completely bare, with no beakers or glass bottles of any kind, something you'd expect in a lab.

There was a metal safe at one side of the room. As he approached it, Ryan was surprised to find the safe unlocked and empty of any contents.

Frustrated at his lack of success in collecting criminal evidence, Ryan realized Jessica Shaw had seen this coming.

Chapter 53

Alaska

Nicholas Drago was in his home office at his computer when he heard a knock at the door. "Come in," Drago said, turning his wheelchair so it faced the door.

Thomas Carpenter came into the room, a grim look on his face.

"What's wrong, Thomas?"

"I have bad news, sir."

Drago gripped the tops of the wheelchair rollers with his hands. "What is it?"

"Sir, the men I hired, the investigators who were looking into your daughter's activities, are dead."

"What? What the hell happened?"

Carpenter frowned. "They were keeping an eye on Ms Shaw's home, and as you know, they spotted a man prowling her property. Per your instructions, they went to her aid. From the police reports that were filed, both of our men were killed. They were shot by that Atlanta PI, John Ryan."

"Damn!" Drago yelled. "That's the FBI contractor, isn't it?"

"Yes, sir."

"Was Jessica hurt?"

"Not that I can tell from the police reports. The local cops in St. Croix searched her house, but couldn't find her. The FBI has an All Points Bulletin out for her – she's a suspect in a criminal conspiracy."

Drago shook his head, saddened by the news. *It's all catching up to her*, he thought.

"What do you want me to do now, sir?"

Nicholas Drago didn't respond, his thoughts engulfed by Jessica's predicament. His only child, his only family was in jeopardy. He had to do something. *But what?*

"What do you want me to do now?" Carpenter repeated.

"Get out of here, Thomas! I need to think."

Chapter 54

Miami, Florida

Jessica Shaw stared at the bathroom mirror and barely recognized herself.

She had dyed her black hair blonde and cut it shorter.

Jessica knew she needed to ditch her real passport and have a new one created, one with a fake name and with a picture of her new look. *But how?* she thought. *Who the hell do I know here?* She felt lucky to have escaped St. Croix, but was now in an unfamiliar city. A city where she had no contacts.

She left the bathroom and went to the motel room's window where she peeked around the closed shades. The room was on the second floor and it overlooked a half-empty parking lot. In the distance she could make out the high-rise condos of Miami Beach.

Jessica had picked the cheap motel on purpose – it was one of those places where they took only cash and asked no questions.

Turning away from the window, she sat on the lumpy bed, trying to sort out her next move. She sat there for the next half hour, mulling her situation. When she'd fled her home in St. Croix, she'd heard multiple shots fired and had seen one man fall to the ground. It was a good bet the cops would be on the lookout for her. *How long can I evade them?*

Knowing her options were limited, she made a decision. Swallowing her pride, she took her cell phone from her pocket and punched in a number she'd memorized a long time ago.

When the other line picked up, she said, "It's me, Jessica."

"God, what a relief," Nicholas Drago replied. "I didn't know if you were dead or alive."

"You heard what happened, father?"

"Yes. Thomas got a hold of the St. Croix police report."

"I'm in real trouble."

"I know you are, Jessica. The FBI's got an APB out on you."

"Shit."

"Where are you now?"

"I'd rather not say, father – I don't know how secure this line is."

"Okay. What do you plan to do?"

"I fucking don't know. That's why I called. I need your help, father."

"Come home."

"To your house?"

"Yes, Jessica. You'll be safe here."

She thought about this a moment, hated the idea of going to Alaska. In fact, she hated the idea of asking her father for help. *But what other option do I have?* She gripped the cell phone tightly, trying to decide. "I got a better idea. Wire me some money. I'm getting low on cash, and I'm afraid of using my credit cards, especially if the FBI is on my ass."

"You want me to wire you money?" the man said, his voice hard.

"That's right, father."

"I already loaned you a large amount of money. Remember?" By his harsh tone, it was clear her father was angry.

"Yes, I know. And I appreciate it. But I'm in real trouble now. You're the only person I can turn to."

"Look, Jessica. Here's the deal. You come here and I'll protect you. We can work through your problems. But I want something in return."

"What?"

"I want the formula, Jessica."

"The formula? What formula?"

"The chemical formula for Skyflash. Thomas told me all about your new wonder drug. I want it. I need it. I'm a frail, old man. From what I understand, with this narcotic I can feel like a young, vibrant man."

"Father, the narcotic has some terrible side affects. It can kill you, if you're not careful."

"I can make it work, damn it! I'll hire the best chemist in the world. I'll hire a crew of chemists. I can afford it. They'll figure out a way to make this damn drug work for me. What else do I have to live for, anyway?"

Jessica thought through her father's demand. Sitting there on the lumpy bed of the cheap motel, she realized she had no choice but to go to Alaska and give up the only thing she had left of value: the formula.

"Okay, father. I agree to your terms."

"Excellent, Jessica. You're making the right decision."

Chapter 55

Atlanta, Georgia

"Too bad you didn't find any evidence at the Shaw's house," Erin Welch said, as she pushed aside her half-finished plate of moo-shoo pork.

"I agree," J.T. Ryan replied. "My guess is Jessica Shaw stashed the drugs and files someplace nearby."

The two people were having lunch at the Chinese restaurant on the lobby level of the FBI building. As usual, the place was crowded and noisy, full of Bureau agents, attorneys, and plainclothes cops.

Erin took a sip of her tea. "I've got the police in St. Croix looking. If she hid the stuff on the island, they'll find it eventually."

"Good," Ryan said, in between bites of his egg roll. "You have enough to charge her?"

Erin tucked her long hair behind her ears. "From what you found out, we issued an arrest warrant for suspicion of a criminal conspiracy."

Ryan finished his egg roll, pushed aside his plate, and wiped his now greasy fingers with paper napkins. "But first we have to catch Shaw."

Erin frowned. "Yeah. There is that. We've got an APB out on her, but so far zilch."

He signaled the waiter and when the young man approached the table, Ryan ordered more tea for Erin and another Pepsi for himself. "I just thought of something. Something that I completely forgot about because I was dodging bullets at the time. When the two gunmen got to Shaw's house, they said they were employed by her father. We need to check that out. Maybe she went to him to hide out."

"Okay. I'll start to work on that."

The waiter returned, served them their drinks and removed the empty plates. When the man walked away, Ryan said, "So what's next?"

Erin took a sip of her tea. "We keep looking. It'll be difficult for Jessica Shaw to evade us forever."

"You need me for anything else?"

"Not right now, J.T. I've got to work the case on my end. I'll call you as soon as I have something."

"That's good, because I want to spend some time with Lauren at the hospital."

"Any change?"

"No. I went to see her yesterday."

"Sorry to hear that, J.T."

Ryan nodded, dejected from Lauren's lack of progress. And she had been in a coma so long, that in the back of his mind he was worried she'd never recover.

He removed his wallet from a pocket and took out money for the restaurant meal.

"Oh, no you don't," Erin said. "This lunch is on me."

He shook his head. "No way. I never let a woman pay."

"What are you? A male chauvinist pig?"

"I've been called worse."

"You're intolerable sometimes," she replied with a frown. "But you already know that."

Ryan chuckled. "Yeah, I know. But don't forget, there are plenty of times I'm also charming and witty."

"Maybe you are witty sometimes. But you're not as funny as you think you are."

"I'll take that as a compliment."

"A small compliment, John Taylor Ryan."

Ryan smiled. "I'll take any I can get."

***

Ryan parked his car in the parking lot and walked into Emery Hospital. He'd been there so often that he knew the drill by heart. After signing in at the main desk on the first floor, he made his way up to the special trauma wing on the fifth floor. Then, after checking in with the nurses at the trauma desk, he strode toward Lauren's room.

Unlike many hospitals, the Emory facility was well-lit, excellently maintained, and for a hospital, a relatively cheery place. It was also staffed by some of the best medical professionals in the world. But as he walked down the corridor, there was no mistaking the antiseptic, medicinal scent that hung in the air, something no hospital can ever eliminate, even with the best filtration system.

Ryan found her room and stepped inside.

Lauren was there, lying on the bed with her eyes closed, her body covered to her waist by a sheet, just as he'd left her yesterday. She was wearing a print hospital gown and she was motionless, save for the slight heaving of her chest. He pulled a chair next to the bed and sat down.

He had to admit she looked better than when he'd left for his overseas trips. The respirator had been removed and she was breathing on her own. The bandages on her head were gone and the bruises, which had covered much of her face and arms, had disappeared. She still looked pale, and her long hair was matted, but other than that she appeared almost normal.

But even without makeup and with disheveled hair, she still looked like the most beautiful woman he'd ever seen. And she was certainly the most caring and loving woman he'd ever known. He felt a surge of emotion and fought back tears.

Ryan reached out and lightly caressed her hand. Her skin felt cool, but it reassured him that he could feel her pulse.

"It's me," he said, rubbing her hand. "Can you hear me?"

There was no reply.

"I love you, Lauren."

She said nothing and he settled back on the chair, content to be near her, holding her hand and watching her sleep.

***

"Mr. Ryan. Wake up, Mr. Ryan."

Ryan was startled awake by the sound of the voice. He jumped up from the chair and reached inside his jacket to pull his gun, then saw the nurse standing next to him.

"Mr. Ryan," the matronly nurse said, "visiting hours are over. You'll have to leave."

"Of course. I must have fallen asleep."

The woman smiled kindly.

"Can I spend another moment with her?" Ryan asked.

"Sure. But just a minute."

"Thanks." He sat back down as the nurse left the room.

Reaching out, he gently caressed his girlfriend's face.

Suddenly Lauren's eyes snapped open.

Startled, he pulled his hand away from her face.

Her eyes looked vacant for a moment as she gazed around the hospital room. Then she stared at Ryan. "Who are you?"

Ryan's heart pounded with excitement. "Lauren! You're awake!"

"What's going on? Where am I? Who are you?"

"You're at the hospital, hon. Do you remember what happened?"

She gazed around the room once again, a perplexed look on her face. "Hospital?"

"Yes, Lauren. You've been in a coma." His heart skipped a beat as the seconds ticked by and she didn't reply. He'd heard of coma patients who recovered physically but never regained their memory, the traumatic events giving them amnesia. *God, please God*, he thought, *bring her back to me.*

A minute later Lauren's eyes focused on Ryan and she gave him a wan smile.

"J.T," she said. "Now I remember what happened. The man going berserk. He attacked me and the others. I remember being put in an ambulance and I fell asleep. How long have I been here?"

"Months."

She reached out and took hold of one of his hands. "I love you, J.T."

Ryan's eyes welled up with tears of joy. "I love you too, hon."

Chapter 56

Miami, Florida

Jessica Shaw started up the rusted-out, ten-year-old Chevy clunker she'd bought for cash and pulled out of the parking lot of the motel. She was glad to be leaving the flea-ridden place, where she'd stayed for several days as she hunted for someone to make her a fake ID.

Luckily she now had a new driver's license and passport, although to her eyes the quality of the documents was marginal. Knowing she'd never be able to board a commercial flight to Alaska with the new ID, she was headed to the Greyhound terminal. It would be a long haul by bus, but she had little choice. Her father's plane was undergoing repairs so his people couldn't pick her up. Her clunker of a car would never make it to Alaska. On top of that, she was afraid of using her credit cards, now that the FBI was on her trail.

Jessica drove east on 29th Street, then turned north on Biscayne Boulevard. It was noon and traffic was extremely heavy on the four lane road, typical for Miami in January.

She stopped at a red light and impatiently tapped on the worn steering wheel, anxious to get to the bus terminal.

The light turned green, she gunned the engine, and the rusted-out Chevy surged forward.

Out of the corner of her eye she spotted it, but it was too late. A Dodge pickup truck, crossing the intersection at high speed.

She felt the impact of the crash, heard the crunch of metal, and saw shards of glass flying everywhere all at the same time as the truck T-boned her car on the passenger side.

Chapter 57

Atlanta, Georgia

J.T. Ryan was driving south on the SR 400 highway when he felt his cell phone buzz in his jacket pocket.

Keeping an eye on the traffic around him, he pulled the phone and held it to his ear.

"It's Erin," he heard the woman say. "We finally caught a break."

"That's great, Erin. What is it?"

"Where are you now?"

"On the 400."

"Okay, J.T. Come to my office. I want to tell you in person."

"You got it." He hung up the phone and rested it on the dash. Then he got off at the next exit and made his way downtown.

***

Erin saw Ryan as soon as he approached her glass-walled office and waved him in .

He sat in one of the visitor's chairs across from her and leaned forward. "We got a break in the case?"

A smile crossed her face. "That's right. And it's about time. This case has been a bitch from the start." Erin paused and tented her fingers on the desk. "Got a call from Miami PD. They picked up Jessica Shaw. She was involved in an auto accident down there – a truck crashed into the car she was driving. She wasn't hurt, but the ID she was carrying didn't look right so the cops checked her out thoroughly. They saw our APB about Shaw and put two and two together. She had dyed her hair blonde, but they realized it was Shaw."

"That's great, Erin. Where's she now?"

"She's in custody, on her way to Atlanta."

"Good. I want a crack at interrogating her. My last talk with her was interrupted."

"You'll get it. But I'll be grilling her myself." Erin smiled again. "You're not the only one who's proficient at getting answers from criminals."

Ryan nodded. "Yeah, I know."

Erin leaned back in her executive chair. "I was glad to hear Lauren came out of her coma."

He let out a long breath. "Thank God she did. I was really starting to worry ...." He didn't finish the sentence.

"She still at the hospital?"

"Yes, the doctors want to keep her at Emory for a couple of more days for observation. But they've done a battery of tests. They've given her a clean bill of health."

"That's great, J.T. If I can help in any way, just let me know."

He studied the woman, a little surprised at her remark. "I appreciate that. But I always got the feeling you didn't like Lauren."

"When you were overseas I visited her at the hospital several times. Seeing her like that, helpless in a coma ... I guess my impression of her mellowed."

Ryan smiled. "I can't believe it."

"Believe what, J.T.?"

"Beneath your icy exterior, there is a human heart beating."

Erin's eyes flashed in anger. "You bastard!"

"Take it easy," he said. "I was only kidding."

"Sometimes your jokes cross the line."

He held up a hand. "Sorry. I get carried away."

"You do."

She leaned forward in her chair and tented her hands on the desk. "There's something I need to tell you, and it isn't good news."

"Sounds serious."

"It is, J.T. The FBI Director is on the warpath again, and this time my job's in real jeopardy."

"I thought you had something on him, some dark chapter from his past."

"I did. But Stevens is a slimy bastard. A real snake in the grass and he's been able to slither away from that issue. With that threat gone, he's really gunning for me."

"You're an intelligent woman, Erin. I know you'll figure out a way to outsmart him."

She looked pensive. "I hope so. I really hope so."

Chapter 58

Atlanta, Georgia

Jessica Shaw was led into the small interrogation room by two FBI agents and pushed down on a chair. Then her shackled hands were locked to the metal loop on top of the rectangular table.

The two men left and she glanced around the room, noticed the opaque glass panel on the opposite wall. She had never been arrested before but had seen enough television cop shows to know that her every movement was being recorded by CCTV surveillance cameras.

Jessica was wearing a baggy, orange jumpsuit, just like she'd seen on the television shows. She was scared; had been scared from the moment of her arrest in Miami. She was a long way from her Rolls-Royce lifestyle, she realized. A long way from her beautiful home and all the trappings of wealth. The uncomfortable metal shackles, the scratchy jumpsuit, the fact she hadn't been able to bathe properly for days, the crappy jail food – all of it reminded her how far she'd fallen.

Fuck it, she thought. *I've got to snap out of this. Got to stop feeling sorry for myself. Figure a fucking way out.*

Just then the door opened and a good-looking woman walked in. She had long blonde hair pulled into a ponytail and was wearing an expensive, well-tailored gray business suit. The woman sat in the chair across from her and tented her hands on the table.

"I'm Assistant Director in Charge Erin Welch," the woman said.

"I don't care who you are," Jessica spat out, putting on a show of bravado she didn't feel. "I want to see my lawyer."

"Feisty, aren't you, Ms Shaw."

Jessica shook her shackled hands, the metal links clicking loudly against the loop. "Why am I here? Why was I arrested?"

"You're being held on criminal conspiracy charges. A drug conspiracy involving Colombian drug lord Jose Garcia."

"You have no proof of that!" Jessica shouted. "I'm sure that Ryan guy searched my house. Did he find anything?"

"We're still looking, Ms Shaw. We'll find it."

Jessica gave the other woman a hard stare. "See. You have nothing on me."

"That's not true. You were carrying a forged passport. That's a Federal offense. We also have you for violating U.S. Postal regulations in St. Croix."

Jessica's eyes flashed in anger. "Those are bullshit charges. My lawyer will get me out on bail for those."

The FBI woman leaned back in her chair. "Maybe. But there's something else. When we started investigating you, we noticed irregularities regarding your husband's recent death."

Fear crept up Jessica's spine and she felt a surge of bile in her throat. "Irregularities? What are you talking about? Paul's death was due to natural causes. The coroner said it was a heart attack."

"The death looks suspicious, Ms Shaw. An overdose of the illegal drug you're involved with, Flash, can lead to death by heart attack. We're having Paul Shaw's body exhumed. A proper autopsy will be performed."

"You can't do that!"

"You're wrong about that. An autopsy will be done."

Jessica shuddered as the chill of fear grew.

She heard a ringing sound and saw the FBI woman remove her cell phone from her jacket. The blonde held the phone to her ear and after a moment stood up and left the room.

When Welch came back a few minutes later, she had a broad smile on her face. "I just had a very interesting phone call, Ms Shaw. Care to know what it was about?"

Jessica shook her head forcefully. "I don't give a shit, you bitch. Just un-cuff me and let me call my lawyer. I know my rights."

Erin Welch continued smiling. "The call was from the St. Croix police department. They found the storage unit you rented. They found a stash of illegal drugs and boxes full of your files." The blonde placed both hands on the table and leaned in close to Jessica, her eyes boring into hers. "You're not going anywhere, Ms Shaw."

Chapter 59

Atlanta, Georgia

J.T. Ryan unlocked the front door of Lauren's modest, brick-front, two-story home in the northern suburbs and walked inside.

He flicked on the light in the foyer and closed the door behind him. The house, unused during her long stay at the hospital, smelled musty. Despite the cold outside, he opened several windows to bring in some fresh air. He'd close up in a few minutes and put the heat on.

After placing the bag of groceries he'd bought on the kitchen counter, he began putting away the food. Lauren was being released today from the hospital and he wanted to get her house ready for her return.

Ryan felt good. In fact, he felt great. Lauren was finally coming home.

On top of that, Jessica Shaw had been arrested. He was certain it was just a matter of time before the Flash case was completely resolved. Then he and Lauren could go on their long-delayed vacation to Italy.

With a spring in his step, Ryan went through the rest of the house, making sure the place was as ready as he could make it. He'd even considered cooking a meal for her, but knew his culinary skills were limited. He decided instead to get takeout food once he'd picked her up from the hospital.

After a last look around, he left the house and got in his car.

***

Ryan parked his Acura in the hospital parking lot and, going inside, signed in at the first floor desk. Then he made his way up to the trauma wing on the fifth floor.

As soon as he stepped off the elevator, he knew something was wrong. He saw two hospital security guards racing down the hallway, while a third was talking loudly with the nurses at the trauma desk.

Ryan strode to the desk. "What's going on?" he asked.

The head nurse, a woman he'd dealt with frequently turned toward him. "Mr. Ryan. I'm glad you're here."

"What is it?"

"She's gone, Mr. Ryan."

"Who's gone?"

"Lauren Chase. She's missing."

"What do you mean she's missing?"

"Our security people have searched the whole wing and the rest of the hospital, Mr. Ryan. We can't find her anywhere."

"That's crazy. I just saw her yesterday."

"I know. Do you think she might have left on her own?"

"Absolutely not," he replied. "She knew I was picking her up today. We talked about it. Are you sure she didn't wander off – went to the cafeteria to get something to eat?"

"We don't think that's what happened, Mr. Ryan." The nurse's eyes clouded with concern. "There's something else. In her hospital room, we found signs of a struggle. A broken glass. Some blood."

"Oh my God. Have you called the police?"

"Yes, of course. They're on their way."

Ryan's heart raced. *What the hell happened?* he thought, his mind churning. *Did she get confused, maybe fell off the bed and hurt herself, then wandered off? Was she kidnapped?*

Suddenly he felt his cell phone buzz in his jacket pocket. Stepping away from the nurses desk, he took the call.

It was a text message and it read:

RELEASE JESSICA SHAW.

OR WE KILL LAUREN CHASE.

Below the text was a proof-of-life photograph. It was a picture of Lauren standing in front of a white wall. She was wearing a hospital gown, she was gagged and blindfolded, and there was a cut on her forehead. She was holding up the front page of the *Atlanta Journal.* He looked closely at the newspaper's date – it was dated today.

Chapter 60

Atlanta, Georgia

J.T. Ryan slowed his car, pulled it to the curb, and turned it off.

Ryan was exhausted. He'd spent the last six hours, along with the Atlanta police department, searching every square inch of the hospital and the nearby areas, looking for clues to determine Lauren's location.

They'd found nothing.

Emory's security cameras had spotted no suspicious activity. Ryan was sure the kidnappers had been dressed as doctors or orderlies, enabling them to blend with the staff.

Ryan and the cops had broadened their search, inspecting the parking lots and nearby neighborhoods and business districts with no success. Worse than that, the phone the kidnappers had used was a burner, one those cheap cell phones that can't be traced; the kind you can buy at any Wal-Mart or Target store. It was clear the criminals were pros.

He drummed his fingers on the steering wheel, trying to assess his next move.

Taking out his phone, he called Erin Welch again. And again it went to voice mail. He'd called her numerous times already, and even talked to the FBI switchboard attendant, who'd told him Welch was in a meeting and could not be disturbed.

Realizing that continuing to drive around the hospital area would yield no more results, he decided to go to the FBI building downtown. Maybe with Erin's help his search would be more productive. He turned on his car, pulled away from the curb and drove directly there.

***

After going through the FBI building's security on the first floor, he took the elevator to Erin's level and strode down the corridor.

Looking through her glass-walled office, he saw she was inside. She was hunched over her desk, packing items in a box.

Ryan stepped inside the office, noticed several more boxes on the floor.

"I need your help and it's urgent," he blurted out. "I tried calling, but it kept going to voice mail."

Erin stopped packing the box and looked up at him, an angry expression on her face. Her eyes were red-rimmed, as if she'd been crying earlier.

"It's not a good time, J.T. It'll have to wait."

"It can't wait, damn it! Lauren's been kidnapped."

Erin's expression changed from anger to confusion. "What?"

"That's right. Somebody abducted her from the hospital. I've searched everywhere I could think of and found nothing."

"You're sure she was kidnapped? She just came out of a coma. Maybe she got disoriented and left on her own."

"I thought that too, at first," he said, pulling out his cell phone and scrolling to the kidnapper's text message. "Until I got this." He handed Erin the phone so she could see it.

"Christ," she said, slumping on to her executive chair. "The kidnappers want Jessica Shaw. So it's definitely connected to the Flash case."

"That's right. I need your help finding Lauren. I spent six hours with Atlanta PD, trying to locate her and came up empty."

"God damn it!" Erin yelled angrily, her face flushing. "This couldn't have happened at a worst time!"

Confused, Ryan said, "What do you mean?"

She rubbed her temple, as if she had a migraine. "They suspended me, J.T. They fucking suspended me." Her gaze flashed in anger. "The fucking FBI Director. Director Stevens. He finally did what I suspected he'd do."

She grimaced and her eyes watered, but she was a strong woman and she fought back the tears.

"I can't believe it, Erin."

"Believe it. That slimy bastard!"

"Do you have any recourse? You have a stellar record at the FBI."

"Sure. I'll file an appeal. But that takes time. And there's no guarantee the suspension will be overturned. Stevens, as the Bureau's director, has a lot of leeway in his decisions. In the meantime, they took away my FBI badge and my service weapon." She pointed to the boxes on the floor. "Now I'm just packing up my personal items because I lose this office too. Like I told you a while ago, Stevens is a real viper. A slimy bastard that kisses his boss's ass and beats down his own subordinates. If you're not one of his 'yes' men, he treats you like dirt."

"I'm sorry, Erin."

She took in several deep breaths and let them out slowly, trying to compose herself. "I'll help you as much as I can to find Lauren. But I'm not the ADIC here anymore. In fact, this is my last day here at the FBI building, until I can get this damn suspension overturned. Which will be difficult." She paused and took another deep breath. "My replacement is flying in from Washington. He'll be here tomorrow. And he's another slimy bastard, just like Stevens. Don't expect any help from him."

Ryan shook his head, sad and angry about what had happened to Erin, one of the best Bureau agents he knew. At the same time he recognized that finding Lauren was going to be a lot tougher without Erin's assistance. He slumped on the visitor's chair in front of her desk.

"What happens to the Flash case, Erin?"

She shrugged. "I don't know."

She looked pensive a moment, then reached into her desk and pulled out a file folder. She slid the folder across the desk. "Take this. It's a copy of some of the files on the case. In there is info from St. Croix's police department. I told you the cops down there found a storage unit with Shaw's records. Maybe this will give you a starting point. Since Shaw's arrest and Lauren's kidnapping are connected, maybe you can piece together some clues to her location."

Ryan opened the file folder, took out the sheets and put them in his jacket pocket. "Thanks, Erin. Where's Jessica now?"

"A holding cell downstairs."

"I want to interrogate her."

Erin shook her head. "No way. Not now. I don't have the authority to make that happen. I'm not in charge anymore. And since I hired you, it's a good bet the next ADIC won't trust you one bit. Don't be surprised if he cancels your contract with the Bureau."

Ryan nodded. He'd worked with enough government agencies to know that what she said was true.

Just then there was a knock on the office door and both Ryan and Erin turned to look. Two men wearing dark suits were standing in the open doorway. The men had their FBI badges clipped to their lapels.

"Sorry, Ms Welch," one of the men said, "but we need to escort you out of the building."

An angry look crossed Erin's face. "Is that really necessary, Bill?" she said to the FBI agent.

"Yes, ma'am. I have very specific orders."

"Whose orders, Bill?"

"Director Stevens."

Chapter 61

Lauren Chase awoke slowly, coming out of what felt like a very long sleep.

Sitting up on the cold concrete floor, she stared around the small, almost pitch black space. The only dim light in the room came from a sliver of illumination from underneath what appeared to be a door in front of her.

Feeling a jolt of pain from her forehead, she touched the area gingerly and felt a bandage there. Although it was dark in the room and she could not see what she was wearing, the garment felt like a flimsy hospital gown underneath a long, heavy coat. Her feet were bare and she shivered from the cold.

Standing up unsteadily, Lauren approached the door and fumbled around until she located the knob. The door was locked.

She felt her way around the small space, touching the walls as she moved. It took no more than a minute, as the room was small. *A closet?* she thought. *Where am I? What's going on?* The last thing she remembered was being at the hospital, looking forward to going home with J.T.

Then her recent memories flooded back. Two big men wearing blue hospital scrubs had rushed in her room, tied her up, gagged and blindfolded her. She had felt a sharp pain in her arm from an injection. Lauren remembered fighting back, but they were too strong. One of them hit her and she blacked out.

The next part was a blur, as if she'd been drugged. She vaguely recalled hearing loud noises. *A plane's engines, maybe?* After that she had fallen asleep and awakened here.

Lauren listened closely for any sounds, but heard nothing in the small, dark room. It smelled musty and she'd felt cobwebs as she'd touched the walls. *Where am I? Am I going to die here?*

Sitting back down on the cold concrete floor, she wrapped her arms around herself, trying to ward off the chill.

A feeling of dread settled in the pit of her stomach.

Chapter 62

St. Croix, U.S. Virgin Islands

J.T. Ryan's flight from Atlanta landed and after deplaning, he rented a car at the St. Croix airport. Instead of checking into a hotel, he drove directly to the police department in Christiansted. Ryan had called the detective assigned to the Shaw case yesterday and had set up a meeting with him.

Parking in the PD building's lot, Ryan signed in with the sergeant at the front desk and was shown to Detective Martin Clay's desk. The detective wasn't there at the moment.

Since Christiansted was a small town, the police bullpen was a compact space, with only a few desks for the plainclothes officers. Ryan saw several uniformed cops milling about the room, but none looked particularly busy. St. Croix, the PI knew, had a reputation for a low crime rate and the activity level of the cops confirmed this.

After a few moments a tall, black-skinned, mustachioed man wearing dress slacks and a blue dress shirt walked in. He had a semi-automatic pistol holstered on his hip.

"Mr. Ryan," the man said, as he extended his hand.

"That's right. You must be Detective Clay."

They shook hands and Clay sat behind his desk while Ryan took a chair next to it.

"After we talked yesterday," Clay said, in the lyrical Caribbean accent of the islands, "I called the FBI office in Atlanta." He flashed a broad smile, but his eyes showed no warmth. "They told me that yes, you had been working on the drug case. But that the person in charge of that office, the person who hired you, had been suspended." He flashed the cold smile again. "They said your contract with the Bureau has been terminated."

Ryan nodded. "I can explain."

He gave Clay a lengthy description of what had happened, including Erin Welch's stellar career with the FBI, his own association with the Bureau, plus his background as a U.S. Army Special Forces officer. Then he went on to explain Erin's unjust suspension.

Clay pointed to a framed picture on his desk. It showed several men wearing military fatigues standing in front of an M1A2 Abrams tank. "That photo's from a few years ago – that's me in the center. I was in the Marines. I made staff sergeant by the time I got out." He smiled broadly again, but this time it was genuine. "Since you're former military, I'm going to help you."

Relieved, Ryan said, "That's good. Because I really need your help."

"Okay. Shoot."

"My girlfriend, Lauren Chase, was kidnapped by people involved with the Flash drug conspiracy."

Clay sat up straighter. "I see. Where was she kidnapped?"

"Atlanta."

"The local PD involved?"

"Yes. They're doing everything they can, but I'm the one who has the most incentive to find her."

"Okay. How can I help, Ryan?"

"You guys found Jessica Shaw's storage unit here on the island. You seized her records."

"That's right. All that stuff is locked up in our evidence room."

"You've looked through it?"

"Some of it, yes. But there are a lot of files."

"I want to go through them. I need to find some link to the kidnappers."

Clay was pensive and he didn't respond right away. "We have regulations about seized records. Only authorized law enforcement is allowed into our evidence room."

Ryan leaned forward in the chair and lowered his voice. "Those records are my only connection to finding Lauren's whereabouts. Please, her life depends on it."

"Okay, Ryan. I'll make an exception."

"Thank you," he replied, feeling immense relief.

"When do you want to start?"

"Right now."

Clay stood up. "Follow me."

Ryan followed the man down a long corridor. At the end of the hallway they came to a large, rectangular room, caged at the front. The whole front wall of the space was constructed of heavy-duty chain link. Clay unlocked the metal door and went inside, with Ryan right behind.

The evidence room was lined with floor-to-ceiling metal racks, on which were stacked rows and rows of boxes. When Clay reached the rack at the end of the room he pointed. "Here they are. All of these cartons are labeled 'Shaw, case number #325'."

Ryan stared at the large number of boxes, which were stacked four wide, at least five deep, and reached up to the ceiling. "This is going to take a while," he said.

"Take all the time you need," Clay replied. "But a couple of ground rules. First, you can't take any of it with you. You'll be searched when you're done. And I'll be locking this room when I leave. If you need anything, ring the buzzer by the door. Understood?"

"Yes. Thanks again."

Clay turned and walked away, and Ryan pulled out the closest box to him and set it on the floor. Bending, he opened the container and began.

He spent the next five hours poring over the seized records. Most of the papers were chemical formulas, obviously written by Paul Shaw. There were also files related to the Colombian drug lord, Jose Garcia, but none of it was new material Ryan didn't already know.

Knowing he couldn't go through the mountain of boxes in one sitting, Ryan took a short break at six p.m., had a quick meal at a nearby cafe, and was back at it after a conversation with Detective Clay. The cop agreed to let him continue the search of the records overnight.

After being locked in the evidence room once again, Ryan continued poring over the files. He found nothing useful for the next several hours.

But at one a.m. he found something interesting. It was a file containing handwritten notes by Jessica Shaw. The notes alluded to a contract with a man named Nicholas Drago. The contract stipulated that she would share her future profits from the Flash drug sales with Drago, after the man agreed to loan her a large sum of money. Reading further, he noticed that in several instances, Shaw referred to Drago as her father.

Ryan made the connection immediately.

The gunmen that showed up at Shaw's house to protect her had been sent by her father. Lauren had been kidnapped by someone wanting payback for Jessica Shaw's arrest. *A father trying to rescue his daughter. That's a huge motivation.* Most parents would go to great lengths to save their children. Even kill if they had to.

Elated by his find, Ryan continued reading the files. After another hour he found what he was looking for – where Nicholas Drago lived.

Chapter 63

Juneau, Alaska

Juneau is a difficult place to get to, J.T. Ryan mused, as the Alaska Airlines jet touched down at the airport. The only way to reach Alaska's capital and third largest city was by plane or boat. If you came by car, you'd need to include a ferry ride. He'd left Atlanta that morning via a Delta flight into Seattle, and after a three hour layover, caught this flight into the city.

Grabbing his coat and carryon bag from the overhead bin, Ryan followed the other passengers out of the plane. Besides himself and a few other travelers in business attire, the only other people on board were the crew. *Not surprising,* he thought. *Alaska's not a big draw for tourists in February.*

As soon as he walked out of the terminal a short while later, he realized he needed a heavier coat. An icy cold wind was blowing, making the area's already frigid temperatures even worse. He turned up the collar of his coat and flagged down one of the cabs by the taxi stand.

Ryan took the cab to the hotel he'd booked and as the vehicle made its way there, he noted the stark contrast of the landscape to the warm climates he had been recently: Colombia and St. Croix. The banks of piled snow on either side of the road were a testament to the difference.

They drove past the historic downtown buildings, which had a Western frontier appearance. Ryan knew that in 1880 gold had been discovered in the area, which had brought in a huge inflow of prospectors seeking to make an easy fortune. For the next sixty years, gold was the mainstay of the city's economy, and the Western look and feel of the place remained strong. He had been to the city once before on a cruise, but that had been in June. A port city, Juneau had a wide harbor which easily accommodated large ships. As the cab drove along Marine Way past the cruise-ship docks, he noticed no ships there now. And in fact, many of the restaurants, bars, and shops they passed along the avenue were shuttered, only open part of the year starting in May.

The taxi stopped in front of the Baranof Hotel on North Franklin Street. Ryan paid the fare, got out and entered the landmark place. First opened in 1939, the hotel's art deco lobby of dark woods and period lamps was reminiscent of that era.

After checking in at the hotel, he visited the adjacent clothing shop and bought a heavier coat, thick gloves, all-weather boots, long underwear, and a wool watch cap. Then he went to his room, and once he'd put away his things, he pulled out the map of Alaska he'd bought at the airport.

Spreading the map on the four-poster bed, he studied it carefully. He was looking for his final destination. Ice Point. It was a tiny dot on the map, located north of Juneau. He'd done an Internet search on Ice Point before his trip, but found nothing useful. It wasn't a city, not even a town. More a cluster of homes and a few shops bordering a lake. Access to Ice Point was extremely difficult. Almost impossible at this time of the year. There was a road leading up there, but it was covered with snow and impassable during winter. The only way to get there in February was by plane. Small charter companies and air-taxi services flew throughout Alaska, connecting the remote towns that were scattered in the vast wilderness areas.

Ryan had also done an Internet search on Nicholas Drago. Here again he'd come up empty. Drago, like many people who choose to live in the remote parts of the arctic state, live there for a reason. They want to stay away from other people; under the radar, and off the grid of civilization.

Two days ago Ryan had contacted the Alaska State Police who had given him a similar story. He had explained his situation and asked for their help in locating Drago. Short staffed and chronically underpaid, the state police did the best they could trying to tame the vast, mostly wilderness area of over 365 million acres, an area twice the size of Texas. The police detective he spoke with ran a check on Nicholas Drago. They had no record of him and told Ryan the man probably went by an alias.

Folding the map, he looked at his watch. It was too late in the day to start the search. Using the phone in his room, he called down to the front desk. Reaching the manager, he inquired on the best way to get to Ice Point. The manager gave him a couple of names of the local air-taxi services and Ryan wrote them down. Replacing the receiver, he began filling a backpack he'd brought along with the items he'd need tomorrow.

Once done, he headed downstairs to grab a meal at the hotel's restaurant.

After a dinner of wild salmon, potatoes, and two Alaskan Amber beers, he went back to his room and went to bed. Tired from the long day of traveling, he was asleep in minutes.

Chapter 64

Juneau, Alaska

The next day was bright and sunny, the sky a deep blue with no clouds in sight. It was just as cold and windy, but this time Ryan was better prepared, wearing his heavy parka and the other winter garments he'd purchased.

He hailed a cab in front of the Baranof and instructed the driver to take him to the city airport. Once they reached it, he got out and located the area of the terminal designated for charter planes and air-taxi services. Finding the counter for one of the companies the hotel manager had mentioned, he saw the place was closed. He noticed other air-taxi services were likewise closed, so he went to the few that were open and inquired about going to Ice Point. Unfortunately, none of them were flying in that direction that day, but one of the attendants pointed him toward a small counter at the very end of the terminal building that was open. The attendant explained that February was a slow time of the year for travel which was the reason so few charters were available, in particular to such a remote spot as Ice Point.

Ryan walked to the counter and rang the bell. As he waited for someone to come out of the back room, he noticed the sign hanging on the wall behind the counter. It read *'Arctic International Airways'*, which he found humorous, considering the sign was clearly hand painted and hung crookedly on the wall. Hopefully their plane, Ryan thought, was in better shape than their signage.

Eventually a man wearing a faded bomber jacket, a cowboy hat, and worn dungarees came out of the back room.

"Can I help you?" the man said. He had a full beard and looked to be about fifty years old.

"Yes," Ryan replied. "I need to go to Ice Point."

"Ice Point?"

"That's right. It's north of here."

"I know where it is. Just don't get many people wanting to go there. That's really off the beaten path."

Ryan smiled. "Yeah. I could tell. It's hardly a smudge on the map."

"Okay. I'll take you there. The bearded man pulled out a card from his pocket and scanned it quickly. Then he told him the cost of the trip.

"Sounds high," Ryan said. "But I guess you don't have much competition."

"Not at this time of the year."

"You the pilot, by the way?"

The bearded man nodded. "I'm the everything at Arctic International Airways. Pilot, mechanic, steward, counter agent. I do it all."

Ryan pulled out his wallet and paid the man in cash. After inspecting the PI's ID, the pilot wrote him a receipt for the money and handed it to him.

"Why you visiting Ice Point?" the man asked. "There's not much up there. Just lots of snow."

"I'm looking for someone. Nicholas Drago. Ever heard of him?"

The man shook his head. "Nope."

"That's surprising. Drago's a wealthy man", Ryan said, guessing. "There can't be too many rich people in a place that small."

The bearded man looked away, as if uncomfortable from the conversation. "Look mister. I don't ask questions. I fly a plane. I'm just trying to make a living."

"Understood. When can we leave?"

"I need to gas up the plane and de-ice the wings. We'll take off in half an hour." Then he turned around and went into the back room.

***

To Ryan's pleasant surprise, the Arctic Airways airplane was in much better shape than their cheesy sign. Although the 6-passenger, twin-engine Piper was not new, it appeared to be well-maintained.

They had taken off fifteen minutes ago and were now cruising at an altitude of about 10,000 feet. Besides Ryan and the pilot, there was no one else on board. It was such a clear day that the rugged and beautiful, snow-covered terrain below was stunningly visible. It was very loud in the cabin from the engine noise, a drawback of small planes, but other than that it was a smooth flight.

Ryan settled back in the seat and thought through his upcoming day. He didn't really know what he'd find, if anything. But he was armed and prepared as much as he could be, the backpack on the seat next to him loaded with supplies. His goal was clear – find Drago, and find Lauren. Do whatever it took to get her back.

Ten minutes later he heard the pilot speak over the plane's intercom, his voice competing with the loud drone of the engines. "Mr. Ryan, my oil-engine warning light just came on. I need to land for a few minutes and check it out."

The twin-engine prop plane banked to the left and began a slow descent. Below them was a large, ice covered lake and the plane bled altitude until they were only fifty feet over the shiny, sleek surface. After a final approach, the aircraft landed on the smooth ice and rolled to a stop.

The pilot turned off the engines, opened the cabin door, and lowered the air ladder. "I'll be working on the engines, Mr. Ryan. You might as well get out and stretch your legs." Then the man climbed down the steps and opened the cowling on the left propeller motor.

After zipping up his parka, Ryan took his gloves and watch cap out of the backpack, put them on, then slung the pack over his shoulder. Using the air ladder, he exited the plane. There was a brisk wind blowing and he felt the icy cold air bite into the exposed parts of his face.

Ryan stood on the ice and watched as the pilot worked on the motor. Eventually the man closed the cowling and said, "I made an adjustment on this one. I'll start it up and see if it's okay. Then I'll have to repeat the process for the right side engine."

Ryan nodded and the pilot climbed back in the aircraft and turned on both turbo-props. A moment later the propellers roared as if on full throttle and the Piper began rolling forward. The plane picked up speed, and to his astonishment, Ryan watched as the aircraft lifted off the ice covered lake.

"What the hell," the PI muttered. His confusion grew when the plane climbed at a 45 degree angle, quickly reached an altitude of several thousand feet and banked right. A minute later the aircraft was only a dot against the bright blue sky.

Chapter 65

Ice Point, Alaska

Nicholas Drago was in his wheelchair, watching the roaring fireplace in his study when he heard a woman's voice from behind him. Drago turned his chair around and saw his bodyguard Heather come into the room.

"Sorry to disturb you," she said as she approached. "But I needed to tell you something."

"Of course, Heather," he replied, always glad to be interrupted by the attractive young woman. She was a pleasant contrast to his head of security, Thomas Carpenter. "You can come see me anytime, you know that."

"Yes, sir. I got a call a while ago, while you were taking your nap. The call was from Frank Hardy."

"Who's that?"

"He's a pilot for one of the air-taxi services in Juneau. We were neighbors in the same apartment building when I lived there. Anyway, Hardy was calling to give me a heads up. He told me a passenger was hiring him to fly him to Ice Point."

"Ice Point? Who the hell comes to Ice Point in February? There's nothing here."

"My thought exactly, sir. Then Hardy told me something disturbing. The passenger was looking for you."

"Me?"

"Yes, Mr. Drago. And the passenger's name is John Ryan."

Drago's heart raced. "What? Ryan? That's the Atlanta PI working on the Skyflash case."

"That's right, sir."

"What did you tell the pilot to do?"

"I told him to make sure Ryan never got to Ice Point. I promised him $20,000 for his cooperation."

"Good."

"I just got off the phone with Hardy again. He took care of it. He dropped off Ryan about twenty miles south of here."

Drago tried to visualize a map of the area she was talking about. "What's there, Heather?"

"Absolutely nothing, sir. No homes, no people, no civilization of any kind. Only ice and snow. The only living things are caribou, bears, and wolves."

The old man processed this information, but said nothing.

"I hope I did the right thing, sir."

Drago let out a cold, harsh laugh. "You did good, Heather. Very good. Nobody can survive the arctic wilderness of Alaska in the dead of winter."

Chapter 66

North of Juneau, Alaska

As J.T. Ryan jogged, his boots crunched over the irregular drifts of snow.

He'd been moving north as soon as it dawned on him that the pilot, for some inexplicable reason, was not coming back.

Ryan had made quick progress when he was running over the ice covered lake, but had to slow down as soon as he reached the snow covered banks, trudging around boulders and occasionally sinking into deep drifts. He was in a fairly flat valley area; to the north in the far distance was a jagged mountain range.

He stopped a moment to catch his breath and readjust the pack on his back. Turning slowly 360 degrees, he scanned the frigid, vast wilderness. There were no signs of civilization anywhere. All he saw were stands of icicle-covered fir trees, outcroppings of rocks, ice, and drifts of brilliant white snow in every direction.

The only sound was the howling of the wind, which had picked up in intensity. He took in a large breath, trying to determine if any of the smells might be human. It was a technique he'd learned during Special Forces survival training. Human civilization gave off distinct smells. Campfires. Burning trash. Urine. Body odors. All those smells carried for long distances. But all he smelled was the clean, fresh scent of pine trees.

Ryan's mind raced as he considered his next moves, knowing he would not survive long in the harsh arctic conditions. Already his fingers were numb from the frigid temperatures, even with his gloves on. He rubbed the exposed parts of his face, trying to warm them up a bit. The icy wind felt like it was cutting and burning the skin of his face. After pulling his watch cap lower over his forehead, he unrolled the hood from his heavy parka and pulled it over the cap to help keep the frigid wind at bay. He tightened the hood and tied it snugly so that only his nose and eyes were exposed.

Standing there, he took stock of his situation. In his backpack he had his revolver, extra ammunition, the map, a knife, a compass, a BIC lighter, several bottles of water, and six protein bars. Not much, he knew. He recalled his survival training: a person doing strenuous exercise needs at least a half gallon of water per day and about 3,000 calories worth of food in a warm climate, and twice those amounts in a cold climate.

Ryan looked up at the bright blue sky. The sun was still shining, making the cold temperatures somewhat bearable. But as soon as nighttime came, the temps would plummet. People don't survive out in the open in sub-zero temperatures. And it was not uncommon in Alaska for overnight lows to be 50 degrees below zero.

By the length of time the Arctic Airways plane had flown before landing on the lake, Ryan estimated he was halfway to Ice Point. Since the village was about fifty miles north of Juneau, that meant he still had twenty five miles to go. Definitely doable for a very fit, well trained man in a warm climate. *But in these conditions?* he thought. *If I was a betting man, I wouldn't take those odds.*

A blast of frigid wind blew, pushing him sideways, and he had to widen his stance to keep himself upright, reminding him of the harsh reality of his environment.

For a moment a hint of fear crept in his thoughts. *I'll never make it. It's too damn cold. I'm going to freeze to death.*

Then his Delta Force training kicked in and he pushed away the negative thoughts. He started jogging again over the drifts of snow, heading north.

***

Hours later he came to an ice covered creek. Pressing the toe of his boot on the sleek surface, he tested it for strength. The small river seemed to be frozen solid and he crossed over it. Once again he turned his body 360 degrees and scanned the surroundings. The landscape had changed somewhat. He was no longer in a valley – the flat terrain had given way to a craggy, mountainous setting, dotted with tall firs. Just ahead was an ice-covered sheer face of rock that rose at least 100 feet high.

But it was still as desolate here as before. There were no signs of human life. He'd spotted a few deer and at least one caribou in the distance. He'd also heard the howling of wolves. Once night fell, he knew, the wolves would pick up his scent, as would bears, Alaska's largest predator.

Once again a hint of fear came back and this time it took longer to banish the thoughts. Taking off his backpack, he removed the revolver and placed it in one of the pockets of his parka. Then he put the pack back on.

Ryan glanced up at the late afternoon sky – it was growing perceptibly darker. It would be night soon. And no sun meant even colder temperatures. He knew it would fall well below zero. He had to find shelter. And soon.

Scanning the horizon again, he searched for a suitable spot. His gaze fixed on the ice-covered sheer rock face ahead. And he remembered something from survival training.

Wasting no time, he jogged over the blindingly white powder until he was at the foot of the craggy rock face which towered up to the sky. Large snow drifts, at least fifteen feet high bordered the base of the steep ridge. He trudged along the base of the ridge until he found what he was looking for – a rock outcropping about five feet off the ground. A large snow drift covered most of it. Recalling the specifics of his Special Forces training, he realized it would be an ideal spot to create a snow cave. Unlike an igloo which takes much time and skill to build, a snow cave required much less skill and can be constructed in a hurry.

He glanced around, spotted what he needed: broken pine boughs lying on the ground nearby. Trudging over, he began picking up the branches until his arms were full. Then he carried the wood back to the cliff's face. He laid the pine boughs against the rocky face and packed layers of snow over it.

Going to his knees, he excavated an opening under the branches. Once he'd made the opening, he crawled forward on his hands and knees, and continued tunneling out the packed snow inside until there was an open, covered space about eight feet in length, four feet wide and four feet high. After taking the snow outside the shelter, he brought in more fir boughs and placed them on the snow cave's floor, making it a warmer place to sleep.

An hour later he was done. He turned around inside the snow cave and looked out the man-sized hole at the front of it. A howling wind was blowing in frigid cold air and he knew he had to cover the hole. Taking off his backpack, he pushed it against the opening.

The howling of the wind diminished to a whisper and he breathed a sigh of relief.

But now it was dark inside the cave and he took out the BIC lighter and flicked it on. With his free hand he patted down the fir boughs on the floor so he could lie down more comfortably on the crude bed.

That done, he reclined on his side, with his gaze toward the front of the cave. He checked the time on the glowing digits of his watch. It would be pitch black outside now, and the super-frigid temperatures would have arrived.

Inside the snow cave it was still cold, but since there was no wind blowing it was tolerable. Soon his body temperature and an occasional flicking of the lighter would warm up the small, dark space.

Ryan closed his eyes a moment, tired from his exertions in the harsh conditions. Then in the far distance he heard the howling of wolves and he became instantly alert. Taking out his pistol, he placed it on the ground next to him.

He stayed like that for a long time, wide awake, listening for night predators. But eventually he became drowsy and slipped into a fitful, nightmare filled sleep.

***

Ryan was startled awake by cold drops of water hitting his face. Grabbing the handgun next to him, he glanced around the dim cave and saw what was happening immediately. His body temperature had warmed up the interior space and was beginning to melt the snow on the roof, which was a few feet above his head.

He noticed something else – light was filtering around the backpack which he'd used to block the entrance of the shelter. Checking his watch he realized it was daytime now – he'd been asleep for many hours.

Ryan's body was stiff and cold. He stretched his muscles, flexing his fingers and toes as best he could inside the gloves and boots to regain his circulation.

He was also ravenous. Grabbing the backpack, he took out two of the protein bars and ate them quickly. Still hungry, he ate one more, but decided to leave the rest for later. There was no telling how long he'd be out in the middle of the arctic wilderness. After taking a few sips of water from one of the bottles he'd brought, he packed the bag and slipped it on his shoulders. Then on his hands and knees he crawled out of the snow cave and stood up.

It was a sunny day and the bright light reflecting off the snow banks all around momentarily blinded him. Blinking a few times to adjust his eyes, he pulled his pistol and scanned the nearby area, but saw no wolves or other predators nearby.

After putting the revolver back in one of the parka's pockets, he took out his compass and found the direction for north. An icy, savage wind was blowing, much like the previous day, and he pulled his watch cap lower on his forehead, raised his hood over the cap, and tightened it snugly around his head.

That done, he began trudging north, over the irregular mounds of snow.

***

Ryan walked for hours over the vast, desolate wilderness. The terrain was the same –icicle covered trees, cliffs, and deep drifts of brilliant white powder. There were no signs of civilization anywhere. All he heard was the shrieking of the frigid wind, which bit into the exposed parts of his face, making it numb. Several times he had to stop and rub his face to keep the blood circulating.

An hour later, as he was climbing up a rocky incline, he slipped on the slick ice and fell forward into a deep bank of hard-packed snow and rocks. Scrambling upright quickly, he noticed bright red marks on the snowy ground. He touched his face and felt blood on his cheek. But the skin was numb and he felt no pain.

Just then he heard the howling of a wolf in the distance and he gripped the butt of his pistol, which was inside a pocket. Once again a trace of fear ran down his spine. *I could easily die out here*, he thought. *I probably won't run out of food because I can trap animals, and melt ice for water. No, that won't be the problem. I'll freeze to death instead. Or bears or wolves will find me and attack, and I'll eventually run out of ammo.*

Pushing aside those thoughts, he began jogging over the snow, trying to warm his body by running as opposed to walking. But the terrain was too irregular and slippery, and he had to stop and instead trek north at an even pace.

Two hours later he came to a valley and in the distance he spotted an ice-covered lake. Close to the edge of the lake, among the trees, he spotted something else. A thin plume of smoke reaching up into the sky. *A man-made fire?* he wondered.

His hopes raised, Ryan picked up the pace, heading toward the smoke. Jogging forward, he eventually was able to make out the source of the smoke – a chimney sprouting from a snow-covered, weather-beaten trailer. It was the first sign of human civilization he'd seen since the plane had deserted him, and he raced the rest of the way toward the small, rusty mobile home.

Stopping twenty feet from it, he surveyed the scene. Next to the trailer was a snowmobile with a cargo sled attached to the back. There was no one about, but he noticed animal traps and animal furs hanging from a metal rack on the opposite side of the trailer.

"Don't move or I'll shoot," Ryan heard from behind him.

The PI froze, hearing the racking of a shotgun shell into the chamber. Then he listened as boots crunched over snow and a short, heavyset man wearing a fur coat and a fur hat walked around him and stopped ten feet in front of him. The man was pointing a shotgun at his chest.

"Raise your hands," the man said, motioning with his weapon.

Ryan complied as he studied the man, who was likely the owner of the trailer. By his dark complexion and facial features, he was apparently native Alaskan – an Eskimo or an Aleut, Ryan guessed. He had a thick mustache and beard, both coated with ice, and he spoke with an unusual accent.

"Who are you, stranger?"

"My name's J.T. Ryan. I'm a private investigator. I work ... or I did work for the FBI."

"Are you armed?"

"Yes. I have a pistol in my coat pocket."

The man motioned with his shotgun again. "Take it out. Slowly, and throw it on the ground away from you. Any false move and you're dead."

"I understand." Very deliberately, he removed the gun from his pocket and pitched into a drift of snow.

"Okay, stranger. Now take off your backpack and your coat and throw it on the ground away from you."

"Are your crazy? You expect me to take off my coat? It's freezing out here."

"Do it. Do it now."

Ryan knew he had no choice and reluctantly complied, the arctic wind cutting into his coatless torso.

The man approached him, grabbed the revolver from the ground and pocketed it. Then, still pointing the shotgun at him, he walked 360 degrees around him, obviously looking for other weapons. After that he picked up the coat and backpack and searched them.

"Take out your wallet and throw it my way, stranger."

Ryan did as he was told and the native Alaskan went through the contents. He didn't take the money in the wallet as Ryan expected, but instead pitched it back to him with all of the contents still inside.

"Okay, Ryan. You can put your coat back on. By your ID you're who you say you are."

The PI gratefully shrugged on his parka, zipped it up and pulled the hood over his head. "You must not get many visitors out here."

The native Alaskan flashed a crooked smile – many of his teeth were missing, and the ones left were stained brown. "You're the first one. And I've lived here a year."

Ryan nodded. "You live here by yourself?"

"I used to live in Juneau. After my wife died ... I left ... came out here. Tell me Ryan, what are you doing in the middle of nowhere?"

"I'm working on a drug investigation involving several murders. But the reason I'm here specifically is to find my girlfriend who was kidnapped. I think she's being held at Ice Point."

"Ice Point? That's about fifteen miles from here. You'll never make it on foot."

"It's a long story." The PI shivered as a blast of wind blew by. He pointed to the trailer. "Can we go inside first? I'll tell you everything. It's damn cold out here."

The man smiled the crooked smile again. "Doesn't feel that cold to me. But then I was born in Alaska. By the way, my name's Sika."

"Good to meet you, Sika."

The man lowered the shotgun, turned and started trudging toward the rusted-out mobile home. Ryan followed him after picking up his backpack.

***

Ryan sipped from the tin cup, which was filled with hot coffee laced with Jack Daniels whiskey. He was sitting on the floor of the cramped trailer and across from him was Sika, drinking from his own cup. They sat on animal fur pelts. Besides a lumpy bed in a corner, and a table and a chair in the kitchenette, there was no other furniture in the mobile home. Boxes and animal furs were stacked haphazardly along the bare metal walls.

Ryan was glad for the hot drink and even more appreciative of the wood-fired, pot belly stove in the room, which radiated a comforting heat. It was the first time in days that he'd felt warm. He'd taken off his coat, watch cap, gloves, and boots, and was flexing his fingers and wriggling his toes to regain circulation. His extremities had that tingly feeling common when you warm up after you've been cold for a long time. Luckily, he hadn't suffered any frostbite.

"Like I said earlier, Sika, my girlfriend was kidnapped and –"

The man smiled and raised a hand. "Drink your coffee Ryan. Don't you want to hear my story first?"

It was clear that the man was eager to talk, perhaps because he lived in such an isolated place. Ryan nodded and sipped more of the whiskey-laced coffee.

Sika pointed to the stacks of animal pelts in the trailer. "I'm a trapper. I trap and skin animals then I go to Juneau and sell the furs to the businesses there."

"You said you've been out here a year. Must get lonely."

"It does, sometimes. But after my wife died, I didn't want to be around people anymore. Maybe one day I'll go back there."

Ryan drained his cup. A metal coffee urn was sitting on top of the pot belly stove and he reached over, picked it up, and refilled both of their mugs. "You're obviously native Alaskan. Are you an Eskimo?"

Sika laughed. "Most outsiders think the same thing. But no. I'm Tlingit. Tlingit is a native Indian tribe that originated in this part of Alaska. We're not Eskimo or Aleut, the more well known natives of this state."

Ryan nodded, anxious to get going and continue his search for Lauren. But he knew he'd never make it another 15 miles on foot in the brutal arctic conditions. He needed Sika's help, so he sat and listened for the next half hour as the man described his aboriginal existence, trapping, fishing, and hunting in the wilderness.

After they finished the pot of coffee and the fifth of Jack Daniels, Sika said, "Now tell me your story. You say your girlfriend was kidnapped?"

"That's right. I think she's being held at Ice Point."

"You probably know there's not much up there, Ryan. Just a few people live there."

"Yeah, I know. The man who kidnapped her is named Nicholas Drago. He's probably very wealthy."

Sika rubbed his beard with one hand. "Drago, huh? Can't say I've heard the name. But I do know a few of the folks that live in that village. And they told me there's a rich guy that lives in a big house just north of Ice Point."

"That must be him." Ryan leaned forward on the fur mat he was sitting on. "I saw the snowmobile outside. Can you take me to that village?"

The man said nothing, a skeptical look on his face. It was obvious he didn't want to get involved with Ryan's problems.

"I'll pay you, Sika. I've got cash. I'll give you all I have. I've got to get to Ice Point before they kill Lauren."

Sika rubbed his beard, contemplating what Ryan had said. "All right. I can see you're a man in real need. I'll help you get there. But there's just one thing. I can't take your money."

"Why? I'll be glad to pay you."

The native Alaskan waved a hand in the air. "You're a guest in my home. It's a Tlingit tradition. I help you now. Maybe, sometime in the future, I'll need your help. Then you can return the favor."

"I understand. And thank you. When can we get started?"

A strong blast of wind blew outside, and the metal trailer creaked loudly.

"It's too late now, Ryan. We'll start in the morning."

Chapter 67

North of Juneau, Alaska

The snowmobile howled to life, shattering the early morning stillness. Once again the sun was shining and thankfully the ferocious wind had died down.

Sika, astride the snowmobile, turned the throttle and the vehicle shot forward over the snow. Ryan was sitting in the cargo area of the skid, which was attached by a hitch to the back of the snowmobile. He watched as the Tlingit Indian drove away from the trailer and headed north over the blindingly white terrain.

They took a circuitous route, following alongside a frozen river bed and then through a wooded area, all while avoiding the rocky hills that jutted up around them. Ryan realized he would have never made it on his own – although it was not as windy today, it was still bitter cold, and as he sat on the skid he continually had to flex his gloved hands to keep circulation in his hands. He pulled the drawstring tighter on the hood of his parka to keep the icy temperatures from freezing his face.

He also knew that he probably would have gotten lost in the unforgiving, harsh wilderness. Sika, on the other hand, seemed to know exactly where he was going, not once consulting a map or a compass.

Four hours later the snowmobile slowed down and stopped. They were on a high ridge overlooking a snow covered valley. In the valley was a large ice-covered lake.

Sika, still sitting astride the vehicle, turned his head back toward Ryan and pointed down to the valley floor. "If you look close, you'll see Ice Point."

Ryan got up from the skid, eager to flex his numb arms and legs. He strode to the edge of the ridge and looked in the direction the man had pointed. He saw tiny wisps of smoke coming from the valley floor. The smoke rose from dark spots, which were in stark contrast to a background of white.

"Is that it down there?" the PI asked.

"That's right."

"How long to get down there?"

"About half hour."

Ryan nodded, climbed back on the skid and sat down. The snowmobile's engine roared to life again and they began the final leg of the trip.

After descending the ridge and crossing the ice-covered lake, they entered the village on the only road, a rutted street covered in a slush of dirty snow. It was bordered on both sides by small homes and a couple of businesses. Like Sika had said, there wasn't much here. The snowmobile stopped in front of a weather-beaten wooden structure with a faded sign that read, *'General Store'*.

Climbing off the vehicle, the Tlingit man said, "I'll go inside, get directions to Drago's place. You stay here – people in these parts are distrustful of strangers."

"All right," Ryan replied and watched as the man climbed up the icy wooden steps and entered the general store. He came out five minutes later carrying a sack of groceries, which he set down on the skid.

"Low on food?" Ryan asked.

"No. But you can't go in a place and just ask questions. People get suspicious."

Ryan smiled. "You'd make a good PI."

The other man shook his head. "I like what I do. I'm not looking to change."

"Get directions?"

"Yeah. The owner didn't know anybody named Drago. But he told me there's a rich guy who lives in a big house north of here."

"I'm sure it's him."

"Me too, Ryan. There's nothing else out here."

Sika climbed on the snowmobile, turned it on, and they followed the road out of the village. The road was covered with deep drifts and Ryan guessed that it was impassible for most vehicles in winter. Not even 4-wheel drive trucks would be able to drive on it. The only way in was by snowmobile, snow-tractors, or by air. *Did Drago own a plane or a helicopter?* he wondered.

An hour later they came to a fork in the road and Sika stopped the vehicle. He pointed to the signs posted on the side road which split off from the main one. Tall, ice-covered firs bordered both sides of the side road.

Ryan got off the skid and walked forward to get a better look at the signs, which read, *'Private property. No trespassing.'* He turned back toward the other man.

"This is the place, Ryan."

"Okay. I'll walk the rest of the way."

"The shop owner said it's still a few miles further. I brought you this far. Might as well take you all the way."

"You sure, Sika? It could get dangerous."

Sika laughed. "I'm Tlingit. Not much scares me."

"Okay. But we might as well be prepared. You got that shotgun handy?"

The other man climbed off the snowmobile, opened a storage case on the skid and took out the Mossberg 12-gauge, pump-action weapon. He handed it to Ryan, then got back on the vehicle.

The PI racked the slide on the shotgun and sat back on the skid. As they drove down the side road, he scanned the scene, his gaze darting in all directions, alert for any sudden movement.

Chapter 68

Ice Point, Alaska

Nicholas Drago was in the office of his estate when he heard a knock at the door. Looking up from his computer, he noticed Thomas Carpenter standing at the open doorway.

"Sir, we have a problem," Carpenter said.

"What is it?" Drago replied.

"Our security cameras picked up a snowmobile on our road."

"Can you tell who it is?"

"It's two men and one of them looks a lot like the Atlanta PI, John Ryan."

Drago's pulse raced. "How's that possible? That pilot left him in the middle of nowhere. And anyway, how could he find this place?"

"I don't know, sir."

The old man rubbed the tops of the wheelchair rollers with his bony hands. "Damn. This is the last thing I need."

"What should I do, sir?"

"Eliminate the problem."

Chapter 69

Ice Point, Alaska

J.T. Ryan watched as the snowmobile veered left and then right as it followed the bends of the small road. Eventually the trail straightened and the heavily wooded area which they'd been passing through thinned out somewhat, giving him a clearer view up ahead.

They were in a valley dotted with tall, snow covered trees.

He didn't spot a house or any buildings, and he was beginning to wonder if the shop owner was on Drago's payroll and had given them false directions. In the far distance he could see jagged, white-peaked mountain ranges. The vast wilderness appeared beautiful and serene, much like a photo from a picture postcard; the kind you'd send home to your friends if you were on vacation.

Out of the corner of his eye he noticed a flash in the distance. A split-second later he heard the loud crack of a high-powered rifle.

Suddenly Sika's head exploded.

Fragments of bone, brain matter, and blood flew in all directions. Sika's body slumped backward on the snowmobile's seat and collapsed to the ground, rivulets of bright red blood staining the pristine white snow.

Clutching the shotgun with one hand and his backpack with the other, Ryan scrambled off the skid just as more shots rang out. Spotting nearby tree cover, he raced in that direction in a zigzag pattern, while small plumes of snow jumped up from the ground around him as the bullets tried to find their mark.

Reaching the trees seconds later, he crouched behind a large fir, his heart pounding. Several more shots rang out, the sounds echoing throughout the valley. The rounds thudded into nearby tree trunks, but none hit the tree he was using for cover.

Over the next several minutes the rifle fire continued, but the bullets were scattered over the whole of the wooded area. Obviously the shooters couldn't spot him. Then the shots stopped.

Shrugging on his backpack, Ryan held the shotgun with both hands and peeked quickly around the thick trunk – he saw no movement in the distance, only heard the whistling of the wind, the rustle of leaves, and the call of birds.

Moments later the sounds of nature were interrupted as one, then two snowmobile engines came to life. The whine of the vehicles was faint at first, but grew louder quickly. Ryan began running, sprinting over the snowy ground, deeper into the woods.

***

Daytime had faded into night, the arctic cold descending like a heavy blanket, seeping through Ryan's parka, gloves, boots, and cap as if he were wearing only a T-shirt and shorts. The part of his face that was uncovered was numb to the touch and he feared he'd suffered frostbite.

Ryan knew he'd never stay alive if he spent the whole night outdoors. He had to make his move now, before his fingers, face, and the rest of his body froze in place. He'd spent the day evading the two snowmobiles as the fast-moving vehicles crisscrossed the vast property. He'd been fortunate to elude them and finally locate Drago's estate. Ryan felt terrible about Sika's death; if he accomplished his objective and found Lauren, he planned to come back to where Sika had been killed and bury the body.

Crouching within a stand of firs, he was gazing at Drago's home now. He was about a half a football field's distance away from it. The massive, three-story house, constructed of brick and marble in a Victorian style design, looked oddly out of place in the desolate wilderness. It was one of those 'statement' homes. And the 'statement' said money. Lots of money.

There were vehicles parked in front of the home – trucks, Jeeps, a snow-tractor, and several snowmobiles. In a long, flat area west of the house he spotted an airplane hanger. The moonlight was strong enough that he could also make out a runway near the hanger.

Ryan focused his attention back to the home – all of the interior lights appeared lit, as were the outside floodlights. It was clear by the comings and goings of the vehicles as they moved around the property that they knew he was out here somewhere. Drago's guards were ready for him. There was no element of surprise.

Ryan thought back to the first shot that rang out, the one that had killed Sika instantly. The shooter, who was definitely firing from far away, was a skilled sniper. The question in Ryan's mind was how Drago and his men had been alerted to the intrusion on to the property. The PI had seen no security cameras. But anyone who could afford a home like this had plenty of money for extensive and high-quality security. Ryan had to assume that the entire estate and the grounds were protected by cameras with 24/7 monitoring.

While he continued to crouch, he stretched in place to keep his muscles from stiffening from the mind-numbing temperature. He knew he had to reach the house undetected. Otherwise a firefight would erupt and he was seriously outnumbered and outgunned. He had the 12-gauge shotgun with eight shells. And he had his revolver, with a total of 18 bullets. Not too bad if he were facing three or four men. But so far he'd counted ten guards. To his surprise, two of the guards were women.

Ryan's mind churned as he tried to come up with a plan. After discarding several options, he fixed on one final plan. In order to evade the cameras, he'd have to crawl to reach his destination undetected. He shivered, knowing that moving over the icy ground for such a long period of time would make him even colder than he already was. But he had no choice.

Not wasting any more time, he stretched out on the ground on his belly and, cradling the shotgun with his arms, he began crawling.

Chapter 70

Ice Point, Alaska

Nicholas Drago rolled his wheelchair into his home's foyer and found Thomas Carpenter and Heather talking there. Both were armed with MP5 submachine guns and semi-automatic pistols.

"Have you found him yet?" Drago shouted.

Carpenter turned toward him. "No, sir. Not yet."

"Why the fuck not, Thomas?"

"I'm sorry, sir. Ryan is a difficult man to track down."

"Don't give me a fucking excuse," Drago yelled. "I pay you for results."

"Yes, sir."

Drago stabbed a finger in the air in Carpenter's direction. "Get back out there, damn you! Kill Ryan."

Chapter 71

Ice Point, Alaska

By the time J.T. Ryan got close to the airplane hanger west of the home, he was exhausted and extremely cold. He ignored that and focused on the task ahead. He knew he couldn't overcome ten guards – it was too many. Ryan had to even the odds. And the best way to do that was to create a diversion.

Only one guard patrolled the grounds around the hanger, a man wearing a fur-lined coat and hat and carrying what looked like a compact submachine gun. Ryan approached the building from the back and stopped crawling when he got within fifteen feet of the back door.

Leaving the shotgun on the snowy ground, he got up and hid behind a tree. Then he took out his KA-BAR knife and waited. A few minutes later the guard appeared around the corner, as he made his circuit of the back of the hanger.

The PI waited until the man was facing away from him and then sprinted forward. He grabbed the guard roughly by the neck and slashed the knife across his throat. The man resisted for a second, uttered a gurgling sound, and dropped to the ground. Ryan knelt down, wiped the blood off the knife with the snow, and quickly searched the dead man's pockets. Finding the loop of keys he was hoping to locate, he took them, along with the guard's MP5 submachine gun, which he slung over his shoulder. Then he raced to the back door and after trying several of the keys, found the right one and unlocked the door.

He stepped inside the cavernous, high-ceiling building. It was dark in the hanger, but instead of flicking on the overhead lights, he took out his flashlight and began looking around the room. Parked at one side of the open space was a Gulfstream jet.

In a nearby storage cabinet he found a filled can of gasoline and a stack of towels, which he carried and placed on the concrete floor next to the plane. The brightly painted pearl-white and blue Gulfstream business jet was a G150 model. The plane could carry up to 8 people, but was still small enough to land on shorter runways. The jet was spotlessly clean.

Not familiar where the gas tank was located on this specific aircraft, Ryan walked around until he found it. After prying off the plane's gas tank locking plate and unscrewing the lid, he began rolling up the towels and dipping them into the filled can of gasoline. Once they were thoroughly doused, he tied the towels into a long rope. Then he inserted one end of the towel rope into the plane's gas tank and stretched out the rest along the floor. Taking out his lighter, he flicked it on and lit the towel rope at one end. That done, he unslung the submachine gun and raced out of the hanger.

Chapter 72

Ice Point, Alaska

Nicholas Drago heard shouting outside his home and he rolled his wheelchair to a nearby window and looked out.

He was shocked at what he saw – flames rising from the airplane hanger, the blaze lighting up the nighttime sky. Two of the guards' trucks were converging on the building and several other vehicles were headed in that direction.

Drago's heart sank. He loved that plane. It gave him the freedom to travel at will. He was certain that bastard Ryan was responsible. *Damn it! I want him dead!* his brain screamed.

Then he began shouting at the top of his lungs. "Heather! Where are you! Heather!"

Chapter 73

Ice Point, Alaska

Crouching among the stand of trees closest to the hanger, Ryan lined up the sight of the MP5 submachine gun, the weapon pointed toward the front of the building. His finger was on the trigger, but he didn't pull it, wanting to maximize the damage.

Two large Ford trucks had already pulled up to the front of the building. The vehicles were the 4-wheel drive type, with high ground clearance, oversized snow tires, and heavy-duty bumpers. The drivers climbed out of the trucks and clearly wanted to go inside to douse the flames, but the fire was too intense.

Ryan counted out the seconds.

A moment later two snowmobiles drove up and their drivers climbed off.

Ryan clicked the weapon to full-auto and pulled the trigger, the MP5 spraying a full 30 round clip into the area where the guards were standing. Three fell to the ground immediately, while the fourth clutched his leg and yelled in pain.

Dropping the submachine gun, Ryan took out his revolver, and aiming with both hands, fired one shot. The wounded guard dropped to his knees and toppled forward. So far the PI had killed five of them. Five to go.

Ryan ran to the inert bodies and once there, grabbed one the dead men's assault rifles. It was an AK-47, and along with the weapon, he picked up extra clips. He was about to sprint toward the estate when a better idea struck him. He strode to one of the Ford trucks, climbed inside, and placed the AK-47 on the passenger seat. Putting on the seatbelt, he strapped it tightly.

Then he turned on the ignition and the large engine roared to life. Pressing the accelerator, the vehicle shot forward. After doing a 180 degree turn, Ryan pointed the truck toward the front of the home. The PI smashed the gas pedal to the floor and gripped the steering wheel tightly.

The large Ford roared forward at full speed, bouncing over the irregular drifts of snow and ice. He was only twenty feet from the house now and he twisted the wheel slightly, aiming for the large front door. The three-story home loomed large and was getting bigger by the second. Ryan fought the urge to close his eyes, wanting to insure the front of the vehicle with its heavy-duty bumper hit the entrance squarely.

In a split second the oversize truck tires rolled over the marble front steps and crashed into and through the massive wooden front door, sending splinters, metal, and bricks flying in every direction. Ryan felt the concussion immediately. He saw shards of glass as the truck's windshield imploded, and heard the howl of the motor and the roar of metal crashing into stone and wood.

Suddenly the truck's engine died. Dazed from the crash, he groggily unstrapped his seatbelt and grabbed the AK-47 from the passenger seat.

He glanced around the well-lit room he had crashed into. It was an expansive foyer with a cut-glass chandelier hanging from the high ceiling. Gilt framed Rembrandt paintings hung on the walls. He saw no one around.

Ryan tried to open the driver's side door, but it was too damaged from the crash, so he climbed out through the broken window.

With the assault rifle pointed forward, he scanned the scene quickly. The complete front of the truck was crushed. Broken furniture pieces littered the marble floor, pieces of glass and wood splinters were everywhere. He noticed a large red spot under one of the truck's front tires and took a closer look. A severed hand lay on the floor. The rest of the human body, a woman, was partially under the truck. He checked the woman's pulse and found none.

His mind racing, Ryan tried to figure out his next move. At least four other guards were left, plus Drago. Now it was five to one. His odds were better.

Putting the AK-47 on full-auto, he advanced cautiously into the home, creeping along a wide corridor. He passed an unoccupied living room and a massive study. A fireplace was burning in the study and he glanced inside, scanning for guards. The room, which was lined with floor-to-ceiling bookcases and furnished with 16th century Italian furniture, was deserted.

Turning around, he went back into the corridor and continued deeper into the estate. Stepping into the lavish kitchen, he heard a creak and froze.

A shot rang out and he felt a jolt of pain in his shoulder; he squeezed the trigger blindly, spraying the kitchen with the AK until the magazine was empty. Ryan took cover behind a granite-topped counter, and quickly changed the clip of the assault rifle. He glanced at his shoulder – the parka was ripped and blood was oozing from a wound. It hurt like hell, but he knew the artery hadn't been hit, otherwise he would have already bled out. He could still function.

Cautiously, he peeked over the counter – laying on the floor by the custom-made, built-in refrigerator was a man's motionless body. A pool of blood was spreading on the Italian marble floor. He listened for voices, heard none. He continued his search of the first floor rooms, including the garage, but found them unoccupied. *Where the hell was Drago?* he thought. *There's two more floors – he must be up there.*

Ryan retraced his steps to the main corridor and looked up the wide marble staircase. There's bound to be guards posted there, out of sight, ready to fire once he reached the second floor. But he had no choice.

With his finger on the assault rifle's trigger, he crept slowly up the staircase. Reaching the top step, he peered around the wall. The corridor led both ways, but to his surprise he saw no men posted anywhere. His adrenaline pumping, he crept into the hallway and proceeded to search all of the rooms. He went into an office, and several bedrooms, but all were vacant.

Going back to the second floor corridor, he glanced up the staircase to the third floor. Standing stock still, he listened closely for sounds. And this time he heard something. People whispering. It was so faint he couldn't make out what they were saying.

It was clear what was happening – Drago was making his last stand on the third floor. All of the remaining guards would be up there.

A bolt of sharp pain ran down his wounded arm and Ryan winced. He grit his teeth until the ache subsided and considered his next move. The PI thought furiously, trying to come up with a way to overcome the remaining men. Clearly he was still outnumbered. He had to create chaos to even the odds. When he was in Delta Force he had all the right tools – flash-bang grenades, tear gas, RPGs, a backup team of soldiers, the whole arsenal. But today he had none of that. He had to improvise.

Then it came to him.

Quickly descending the stairs, he went down to the first floor. Earlier he'd searched the garage and found it vacant. He went there now and scanned the room. Parked at one side of the space was a Mercedes SUV. Slinging the AK over his shoulder, he rummaged through the garage and found what he was looking for – several glass bottles of cleaning solvent, towels, and a few other items. Carrying the items to the area by the SUV, he began to work.

First he emptied the glass bottles. Then he opened the vehicle's gas tank and inserted the long plastic tube he'd located. Inserting one end of the tube into the gas tank, he put the other end into his mouth and sucked. A moment later the bitter taste of gasoline filled his mouth and he spit it out, then quickly inserted the tube into one of the glass bottles. Once that bottle was filled with gas, he repeated the process on the other two. Lastly he inserted the cloth towels into the containers' open ends.

Gathering the bottles in his arms, he cautiously made his way up the stairs to the second floor. Standing by a wall, he peered up the staircase to the third level. Once again he heard whispering. As quietly as possible, he crept up the steps until he was only three feet from the top rung.

Setting the filled bottles on the step he was on, he took out his lighter and lit the towels.

Waiting a moment for the cloth to catch fire, he picked up one of the crudely made Molotov cocktails and, scampering quickly up the last few steps, hurled it against the wall opposite the staircase. The glass shattered and the flaming gasoline doused the lushly carpeted corridor floor.

Ryan heard shouting and he quickly grabbed the two other bottles and threw them in both directions of the third floor hallway. He heard glass shattering, loud screaming, and automatic rifle fire.

He unslung the AK-47 and, still crouching a few feet below the top step, pointed the weapon forward. He waited, his heart pounding. Smoke billowed from the hallway. He heard the crackling of flames, and he smelled the acrid stench of smoke.

A big, burly man loomed over him on the top step and Ryan fired off a three round burst, the bullets tearing into the man's chest. The man staggered to the floor, then tumbled down the stairway. The PI hugged the wall to keep from getting in his way. Ryan climbed to the top step and peered right. The carpet was burning and he saw two men – one was facing his way and carrying a submachine gun, while the second one was trying to stamp out the fire with his boots.

Ryan fired on full-auto, his rounds spraying the far end of the corridor. But the shooter returned fire, the high-caliber bullets whizzing over the PIs head and thudding into the nearby walls, plaster chunks flying in all directions.

Realizing his AK's magazine was empty, Ryan retreated behind the wall. He furiously searched his pockets for the third clip and couldn't find it. *Damn! I must have dropped it during all the shooting.*

Discarding the assault rifle, he pulled his handgun and peered around the wall toward the end of the hallway. Along the burning carpet he saw one crumpled body. As the smoke lifted for a moment, he saw a second prone body, bleeding and inert. No other guards were in sight.

There was a closed door at the end of the corridor. Drago must be in that part of the house. Pulling out a handkerchief, he held it to his nose to filter the smoky air.

Training his gun in front of him, he advanced, avoiding the patches of burning carpet as best he could. When he reached the end of the hallway, he stood to one side of the closed door. Reaching over, he twisted the door knob and pushed the door open.

A blaze of automatic fire erupted, streaming out of the doorway from inside the room, spraying the corridor with rounds. Ryan crouched and hugged the wall by the open entrance but didn't return fire. The rifle fire stopped and he heard a mechanical clicking noise as if a new magazine clip was being inserted.

He was next to a decorative teak-wood table. On the table was an ornate, ancient-looking vase, priceless he assumed. Picking up the urn, he hurled it into the open doorway.

Instantly he heard the loud clatter of automatic fire erupt, the multiple rounds blasting down the corridor, creating large, irregular holes in the plaster walls. He waited for the firing to stop and heard the clicking noise again.

Peering into the room, he fired off three quick rounds, spotted a woman crouching by a bookcase, changing out a clip. He rolled inside the room, took aim, and fired another three rounds, hitting the female guard in the shoulder and chest. She screamed and fell to the floor, dropping her assault rifle in the process.

The PI took cover by a cabinet, reloaded, and scanned the room, which appeared to be an office. Besides the woman, there was no one else in the room. At the far end of the office was a closed, heavy-duty metal door.

He approached her cautiously, holding the gun with both hands. Reaching her, he noticed she was still alive, but badly wounded. Blood was spurting from her wounds and her eyes were unfocused. She was on her back and he knelt next to her. There was a semi-automatic pistol holstered on her hip and he reached over and took the gun.

"Where's Drago?" Ryan asked.

The woman's eyes focused for a moment and she groaned. She tried to say something, but the words were garbled. He knew she didn't have long to live. The woman was an attractive brunette in her mid-twenties. She was dressed in a tight-fitting blouse and a miniskirt, which he thought was odd, considering the circumstances.

"Where's Drago? Where's Lauren?" Ryan asked, his voice hard.

The woman's eyes regained focus and she whispered, "Can't tell you ...."

"Can't or won't? You don't have much time left," he said harshly.

Her eyes clouded over again and she coughed up blood.

Ryan tried a different approach, softening his voice. "What's your name?"

"Heather," she replied as more blood seeped from her mouth.

"Okay, Heather. I really need your help. I need to find Drago and my girlfriend Lauren. You people kidnapped her."

Just then Heather's eyes focused, and as if realizing she was about to die, said, "I might as well tell you ... where Drago is ... I always hated that bastard ...." She stopped, coughed up more gore. "He paid me plenty ... to be his bodyguard ... then he made me ... and my sister Meagan ... his whores ... the bastard ...." More blood seeped from her mouth and she shut her eyes.

Ryan prodded her gently on the arm and she came to. "Tell me where Drago is, Heather."

"The safe room," she said, her voice faint. She lifted a hand and pointed to the metal door at the end of the room.

"That's the safe room, Heather?"

"Yes ...."

He stared at the door, noticed the keypad on the wall next to it. "What's the password, Heather?"

The young woman coughed up more blood. When she recovered a moment later, she whispered, "I never ... wanted to be ... his whore ...."

"What's the combination?"

"6,3,7,4,X,T,Q ...."

"That's good, Heather. Now tell me where Lauren is."

Her gaze lost focus and her eyes rolled up in her head so only the whites showed. He checked for a pulse and knew she was dead.

Chapter 74

Ice Point, Alaska

Nicholas Drago stared at the monitor in disbelief. His home's security cameras had picked up the whole sequence of events. Even though the cameras didn't have audio, the images had been very clear: John Ryan ramming a truck into the front door to gain access and the man killing his guards. Even his beloved Heather was dead.

Drago turned off the monitor in disgust and glanced around the steel walls of the safe room. *No way*, he thought, *that Ryan can get in here. It would take a missile to penetrate these walls.* And besides himself, only one person knew the room's password. Heather. He'd given her the code in case he ever got sick and incapacitated while inside the safe room. But he trusted the beautiful young woman implicitly. He knew he could always rely on her.

Smug from this realization, Drago rolled his wheelchair to the back of the room. In the kitchenette there he began to prepare a meal for himself.

The thought of Heather laying in a pool of blood filled him with grief. He loved her, and she loved him, he was sure, although she'd never spoken the words out loud.

Pushing the grief out of his mind, he took a bite of his salmon sandwich.

Chapter 75

Ice Point, Alaska

After putting out the fire in the home's third story hallway, Ryan returned to the office which fronted the safe room. He approached the keypad, which was to the right of the heavy-duty steel door.

Holding his gun at the ready, with his free hand he input the password on the keypad. He heard a loud metallic click and the thick metal door began to slowly open inward. He jumped away from it and hugged the wall, thinking a blaze of gunfire would erupt as soon as the door fully opened.

To his surprise, nothing happened.

He waited another minute then, his adrenaline pumping, he peeked around the metal door jamb into the safe room.

Instead of finding a group of heavily armed men pointing assault rifles, he saw a balding, frail old man sitting in a wheelchair.

Holding the revolver with both hands, Ryan stepped inside the metal walled room. Scanning the space quickly, he relaxed a bit when he saw no other guards.

"You must be Nicholas Drago," Ryan said, pointing the gun at the old man.

A grim expression was on the man's face. "I am. How the hell did you get in here, Ryan?"

"Heather gave me the password."

Drago's grim expression turned to shock. "She didn't! She loved me."

"Guess you misjudged her." Ryan studied the frail, almost emaciated man. He was wearing a royal blue silk robe over royal blue silk pajamas. A blanket covered his legs and lap. His thin, bony hands gripped the tops of the wheelchair rollers.

"Where's Lauren?" Ryan yelled.

A thin smile spread on Drago's face. "You're too late. I already had her killed."

Ryan ground his teeth in rage and bile rose up his throat.

"You took my daughter, Ryan. So I took someone you cared about." The old man let out a harsh, cold laugh. "That's fair, don't you think?"

"I should kill you right now."

Drago shook his head. "I don't think so. I had my people investigate you. You're not a cold-blooded killer. No. You won't kill me. You're going to arrest me instead." He smiled. "And I'll hire a very good, very expensive lawyer. I'll do time in one of these minimum security places, then I'll be set free. I know how the system works."

The PIs rage grew, knowing what the old man said was probably right. Guilty rich people often get light sentences. And Drago was right about something else. As much as he wanted to, he couldn't kill a defenseless, unarmed man, especially one in a wheelchair.

Ryan took his finger off the trigger and lowered the gun to his side.

Suddenly one of Drago's hands reached under the blanket covering his lap and he pulled out a pistol.

Dropping to one knee, Ryan aimed and fired six shots in quick succession. All of the rounds hit Drago squarely in the chest, bright red blood splattering the royal blue nightclothes.

The old man's body twitched a few times and his head lolled forward on his chest.

Ryan, momentarily deaf from the earsplitting roar of gunfire in the metal room, stood up and checked the man for a pulse.

Drago was dead.

Chapter 76

Ice Point, Alaska

After calling the Alaska State Police to notify them what had taken place, Ryan methodically searched all the rooms of the estate. He was looking for evidence of Drago's and the Shaw's criminal activities. And in the back of his mind, he was looking and hoping not to find, something else. Lauren's remains.

In one of the home's offices he found a treasure trove of evidence. The files contained details of Drago's extensive criminal activities. The PI also found files tying Drago to the Shaw's Flash drug conspiracy. To his amazement, he also found involvement by the U.S. Department of Defense with the narcotic.

While searching he discovered that the house had a basement, a large open space filled with boxes and crates. By the dust and cobwebs covering much of the room, it was clear the basement saw little use except as a storage area.

As he was searching the boxes, he noticed a closed door in a remote corner of the room. Going to it, he tried the knob. It was locked. Taking out his knife, he forced open the door and peered into the pitch black space.

Putting away the knife, he took out his flashlight and illuminated the interior of the small room, which looked like a walk-in closet.

His heart sank when he saw what was in the far corner of the room.

Lauren's body.

Chapter 77

Ice Point, Alaska

The image of Lauren's lifeless body now seared in his brain, Ryan continued to stand there at the open doorway of the closet, frozen in place by the shock of it.

After gulping in air to steady his nerves, he plodded forward and stood over her, his heart aching from the grim sight. She was wearing a long overcoat, unbuttoned, over a flimsy hospital gown. Her bare feet were covered with soot. Her motionless body was on its side, and her eyes were closed.

Lauren's face, as beautiful as ever, was marred by smudges of dirt and a bandage on her forehead. Her long, auburn air, which cascaded past her shoulders, was matted and dirty. But its reddish hue still highlighted the freckles on her face.

Overcome with grief, Ryan turned around and walked toward the doorway of the closet.

He heard a sound from behind him and he swung the flashlight back to the body.

He heard it again – a hoarse whisper.

Racing forward, Ryan knelt by Lauren's body.

"Help me," Lauren whispered. Her eyes, which had been shut the whole time, fluttered open.

His heart pounding with relief, Ryan slid his arms underneath her and carried her gently but quickly out of the room. Even though the pain in his shoulder was intense from the wound, he felt better than he had in a very long time.

Chapter 78

Ice Point, Alaska

"Thank God you're alive," Ryan said.

Lauren, who was now resting in one of the bedrooms of Drago's estate, looked up at him and smiled. "I prayed every day I was here. I never gave up hope, J.T."

He was standing by the bed and she reached out and took his hand. Her skin felt soft and warm.

Ryan sat on the bed. "Drago told me he had you killed."

Lauren nodded. "He ordered one of his bodyguards, a woman named Heather to do it. She's the one who brought me food while I was held prisoner here. A few days ago Heather came to the closet. I thought she was bringing me a meal, but instead she pulled a gun and pointed it at me."

"What happened?"

"I don't know, J.T. I guess she had a conscience. She broke down in tears and told me what Drago had ordered her to do. Then she put the gun away, got me food and water, and left."

A fearful expression crossed Lauren's face and she squeezed his hand tightly. "Where's Drago now?"

"Don't worry, Lauren. He's dead. And all of his guards are dead as well."

"What about Heather?"

"She's dead too."

"I'm sorry about that. She saved my life."

"I know. But we were in a firefight. I had no choice."

Lauren nodded. "I understand. What happens now?"

Ryan reached over and gently caressed her face. "I've already called the Alaska State Police. They're on their way here. In the meantime, try to get some rest. You've been through a lot, hon."

Chapter 79

Atlanta, Georgia

"You're looking at doing some serious time," her lawyer said.

Jessica Shaw stared at the heavyset man in the pin-stripe suit who was sitting across from her in the jail's cramped meeting room.

"How much time?" Jessica asked.

"The Feds have you on a long list of charges, ranging from criminal drug conspiracy, to aiding a murder, and mail fraud. And that's not counting the St. Croix police investigation into your husband's death."

"So. How much time in prison, Nathan?"

"Twenty-five to life would be my guess, Jessica."

She recoiled in shock and she tried jerking her hands in the air, but they were held fast by the manacles attached to the table's metal loop. "No way, Nathan! No fucking way! I'll never make it."

"I'm sorry, Jessica."

She looked away from the man and stared down at what she was wearing: an itchy, baggy orange jumpsuit, the prison garment a constant reminder how far she'd fallen. She hadn't bathed properly in weeks. Instead she'd been forced to take quick, cold showers with groups of rough, low-life women prisoners. Her anger boiling over, she gazed back at her attorney.

"I've paid you a lot of fucking money, Nathan. I expect you to deliver results, not bring me bad fucking news."

"Then give me something. Anything I can use to get you a lighter sentence."

Pushing the anger aside, she mulled this over. She went quiet, her thoughts churning. Eventually it came to her.

Leaning forward on the hard, uncomfortable metal chair, she said, "It's true that my husband and I were involved in the Skyflash conspiracy. But there were other people involved too. What if I give you the bigger fish?"

"Like who, Jessica?"

"The man behind the whole scheme."

Her attorney nodded. "That would work. I could use it to bargain with the district attorney. So, who was behind the conspiracy?"

"General Robert Burke."

"Who's that?"

"He's the general," Jessica said, "who heads up the U.S. Army's Advanced Weapons & Tactics programs. He manages the 'Soldier 2.7' project. That's the project that's experimenting with Flash. Burke is based at Aberdeen Proving Ground in Maryland. He funded my whole operation. He also took kickbacks when he gave me the contract."

"So the Feds could charge him with criminal conspiracy."

"It's a lot more than that, Nathan. I know for a fact soldiers died during the testing of Flash. At least five men died. And he covered it up. The Feds could charge him with second degree murder."

Her attorney smiled, the first time the man had done so today. "Okay, Jessica. I can work with that."

"So, can you get me off?" she said in a hopeful tone.

"Not completely. You'll still have to do time." He waved a hand around the small, concrete-walled room which stank of urine and disinfectant. "But you'll do less time, in a much better place than this."

Chapter 80

U.S. Army Base
Aberdeen Proving Ground
Aberdeen, Maryland

General Robert Burke was in his office working at his computer when he heard a knock at the door. Looking up, he spotted three men in the open doorway. All were wearing military uniforms. One was a captain, and the other two were military police. The MPs were armed with pistols holstered at their hip.

The three entered the room and the officer approached the desk. "General Burke, I'm Captain Reagan. I'm with the JAG office at the Pentagon. Sir, we're placing you under arrest."

Burke's mouth dropped open in disbelief. "Is this a joke, Captain? It's not funny."

"It's no joke, sir. Please stand up. My men need to handcuff you."

General Burke didn't stand, his gaze boring into the other man's eyes. "Do you know who I am?"

"Yes, sir. You're Brigadier General Robert Burke. You're in charge of the Army's Advanced Weapons & Tactics Program."

"That's right! Now what's the meaning of this?"

"You're being charged with a criminal conspiracy and potential second-degree murder charges in connection with the death of Army soldiers. You're also being charged with other felonies, including the taking of financial kickbacks on contracts you awarded."

A trickle of fear ran down Burke's spine. "That's insane. What evidence do you have?"

"We've already interrogated several scientists on your staff, General. They've confirmed what's been happening. We also have the testimony of Jessica Shaw, a co-conspirator in the drug scheme you were involved with."

Burke's mind raced as the implications of all this sank in. "I'm not the only one in the Army who's involved in this," he blurted out quickly. "My superior at the Pentagon was also involved."

Captain Reagan nodded. "If that's true, we'll want the full story. But in the meantime, you're still under arrest, General." He motioned to the MPs, who moved forward. "Now, stand up, sir."

Burke stood up reluctantly and one of the military police clicked on handcuffs. The metal felt cold and tight on the general's hands. A vision of a dark prison cell at Leavenworth crossed his mind as bile rose up his throat.

One Month Later

Chapter 81

Rome, Italy

It was a cool evening with a light breeze, the wind slightly swaying the awning which covered their table. J.T. Ryan and Lauren Chase were at one of the open air restaurants which bordered the Piazza Navona. The piazza was a city square near the Tiber River, and one of Rome's most well-known gathering spots.

Festive lights illuminated the nearby ornate Baroque fountains. At the center of the piazza was the famous *Fontana dei Quattro Fiumi*, the Fountain of the Four Rivers, which was designed by Gian Lorenzo Bernini in 1651. The splash of water from the fountains provided a pleasant background noise, mingling with the street musicians and the conversations of the other diners at the restaurant.

Local couples strolled the piazza, along with camera-toting tourists, eager to snap photos of the scenic area.

Ryan reached across the table and caressed Lauren's hand. With her shoulder length auburn hair, hazel eyes, and freckled face, she looked as beautiful as ever. It comforted him to see her this way. The evidence of her coma and kidnapping were long gone.

"We're finally here," she said, smiling. She waved a hand in the air. "And it's just as romantic as you said it would be."

"I promised you we'd vacation in Rome," he replied, squeezing her hand.

"I know you did, J.T. But with everything that's happened ...." She didn't finish the sentence and her voice trailed off.

"That's all behind us, Lauren."

"It's just – the last several months have been such a nightmare."

Ryan smiled. "That's in the past. The doctors at Emory said you're fully recovered. And the Skyflash case has been solved."

She smiled back.

The waiter returned, bringing the bottle of wine Ryan had ordered. The waiter poured each of them a glass and moved away.

Ryan picked up the goblet and raised it. "To us. To a bright, happy future."

Lauren lifted her glass and clinked it to his. "To us." She took a sip, then said, "So you're completely done with the Flash case?"

"That's right. Nicholas Drago is dead. His daughter Jessica Shaw pled to a deal – she's in prison already, starting to serve a fifteen year sentence."

"How about the Defense Department connection, J.T.?"

"Two Army generals had gone rogue – General Burke and his superior at the Pentagon. They put soldiers' lives at risk. In fact, five died. Instead of allowing enough time to thoroughly test the Flash drug on animals, they rushed it through and used human test subjects. They did it to advance their military careers and to line their own pockets. They were taking kickbacks on the contracts. Both of those generals are now behind bars, awaiting military trials. I'm sure they'll spend a long, long time at USBD. That's the military's maximum-security prison in Leavenworth."

"That's good, J.T. What about Erin Welch? On the flight over you said she'd been able to get her job back."

Ryan nodded. "FBI Director Stevens's past finally caught up with him. A scandal he'd been able to keep quiet came to light and he got fired. Once he was gone, Erin got her old job back as Assistant Director in Charge of the FBI's Atlanta office."

"I'm glad, J.T."

"I thought you didn't like her?"

"I didn't before. But you told me she visited me at the hospital when I was in a coma, and how she followed up with the doctors when you were out of the country. That says a lot about the kind of person she is. Now I realize why you like working with her."

Ryan took a sip of wine, glad that Lauren and Erin would be getting along better from now on.

His cell phone buzzed and he took it out of his jacket and looked at the caller ID. It read, *FBI – Atlanta.*

"This is Ryan," he said, answering the call.

"It's Erin Welch," he heard the woman say. "Sorry to bother you while you're on vacation. But something's come up."

"No problem, Erin. In fact, Lauren and I were just talking about you."

"Nothing bad, I hope."

Ryan laughed. "Actually, Lauren was just saying how much she appreciated you."

"That's good to hear, J.T."

"So. Are you calling to listen to my charming banter? Or is this a business call?"

"When do you get back from Italy?" Erin asked.

"One week from today."

"Okay. When you get in, come to my office at the FBI building."

"You have a new case you want my help on?"

"That's right."

"What's it about, Erin?"

"I can't say over the phone," she answered. "But I can tell you it's big. Our biggest case yet."

END

***

About the author

Lee Gimenez is the author of 11 novels. Several of his books became bestsellers, including THE WASHINGTON ULTIMATUM and BLACKSNOW ZERO. His thriller KILLING WEST was a featured novel of the International Thriller Writers Association.
His books are available at Amazon, Barnes & Noble, the Apple Store, Books-A-Million, Books In Motion, and many other bookstores in the U.S. His books are also available internationally at Amazon and at other websites around the world.
For more information about him, please visit his website at: www.LeeGimenez.com. Feel free to email him at: LG727@MSN.com. You can also join him on Twitter, Facebook, Google Plus, LinkedIn, and Goodreads. Lee lives with his wife in the Atlanta, Georgia area.

***

Other Novels by Lee Gimenez

Killing West
The Washington Ultimatum
Blacksnow Zero
The Sigma Conspiracy
The Nanotech Murders
Death on Zanath
Virtual Thoughtstream
Azul 7
Terralus 4
The Tomorrow Solution

KILLING WEST is available at Amazon, Barnes & Noble, and many other retailers in the U.S. and Internationally. In paperback, Kindle, and all other ebook versions.

THE WASHINGTON ULTIMATUM is available at Amazon, Barnes & Noble, and many other retailers in the U.S. and Internationally. In paperback, Kindle, and all other ebook versions.

Lee Gimenez's other novels, including

- Blacksnow Zero
- The Sigma Conspiracy
- The Nanotech Murders
- Death on Zanath
- Virtual Thoughtstream
- Azul 7
- Terralus 4
- The Tomorrow Solution

are all available at Amazon, Barnes & Noble,
and many other retailers in the U.S. and Internationally.
In paperback, Kindle, and all other ebook versions.

CPSIA information can be obtained
at www.ICGtesting.com
Printed in the USA
LVOW11s0346181217
560134LV00003B/323/P

9 780692 454039